Stirring Up a Love Story

Amelia Berry grew up on the North Yorkshire coast and now lives in Worcestershire. She has been writing professionally since 2013, and is also published as Ally Sinclair, Alison May and, in collaboration, as Juliet Bell. She is a former Chair of the Romantic Novelists' Association, and currently works as an associate lecturer for the Open University.

Also by Amelia Berry

The Highland Cookery School

A Recipe for Love
Cooking Up a Christmas Storm
Stirring Up a Love Story

Amelia BERRY

Stirring up a Love Story

canelo
HERA

First published in the United Kingdom in 2026 by

Hera Books, an imprint of
Canelo Digital Publishing Limited,
20 Vauxhall Bridge Road,
London SW1V 2SA
United Kingdom

A Penguin Random House Company
The authorised representative in the EEA is Dorling Kindersley Verlag GmbH.
Arnulfstr. 124, 80636 Munich, Germany

Copyright © Amelia Berry 2026

The moral right of Amelia Berry to be identified as the creator of this work has been asserted in accordance with the Copyright, Designs and Patents Act, 1988.
All rights reserved. No part of this publication may be reproduced or transmitted in any form or by any means, electronic or mechanical, including photocopy, recording, or any information storage and retrieval system, without permission in writing from the publisher.
No part of this book may be used or reproduced in any manner for the purpose of training artificial intelligence technologies or systems. In accordance with Article 4(3) of the DSM Directive 2019/790, Canelo expressly reserves this work from the text and data mining exception.

A CIP catalogue record for this book is available from the British Library.

ISBN 9 781 83598 055 2

This book is a work of fiction. Names, characters, businesses, organizations, places and events are either the product of the author's imagination or are used fictitiously. Any resemblance to actual persons, living or dead, events or locales is entirely coincidental.

Cover design by Diane Meacham

Cover images © Dreamstime.com, Getty Images / iStock, Shutterstock.com

Printed and bound in Great Britain by Clays Ltd, Elcograf S.p.A.

Look for more great books at
www.herabooks.com | www.dk.com

For Evi and Miri.

I'm not sure I could have written this one without you

Prologue

15 years earlier

Darcy Lowbridge opened her eyes at the sound of the heavy wooden bedroom door swinging open on its ageing hinges. 'How are you feeling?'

She wriggled her way up to sitting, pulling the covers up to her chest against the draught, and shook her head. 'Stay back. You don't want to catch this.'

Her husband was carrying a tray. 'Can you manage something to eat?'

Darcy hadn't felt like anything more than a sip of water for days, but as she rubbed the sleep from her eyes, she nodded. 'I think so.'

He placed the tray down on the bed. 'Just a poached egg.'

'You made it?'

He nodded. 'Flinty has gone to the shop, so I was allowed.'

Darcy managed a smile at that. Flinty had been the housekeeper at Lowbridge Castle for years before Darcy had arrived, long before Alexander had inherited from his father and become the baron, and it was very clear that the kitchen was her domain.

She sliced into the yolk of the egg and watched the soft yellow flow over the buttered toast. 'Thank you for this. It's exactly what I needed.'

'I'll let you enjoy it then.' Alexander stepped towards the door.

'Stay,' she whispered.

He moved back instantly and sat gently on the end of the bed. 'Are you all right?'

'Apart from this stupid bug?'

He nodded. 'You moved all this way. And you're living here and you have a stepson and… I hope you're happy.'

Darcy shook her head at the ridiculousness of the question. Moving from New York to the Scottish Highlands to marry a man fifteen years older than her, with a teenage son and a vast country estate to manage, was the most reckless thing she'd ever done. No part of her life was what she'd imagined it would be at this point even twelve months ago. She swallowed the mouthful of soft egg, and crunchy toast. 'I'm perfectly happy. I'm with you.'

Chapter 1

'So the girl from the village loved the baron and he loved her, and he built the very first Low Bridge across the river so he could visit her. And even after she was forced to marry the fisherman's son he would creep into the village to see her – until one day her fisherman husband went out to sea and never came back. That meant the girl was free to marry her baron. Not very long after the wedding she had a baby, and nobody was ever quite sure whether the son she had was really the baron's or whether he was the fisherman's boy. Either way, the baron loved him and raised him as his own, and to this day Lowbridge Castle and Lowbridge village are linked together, part of the same family.' Darcy Lowbridge forced a smile as she finished the familiar story. She'd never, personally, been quite convinced it was true, but it was a good tale and visitors lapped it up, including the small crowd currently gathered around her in the courtyard of Lowbridge Castle. 'And, well, that's the end of the tour. Please do feel welcome to take a walk around outside. There's a path right up to the clifftop which takes you past the walled garden, and we've also got our tea room' – she pointed towards the tables set up at one side of the courtyard – 'with plenty more seating inside and we sell produce and seedlings from the stall outside the coach house. Please just ask if you have any questions at all.'

An American couple hung back as the group dispersed. 'And you're really the lady of the manor, honey?'

Darcy nodded at the familiar question. 'Well, I married the laird, so...'

The woman's eyes almost popped out of her head. 'That attractive young man in the garden?'

'No.' Darcy stifled a giggle. 'I married his dad. Adam's my stepson. A little bit young for me, don't you think?'

'Well, I did not like to say.' The woman laughed. 'So where's your husband?'

'He passed away.' Darcy answered quickly. She always did. Say it fast and don't dwell. 'So Adam's the laird now.'

'And you never wanted to go back home?' the woman asked. 'New York, from your accent?'

'Oh no,' Darcy answered on autopilot. 'Lowbridge is home now.'

The couple wandered away. Around them, the whole castle estate was bustling. Flinty and Nina had come over from the village to serve teas and scones over the bank holiday weekend. Darcy made her way to their serving counter, newly set up in the corner of the dining hall. 'Anything I can do?'

Flinty bustled her away. 'All in hand, love.'

Veronica, Darcy's mother-in-law and rival dowager lady, was just setting out from the other side of the courtyard with a bird-watching group who'd signed up for their new coastal wildlife walk. They strode past Darcy at an impressive pace. 'Come along,' Veronica called. 'No dawdling.'

It was possible that the chat they'd had about the bird watchers being paying guests, who were supposed to be treated with enthusiastic respect, hadn't been entirely taken on board by the older dowager.

Bella would be busy in the cookery school, which ran like a well-oiled machine these days. Adam would be in the garden. Neither of them needed Darcy under their feet. Their newest recruit, Molly, came past her, carrying her cleaning kit at her side. 'Coach house rooms are all done,' she announced, checking the time on her phone. 'I'm going to grab a coffee and then I'll be ready to sort the cookery school washing-up.'

'I can do that,' Darcy offered.

Molly shook her head. 'Don't bother yourself. It's what I'm here for.'

Darcy made her way inside and headed to the estate office. She caught herself as the door swung open and realised she hadn't hesitated, for her customary moment, outside the door. She always hesitated. Not always, but ever since Alexander passed she'd involuntarily stopped for a second at this door. Of course she didn't expect to see Alexander in the office. She wasn't mad, and the feeling wasn't as simple as expectation. It was something deeper and stranger than that. It was more that until she opened the door the possibility of him continued to exist. She could hold on to the picture of him sitting at the desk, probably ignoring a stack of estate work, head bent instead over one of his books, lost in his reading. Every time she opened the door and he, of course, wasn't there, that image cracked and faded a tiny bit more. But today she hadn't paused at all, and the absence of the constant awareness of his absence sat heavy.

She'd made the best of things, since he died. That was what everyone said. Darcy had been a real trouper. She'd rolled up her sleeves and got stuck in, taking over the bookkeeping and a lot of the admin for Adam and Bella, supporting their new approach to running the Lowbridge estate. For the last few months this had, effectively, been her office, although she'd never quite thought of it that way. She stepped through the open door.

Fiona MacCellan, Lowbridge's new... Darcy paused. They still hadn't agreed on a job title. Fiona was their new manager but what precisely she managed was amorphous and open to debate. She looked up as Darcy came in.

'What do you think of "guest experience"?'

'What?'

'Guest experience manager,' Fiona explained. 'I think it's got a ring.'

Darcy shrugged. 'Bit corporate maybe? And you do more than that. There's all the marketing and social media and...'

'I'll add it to the list.' Fiona pulled a Post-it note from a pad on the desk and stuck it to the front of the shelf behind her, along with at least ten others. 'So what can I do for you?'

'I wondered if anything needed doing. I was going to send out confirmations for next week's cookery school places.'

'Oh.' Fiona smiled. 'The new booking system does that automatically.'

'Right. Yeah. Course it does.' Darcy knew that. 'Well, we need to invoice Kenny for his group this week.'

'Done.' Fiona glanced down at the floor. 'Sorry. I didn't realise you were going to do that.'

'No. It's fine. So long as it gets done, right?' Darcy had no wish to make Fiona feel bad. 'That's what matters. Right. Well, I guess I can...' She gestured out towards the door.

'Yeah. Take a break. You can go for a ride.'

'Yeah. Maybe.' Darcy felt like she was being told to go for a ride a lot recently. It put her in mind of a much-loved, but also slightly needy, child being sent to play in her room while her parents talked about adult things beyond her understanding. She'd already been out for a ride along the cliff this morning. She didn't think her very lovely, but not as young as she once was, pony would thank her for a repeat performance quite so soon.

—

Nathan Thomas tapped his hand against the arm of the stupid beige chair and stared down at his knees. He knew the beige and cream room was supposed to be calming but the plainness made him twitchy and thankful for the sounds of traffic and an ambulance siren getting closer and further away to anchor him into reality. Diagonally across from him, the Owl tilted his head slightly to one side.

Nate had started calling his current therapist the Owl at their very first meeting. His actual name was something not a million miles from that, he thought. Oliver? Ollie? Owen? Owen. That wasn't the reason he'd got set as 'the Owl' in Nate's imagination though. There was something owlish in his beige, tweedy, bespectacled demeanour. He was waiting for Nate to break the silence. Nate's fingers continued to drum against the seat.

'So what were you feeling immediately before this all happened?'

'Well, angry.'

'Right.' The Owl nodded. 'Were you able to try any of the things we discussed to manage that feeling?'

Nate didn't want to think himself back to last night. He knew he'd screwed up. He knew he was on his last chance.

He knew he was only here because, despite last night, Guy Fforde was still paying for his counselling. It was possible the anger management element wasn't entirely working.

He shook his head. 'It weren't anger like that.'

The Owl leaned forward slightly. 'Tell me what it was like?'

'It wasn't like before.' Nate knew he'd had trouble controlling his temper in the past, but he'd been good for a couple of years now. He could see the red mist coming and take a breath, or ten, and talk his way down well before he lost control. What he'd been feeling lately was something else. 'It was just…' He shook his head. 'I dunno. It was busy all weekend.'

The Owl nodded. 'Bank holiday.'

Three days of full dining rooms and stressed-out services. That was the job though, and the job was who Nate was.

'So what happened last night?'

He really didn't know. 'It was like I couldn't think. I was doing the salmon. And you have to cook it fast, right?'

The Owl nodded.

'So you flash the skin under the salamander, but it doesn't need long, and I…' Nate couldn't explain it. 'I could see it was burning, and then Jules came over and went spare, and I walked out.'

The Owl closed his notepad and put his paper and pen down on the low table between them. 'You know we've talked before about fight and flight responses?'

Nate sighed. He tended to go into crisis mode when it wasn't necessary. He didn't do that any more. 'I didn't fight though, did I?'

'That's not the only stress reaction.'

'You're saying I've just shifted to flight?'

'Not exactly,' the Owl replied. 'Really we should talk about fight, flight and freeze reactions. Sometimes when we're overwhelmed we just freeze up. Does that sound like what you're describing?'

Nate stared at the floor. 'Maybe.'

'Do you remember last week we talked about burnout?'

Of course Nate remembered. 'That's like junior doctors and stressed-out students and that though. I'm tough.'

'You are.' The Owl looked serious. 'That's probably the only reason you're still standing now.' He paused. 'Have you considered the other suggestion Mr Fforde made?'

Of course Nate had thought about it. He'd thought about the embarrassment of being shipped off because he couldn't take the pace. He'd thought of the fake sympathy he'd get from colleagues all secretly delighted to have him out of the way of their own paths to career glory. He'd thought about being miles away from the only place he'd ever felt at home – in the heat of a restaurant kitchen in the middle of service. 'I'm not a quitter.'

'Taking a break, or even taking the chance to have a change, isn't necessarily quitting.' The Owl leaned forward slightly. 'And quitting can be a good thing, if it makes space in our lives for something new. I believe the post you're considering is maternity leave cover?'

Nate nodded, even though he wasn't considering it at all, but maternity cover was, indeed, what Guy had said. A favour for someone he really rated as a chef was what he'd called it.

'So a few months probably. Perhaps a year at most.'

A year. A whole year away from London. A whole year out of Guy Fforde's kitchen. A whole year for everyone else around him to take their shot and move up. When he came back he'd be starting over. 'I can't do a year.'

'Well, it might not be that long, but you could find out.'

Nate didn't reply. If he went back to Guy and said he'd consider it, that would be a done deal, wouldn't it? It would be Nate admitting he couldn't cope. And he could cope. That was who Nate was. He wasn't someone who took time out.

The Owl was still talking. 'Look. The maternity cover job is just one option. Maybe it's not the right change right now, but really, Nate, how long can you keep going like this?'

That was an easy question to answer. He was on a path. He'd made senior sous chef in one of Guy Fforde's kitchens before he was twenty-five. Head chef next and opening his own place by thirty. Michelin star at his own restaurant within another couple of years of that. Then maybe he'd slow down.

The Owl was still looking at him. 'How long can you carry on?'

'As long as it takes.'

Chapter 2

Bella was on the phone in the kitchen when Darcy came back in.

'Yeah. Yeah.' Bella's voice was tense. 'I do understand. It's just not very convenient.' She paused. 'No. Of course I do get that. All right. Bye then.' She hung up the phone.

'Everything OK?'

'My blood pressure's still a bit high. The midwife wants me to rest more. She suggested starting my maternity leave a bit earlier.' She rubbed her hand over her growing belly. 'I feel fine.'

She was seven months. If asked she told people she was going on maternity leave at thirty-eight weeks. Six weeks from now. It sounded like the call from the midwife might be suggesting a change from that plan, and Darcy was already doubting that Bella really intended to step back at all. 'And have you contacted any of the people who applied for the cover job yet?' she asked.

Bella picked up a folder from the worktop. 'These are the applications, but none of them blew me away. I said I'd go through them with Fiona on Friday.'

'Well, I can do that.' They didn't need Fiona for everything, did they? Darcy poured herself a glass of wine and Bella a glass of apple juice and made herself useful. Fifteen or so CVs from chefs, cookery teachers and cooks from across Scotland and the north of England. She skimmed through the first couple. Both only just out of catering college. Perhaps not enough experience yet to take on teaching others. She moved on. 'What about this one?'

Bella glanced over the CV. 'No real restaurant experience.'

'Do they need that?'

She shrugged. 'It looks good on our publicity.'

Darcy flicked to the next CV. 'This one's worked in restaurants in LA, and Tokyo and London.'

Bella shook her head. 'Never for more than six months.'

'Well, we're not looking for anyone long-term.'

'Feels fishy. What if he got caught nicking from them or something?'

'And what if he didn't?' Even as she asked the question, Darcy knew what Bella's response would be.

'Not chancing it.'

'OK.' She didn't disagree, really. Lowbridge was a special place. They didn't want the wrong someone swanning in and upsetting it all. Darcy flicked through another three résumés before she paused again. 'This one looks really good. Restaurant experience, and she's taught in a catering college.' She flicked to the covering letter. 'Says she's nearing retirement and is thinking about moving somewhere more rural and this would be a great chance to try that out.'

Bella scanned the CV carefully. 'I can't see anything wrong with her.'

'And yet, you're not on the phone biting her hand off?' Darcy pointed out. She knew exactly what was holding Bella back. 'I know the cookery school is your baby, but you're having an actual baby, so at some point you will have to go on maternity leave and someone else will have to take over.'

She stopped at Bella's expression.

'Not take over,' Darcy corrected her herself. 'Just hold the reins for a while. And the sooner they get here, the more chance you'll have to make sure they're doing it right, before you're busy with the baby.'

'I know.' Bella closed the folder of applications. 'But none of these feel right.'

Darcy remembered a conversation from the week before. 'Didn't you say you'd had someone recommended?'

'Yeah.' Bella half smiled. 'Guy said he knew someone who could use a few months away from London.'

Darcy felt herself bristle slightly. 'So, what? We're a holiday camp for tired chefs?'

Bella shook her head. 'No. Well, maybe. I trust Guy though. He gave me my first chance in a proper restaurant kitchen.'

Darcy didn't like the idea of some fancy London chef dumping his wayward employees on them, but they needed someone, and watching Bella waddle over to the stove to start on dinner, she thought they really needed someone quite soon. 'Maybe you should give him another call?' she suggested.

Nate came out of the Tube and walked back along Whitehall Place towards La Mer, Guy Fforde's oldest restaurant and still the one that held his heart. The streets here were what Nate thought of as fantasy London. Cool grey-white stone, grand frontages and discreet doormen on the step to invite you in, or politely discourage entry to the wrong sort. Working for Guy Fforde was Nate's entry into a different world. He had a place here. So long as he knew his place, the angry voice in his head pointed out. That would change when he had his own restaurant, and the guy in the hat on the door had to show him proper respect.

He pulled his hood up and kept his head down as he hurried into the restaurant, through the dining room and towards the kitchen door. Bloody Jules was at the pass. 'You're late. He's upstairs and he wants to see you.'

'How can I be late if I'm not expected back?' Nate muttered. Jules' text message the night before had made it very clear that she didn't want to see him in the kitchen at La Mer ever again.

'Not up to me, is it?' She glared at him. 'Unfortunately.'

Nate made his way up the stairs to the office on the mezzanine to find out if he still had a job.

Guy was behind his desk, slim wire-framed glasses on his nose, poring over a draft menu printout, fountain pen in hand to make corrections. He glanced up. 'Nathan.' A single word of acknowledgement and a nod at the empty chair between them told Nate that he was to wait.

Guy finished his inspection of the menu and turned his attention to Nate. 'You walked out of service.' No question. No approbation. A simple statement of fact.

Nate nodded.

'Should I take it that you no longer wish to work here?'

That was the very worst thing Nate could imagine. La Mer was everything to him. 'No. I do. I really do. I love my job.'

The mobile lying on Guy's desk rang. He glanced at the screen and half smiled. 'I shall have to answer this. Hello, Bella.' He nodded a couple of times. Nate couldn't make out what was being said on the other end of the line. 'Actually, he's here with me now. Let me call you back.' He turned his attention back to Nate. 'Have you thought any more about the job I suggested?'

Of course he had. If he tried to stop thinking about it, someone – Guy, Jules, the Owl – reminded him quickly enough. 'You want rid of me?'

'That's not what I said.'

Nate didn't want to leave La Mer. He didn't want to leave London. He didn't want to be anywhere other than right here. 'I'd rather stay.'

Guy leaned back in his chair. 'You don't think a break might…'

'You sound like that sodding therapist.'

'The sodding therapist this business is paying for?'

Nate nodded silently.

'Which I am very happy to pay for,' Guy clarified, 'but I would hope that you might listen to his advice. And mine.'

'You never take time off.'

Guy's expression didn't change. 'No. But that is perhaps not an example you ought to be following. I've always encouraged my team to use their annual leave, take compassionate leave, sick leave, whatever when appropriate.'

'You think I'm sick?'

'No. But I do think that you might end up sick if you don't make a change. At least for a little while. View it as a sabbatical.'

'A what?'

'A sort of working break? Focus on developing your own recipes, your own style, come back ready to take the next step.'

Nate's body sprang to attention. 'The next step?'

Guy nodded. 'This is between us, but I'm thinking about stepping back. Not straight away and not retiring or anything, but I want some time to do other things. Carousel and Diablo are already being run for me day-to-day.' He glanced around the office. 'This place will be next.'

La Mer. La Mer was a two-star restaurant. It was Guy Fforde's flagship, started by his uncle and transformed from a well-loved, but unexciting, French bistro into the culinary powerhouse it now was. The idea of being head chef at La Mer was beyond what Nate could have hoped for as his next step. He'd assumed he'd have to take a step down the food chain to take charge of his first kitchen. He must have misunderstood. 'You mean you'll be looking for a head chef here?'

Guy nodded.

'But… but Jules has been here longer than me. Or Olly at Carousel. Wouldn't he want to come over?'

'She has and he might.'

'Right.' So this wasn't a job offer. Of course it wasn't.

'But you have something they don't.'

'Apart from anger issues?'

Guy waved a hand. 'Look, you're all talented chefs. Jules has a lot of experience but neither of you have run your own place full time. Olly would be a very safe pair of hands.' Guy looked at him. 'I honestly haven't made my mind up. I worry that Jules would end up even more as an HR manager and lose sight of the food. I worry that Olly wouldn't innovate and keep pushing forward.'

'And what about me?' Nate didn't have to ask. He knew all the worries about him. His temper. He was immature. He was unreliable.

'I just wonder if you've really found out who you are.'

That was crazy. Nate knew who he was. He was the wonderkid of the London restaurant scene. Technically one of the best – if Guy really was stepping back then possibly the best. He'd soaked up everything he'd been taught, in every kitchen he'd worked in.

'I think this would be a great chance to get back to basics and cook without an audience. You might surprise us all.'

Nate didn't need to do any of that. He knew exactly what sort of chef he was, and so did Guy. He'd trained him after all. He folded his arms. 'What if I say no?'

Guy paused. Guy seldom paused. He was a man who always had all the answers. 'I think that would be an unwise decision,' he eventually replied.

'So I don't have a choice?'

'As I say, there's always a choice.'

But the choice was between this and the very real risk of unemployment. The carrot of the head chef's job dangled in front of him. The stubborn kid inside Nate, sick of constantly being shipped from one place to the next, stuck out his chin. 'I can't just up sticks.'

Of course, he really could just up sticks. His housemates barely saw him anyway and would have sublet his room within a week of noticing he wasn't there. Guy was far too polite to point that out. 'So take the rest of the week to get things sorted out.'

Nate knew when he was beaten. He hated it, but he knew it. 'It's temporary though?'

'Maternity cover.' Guy smiled. 'I think it'll be good for you.'

Nate nodded silently.

'I'll tell her to expect you next week.'

A week. A week and then his punishment began.

Chapter 3

Darcy steered her way carefully over the Low Bridge and along the track down to the shore. She didn't take Larry out very often these days. He was well past retirement age in horse years, but he would still tolerate being ridden, by Darcy at least, so long as the route was short and the pace was slow. She knew that. A short wander over the bridge and along the shoreline and back again was about his limit, but Darcy had still chosen to ride Larry today rather than the much sprightlier Liberty, so they walked slowly alongside the loch. When she'd first moved here this had been one of her favourite things to do. To move slowly felt like an antidote to the insanity of New York City, and she'd loved that. Lowbridge was a place she could simply be.

Now just being felt like being caught at standstill. She wasn't the lady of the manor any more. Adam didn't need a stepmom. And Alexander was gone. Without him would anyone other than her beloved Larry really notice if Darcy wasn't here any more either?

She patted his neck and carefully encouraged him around in a wide semicircle to make his way back home. A short walk out was probably good for him and Darcy could give him that. She encouraged Larry back over the bridge and up the shallow bank onto the lane. 'Nearly home now,' she murmured. They walked their way down the verge at the side of the road. In her heart Darcy knew Larry wasn't going to be with her that much longer but she pushed the thought away. She'd lost too much already. Life seemed to being getting constantly smaller lately. She hadn't noticed until now. Even when Alexander had died, there'd been so much activity – Adam coming home to take over the estate and bringing Bella with him, the cookery school starting, and then Bella announcing she was pregnant. Things kept happening, but they weren't Darcy's things, were they? She was a stone in the bed of a fast-running stream. Bright, wild, vital life was going on all around her, but Darcy didn't seem to be part of the flow.

She eased Larry towards the coach house at the entry to Lowbridge. There was a motorbike parked right outside. Darcy had never seen that there before. Nobody in the village rode a motorbike and the students for this afternoon's cookery school had all come together in the minibus from Kenny's Highland Experience tour, which was parked just beyond the bike.

Darcy walked Larry through the archway and across the castle courtyard towards the far corner that led through to the station. The bike was out of place. Maybe, after she'd got Larry settled, she'd come back and check that out.

—

Nate lugged his backpack round to what he assumed was the front door of the building that a very new-looking sign assured him was Lowbridge Castle, home to the Highland Cookery School. Obviously he'd put the address into his sat nav and he'd registered the C word there in the middle of it, but his brain hadn't quite engaged with it. He'd thought it was going to be a castle like a hundred places had a Castle Street or a Castle Hill. He thought the bingo hall down the road from his last foster placement had been called the Golden Castle. That definitely had not been a castle. This, equally definitely, was.

Nate stuck out his chin. He could work in a castle. He was here to cook. He could cook to impress anybody. The fact that this was Lord Something-or-Other's massive castle didn't change that. Food was food and Nate was good at food. He'd probably be able to teach some stuffy old aristocrat from the arse end of nowhere a thing or two.

He lifted the knocker and let it fall to the door with a loud clear bang. Nobody came. He tried again. Nothing. Should he just walk in? Would archers appear on the battlements and shoot him down if he did? Even in Nate's whirling imagination that seemed unlikely, but it seemed very likely indeed that there was some unspoken etiquette about walking into a castle that he was supposed to know.

He walked back around to where he'd parked the bike and went through the archway that seemed to lead to what he determinedly decided to think of as the back yard. As he turned the corner, he caught sight of what appeared to be the back end of an actual horse disappearing through another archway at the farthest side of the compound. Chasing a horse to ask if it knew where he was supposed to go was not a good option, but given the ridiculous number of doorways this place had leading off the square of cobbles he was currently standing on, it was probably the only option he had. And the horse would have a rider – right? Even in castles horses didn't just wander around the place unaccompanied, did they?

He set off towards the disappearing animal.

'Oi, lad!'

The voice behind him made him stop and turn. The woman striding towards him was older, wearing a tweed skirt and wax jacket that looked like it had been handed down the generations. Her grey hair still retained a hint of ginger.

She frowned as she saw his face. 'You're not the lad.'

Nate presumed not. 'Aren't I?'

'Well, don't you know?' she shot back.

'I guess I'm not.'

'Right, well, who are you then?'

'I'm Nate Thomas.'

The woman shook her head. 'No. I don't think we have one of them.'

For goodness' sake. 'I'm the chef.'

'Bella's the chef, lad.'

That name was finally familiar. 'Yes. Right. But she's going on maternity leave. I'm covering for her.'

The woman looked uncertain for a minute. 'Maternity?' she muttered.

Nate nodded.

'Right, well. You'll not be wanting to do that out here then. You'll be wanting the kitchen.'

'Yes!' Finally.

The woman turned back in the direction she'd appeared from. 'Well, don't dawdle, lad.'

―

Darcy came back into the castle from the courtyard. Adam and Bella would be in the kitchen. Bella lived in the kitchen. Darcy would join them for an evening drink after she'd changed. On the way upstairs she stuck her head round the door of the estate office. Fiona was sitting behind the desk.

21

'You're working late?'

The speed with which Fiona closed her laptop suggested she may not have been working at all.

Darcy frowned. 'What are you doing?'

'Nothing.' Fiona picked a piece of paper from the desk. 'Just finishing...' She looked at what was in her hand. '...this empty envelope.'

Darcy laughed. 'What are you really doing?'

'I was...' She turned her laptop to Darcy and opened it up. The screen flickered into life on the page Fiona had been looking at – a Facebook profile for Isla McKenzie.

It took Darcy a moment to catch up. 'John McKenzie's wife?'

Fiona nodded.

John McKenzie owned the large estate that bordered Lowbridge, and was largely made up of land he'd bought from Fiona's father. Until a few months ago, Fiona had been his business manager.

'I'm cyberstalking my ex's wife.'

'Wow.' Darcy had heard rumours that Fiona and John had been more than colleagues, but she'd never had it confirmed from the horse's mouth before. 'I thought they'd split up.'

Fiona shook her head. 'Well, I never knew she existed so you're one up on me.' She scrolled down the page to a set of pictures showing Isla and John very much together on a golden beach somewhere. 'We were both wrong.'

'I'm sorry.'

Fiona closed the window. 'I know I'm better off, so much better off, now. I can't believe I fell for someone like that.'

'The heart wants what it wants.'

'Maybe I need to get on the apps? Look for someone new?' Fiona suggested. 'We both could.'

Darcy felt her whole body freeze. She couldn't go on dating apps. She was married. Not married though. Of course not. It had been a year. A whole year. But.

'I'm sorry. I didn't mean...' Fiona looked stricken. 'It's too soon. I get that. I shouldn't have said.'

Darcy physically shook herself out of the inertia. 'It's fine. You should do that though. It might be fun.'

—

Nate followed the stranger to the corner of the yard and in through a wooden door that was propped open. She led the way past what looked like two small prep kitchens, and into what appeared to be a large domestic kitchen. There was a large range cooker, big island unit and cupboards with slightly tired-looking wooden doors. The pans, though, were gleaming clean and good quality, and a roll of chef's knives lay open on the worktop next to the main sink. Even so, it was hardly what he was used to.

A young dark-haired woman was sitting at the island, perched slightly awkwardly on a high stool. A man was at the sink, up to his elbows in suds. 'You know we can probably afford a dishwasher now?' he said, without looking around.

The woman smiled. 'But then what would we need you for?'

'Rude.'

The stranger he'd followed inside interrupted them. 'I found a lad.'

The woman finally noticed him. 'Oh! Sorry. Are you Nathan?'

'Nate.'

'Brilliant.' She stood, turning to reveal a very pregnant belly. 'I'm Bella. Guy has been singing your praises.'

Nate nodded. Was that true? What would Guy have said about him? What was this Bella expecting? 'Yours too,' he muttered. That wasn't true. He'd said Bella was someone he'd worked with at the start of her career and that she was a great cook, but beyond that he hadn't said much. His bid to get Nate into purgatory in the middle of nowhere was more about how Nate needed to do better than about why it might be a good place to go. And that was what he had to do. He had to prove that he was everything Guy expected him to be so he could get out of here as quickly as possible.

'Right. Let me feed you. Just dump your bag somewhere. You must be starving.'

He was, but he still shook his head. 'You don't have to...'

'Of course I do.'

'No. You don't.' The man at the sink dried his hands off on a towel and held one out to Nate. 'I'm Adam. And I don't want to be rude but she's supposed to be resting.' He gave Bella a fairly definite look. 'The whole reason he's here is so you don't have to spend all day cooking.'

'This isn't all day.' Bella shook her head. 'I'm fine and cooking isn't work.'

'Cooking is loads of your work.'

'That's teaching cooking and taking bookings and stuff. This is just making dinner for our guest.'

'I'm not really a guest,' Nate pointed out. He nodded at his very large rucksack. 'Hopefully I'm staying, and I do need to learn my way around the kitchen.'

Bella looked at him. 'It's fine. You've had a long journey. I'll make you something.'

'Really, I don't mind. It sounds like you're supposed to be resting.'

'It's just a quick supper.'

'It'll give me chance to get familiar with where everything is.'

'You can watch me.'

'I'm happy to make myself something.'

Nate became aware that Adam's eyes were flicking from him to Bella and back again. Eventually the other woman, the older lady he'd followed into the kitchen, snapped. 'Oh for goodness' sake, *I'll* make him something.' She glared at Nate and then across to Bella. 'Sit down then.'

Bella did as she was told. Nate hesitated. He hadn't come all this way to be told what to do by some octogenarian stranger. The familiar sensation of wanting to kick back in the face of being bossed around bristled across his skin. He took a breath like the Owl had told him. He was here to prove to Guy that he had his issues under control.

The woman folded her arms. 'Both of you.'

Nate sat down.

The woman opened the fridge. 'Right. What have you got?'

'I was going to do salmon.' Bella made to get up again.

'Good. That'll be quick in the pan.' She glanced at Nate. 'You like salmon.'

It didn't appear to be a question. He nodded silently.

'You're harvesting asparagus already, lad?'

Nate frowned. How would he know?

Adam answered. 'There's some in the pantry.'

The woman set off towards the door they'd come in through. She paused. 'Well, come along then, new lad. Make yourself useful.'

'I thought you wanted me to sit down.' Nate could hear the whine in his voice.

The woman shook her head. 'Only when you're not being useful.'

He followed her down the short corridor to a surprisingly well-stocked pantry. There were vegetables, many with a hint of soil still clinging to them, and boxes labelled with names like *Cakes for Any Occasion*, *Simple Italian* and *Beginners' Basics*. 'Is this all the stuff for the cookery school?'

The woman looked at it and seemed to freeze just for a second before she nodded. 'That'll be right.' She stared at the labels. 'See if there's a spot of brown sugar in that one, lad.'

She was already clutching paprika and cayenne pepper.

'You're doing a dry rub?'

'Aye, well, you just wander in expecting feeding, there's not a lot of time to marinade, is there?'

Nate supposed not. 'I just didn't think…'

'Didn't think what?' Her tone was sharp. Honestly, Nate hadn't thought he was going to see much seasoning beyond salt and a twist of black pepper on special occasions. 'Thought the old bird won't be up to much in the kitchen, did you?'

He shook his head. 'Not at all.'

'Good.' She thrust the things she'd collected so far into his hands. 'Now take that back through and ask Bella to show you how to mix the rub.'

'I know how to…'

She shook her head. 'Don't be daft, lad.'

Back in the kitchen, Nate set about seasoning the salmon while the woman chopped vegetables besides him. 'You're not doing too bad with that.'

'It's not my first salmon,' Nate muttered.

'If you say so, lad.'

'Nate.'

She glanced at him. 'What's that?'

'Nate. My name's Nate.'

'As you think, lad.'

Adam pulled out a stool at the island next to Bella. 'Flinty's been calling me "lad" since I was born. You just have to accept it.'

Nate nodded. He could do that. Some old woman he barely knew not remembering his name didn't mean anything. It was fine. It wasn't like another new teacher or new social worker having to check their notes when he came in the room and calling him Nathan however many times he told them it was Nate. It was just one person. The Owl would tell him to breathe. 'You're Flinty then?' he asked.

'That's what everyone calls me,' she confirmed.

Twenty minutes later, Nate was tucking into his salmon.

The food was good. Of course it was good. He'd taken control of the seasoning while Flinty wasn't looking. Her presentation wasn't what Nate would have opted for, but she'd refused to let him clean up the plate, muttering about his cheffy nonsense. He closed his eyes for a second. 'This needs something more. Garlic maybe?'

'Don't let Flinty hear you say that,' Adam cautioned.

'I'm just saying.'

'Well don't.' He grinned. 'Not if you value your life.'

'Is she here?'

The voice that cut through the hint of tension came from the corridor and was female and imperious. The woman that followed it into the kitchen matched the voice.

Adam jumped up. 'Grandmother! This is Nate. Our new chef.'

The woman stopped, looked him up and down, and nodded. 'Veronica Lowbridge. Dowager.'

Nate nodded like he knew what that meant. 'Nice to meet you.'

'So is she here?'

'Who?'

'Margaret.'

Adam shook his head. 'Oh, Flinty? She was here a minute ago.'

'The Land Rover's still parked outside the coach house.' Veronica frowned. 'She's probably off sorting some mess out somewhere.'

'Well, we can help you look for her,' Adam offered. Bella hopped off her stool. Nate made to follow them. Adam waved him back. 'You finish your dinner, mate.'

Alone in the kitchen, Nate took a moment to try to decompress. He'd met four new people in a little over thirty minutes, and the next few days were going to be more of that again. New people. New places. An unfamiliar kitchen. Nothing where he expected it to be. This was the sort of situation where he could easily get edgy, but – whatever Guy said about needing to find his style – Nate knew that really he was here to get him out of the way until he'd proved that he could keep that edginess, that feeling that started in his gut and grew until it felt like an unscratchable itch on his brain, under control. He was, as his grandmother would have put it, being tested.

'Where's the lad?' Flinty, the apparently missing woman everyone else was looking for, came into the kitchen from the door Nate assumed led to the rest of the house.

'Adam? I think he's looking for you.'

She shook her head. 'He should be in bed by now.'

It was after nine, but Adam looked a bit past needing anyone to tell him when it was bedtime. 'I think he went out...' Nate gestured towards the far door that led to the corridor and the outside world. 'There was another lady who was looking for you too. Veronica?'

'Veronica.' The woman smiled. 'She's the lady, you know.'

She was *a* lady, certainly. Nate nodded. 'Well, she was looking for you.'

'Good. She'll be wanting to go over...' The woman looked around and stopped on Nate. 'Are you a friend of Adam?'

'I work here. Just arrived.'

'Right.' She nodded briskly. 'The new lad.'

'We met before.' He gestured at his half-cleared plate. 'You cooked salmon for me.'

Her face showed no flicker of recognition, but she nodded again. 'Of course. I'm not stupid.'

'No. Of course you're not.'

Footsteps in the corridor. 'Margaret!' Veronica led the searchers back into the kitchen. 'Where were you?'

'I've been here. Where else would I be?'

'At home? An hour ago?' Veronica's tone was exasperated.

'Aye, well, I'll be on my way now then.'

The two older women made their way off. Bella frowned. 'What was all that about?'

Adam shrugged. 'No idea.'

Nate didn't say anything. He had a very strong idea what he'd just seen. He'd seen it before, but he wasn't here to get involved. He was here to pay his penance and then make it back to London refreshed and better than ever. At least being here would be a rest. Teaching a few tourists how to spatchcock a chicken would be a walk in a park compared with seventy-five covers for pre-theatre dinner on a Friday night.

'Come on,' Adam said. 'I'll show you your digs.'

Nate followed Adam back outside and through the archway he'd arrived by. 'You're out in the coach house. We were going to put you in the Dower House but Fiona...' Adam grimaced slightly. 'You'll meet Fiona. She's our business manager.' He paused. 'Or something like that. We haven't quite found a job title she and Bella both like. Anyway, Fi went very quiet and very stern-looking at the idea of giving one person a free four-bedroom cottage that we could be renting out to tourists, so you're in here. Hope that's OK.'

Nate didn't really care where he slept. So long as there was a bed and somewhere to take a piss and have a shower, he wasn't that interested in the comforts of home.

'It'll mean you're next to residential students, but we've put you upstairs at the end of the corridor so they won't be traipsing past your room,' Adam added.

'Fine. Whatever.' It wasn't like he was going to be here for a long time.

The room was clean, looked freshly painted, and had a bed, wardrobe, chest of drawers and small desk. What else could he need?

'The bathroom is straight across the hall. You're sharing with one other room, I'm afraid, but we've put a note on to always book that one out last so most of the time you should have it to yourself.'

'It's fine.' It was a lot better than the attics and sofas he'd made do with during his stages in Paris and Nice.

'We do appreciate you coming. I mean, it must be a big change from a fancy London set-up.'

Just a bit. Nate shrugged. 'Favour for Guy, really, innit? He must be fond of your girl.'

'Yeah. I know Bella is fond of him. She reckons he helped her a lot when she was starting out.'

That sounded like Guy. Nate wondered, for a moment, how many waifs and strays had come before him, and then, for a more anxiety-spiking moment, how many would come after him. He'd been in Guy's orbit for nearly eight years now. He couldn't expect to stay flavour of the month very much longer.

Adam was still talking. 'So that's the plan? If that's OK with you.'

Don't style it out. Don't pretend. Guy had noticed pretty early on that Nate had a tendency to get distracted by his own thoughts, or by a random glint of light, or a buzzing from the lights, or, well, anything really. He'd also noticed that Nate was convinced that he'd be in trouble if he admitted to having missed anything so often tried to wing it and hide his failure to pay attention. That never helped. 'Sorry, mate. I missed that. What was the plan?'

'No worries. Tomorrow, Bella has a half-day parents-and-kids' cake-decorating class thing from nine thirty until half-twelve. The plan is that you'll sit in and get a feel for how things work and then after lunch she'll go through the schedule for the next few weeks and go through what's already planned and what you can take over and all that. Sound good?'

Parents and kids cake decorating sounded horrific. Why had they even bothered getting a proper chef at all? This wasn't cooking. It was playtime for grown-ups. Nate took another deep calming breath. He wasn't here to complain. He was here to show that he could suck it up, take his time out and come back stronger. 'Great,' he replied. 'Sounds great.'

—

Darcy perched on the edge of her bed and found herself, strangely, unable to move. Not physically unable – all her limbs were in tip-top working condition – but heavy with the effort involved. She wondered for a moment if she was sad. She was allowed to be sad. Grief, she'd been told by many a well-intentioned soul, wasn't linear. She would feel worse before she felt better.

Darcy didn't think she felt sad. She didn't really feel anything. She could just stop here and somehow, she thought, the world would carry on without her. In her mind vines wrapped around the castle and snuck in through the windows, growing around her room, until they swallowed her whole. While outside life skipped on until the strange American lady in the tower was nothing more than a fairy tale.

How ridiculous she was being. She shook her head, forcing a movement to shake away the inertia. She wasn't about to be cocooned. She was about to stand up, pick up her wrap and go down to the kitchen where she would pour herself and Adam a glass of wine, and Bella a glass of sparkling apple juice, and they would chat about the day, and all would be well. Darcy would be well. She took a breath, pressed her hands into the mattress and pushed her body up to standing. *There. You see. Perfectly well.*

Downstairs, Bella was wiping down the already spotless kitchen. Her laptop was open on the island. Darcy poured them both a drink, grabbing a third glass for Adam, who came in from the courtyard a moment later.

'New boy's all installed in his room.'

New boy? Oh. Of course. Another change. Another ripple of the world moving on around her while Darcy stood still. 'I should have come and said hello. Sorry,' Darcy apologised.

'It's fine. You'll meet him soon enough. Flinty and Veronica were here,' Bella added. 'So he got a good introduction to Lowbridge.'

'What's he like?'

'Young.' Bella laughed.

'He's about five years younger than you, if that,' Adam objected.

'I know but he's all shiny and ambitious, isn't he?'

'Yeah. He is a bit.' Adam paused. 'Not sure how he's going to fit in with… everyone here.'

'Fiona'll love him,' Bella pointed out. 'She can put fancy Michelin restaurant chef blurb on our adverts.'

'And the rest of the village?' Darcy asked. The community of Lowbridge was very special to her. They'd taken her in when she arrived as the new lady of the manor, but they could also be a little overwhelming to the unwary.

'Oh, they'll eat him alive. We should probably keep an eye on him.'

'Or just tell Veronica to make them play nicely.' Darcy's mother-in-law was a real force to be reckoned with.

Bella laughed. 'Yeah. That would probably work too.' She glanced at Adam, and Darcy caught them both looking at her and then back to each other.

'Darcy,' Adam started.

Her stomach clenched a little. She knew where this was going. 'Yes?'

'Tomorrow?'

Yes. Tomorrow. One whole year. She reminded herself that Alexander hadn't only been her husband. He'd been Adam's father. 'Yes.'

'A year, since...'

A year since the love of her life died. Tomorrow morning at 11.30 a.m. it would be one year exactly since she'd shouted through to the estate office to ask if he had the phone number for the plumber and got no answer. It was such an inane way to find out your husband had died – marching into his office in exasperation at being ignored. Such a silly way to lose someone. And she was stuck with it. She would always associate looking for a phone number, calling out the question, feeling irritated at the plumber for sending the wrong invoice – she would associate all of those random mundane little things with the moment when her heart turned into stone.

'I wondered if you wanted to mark it at all? Whether we ought to...' Adam shrugged. 'I don't know. Do something. I don't have any plans.'

She supposed they should. That was what people did, wasn't it? One year on, they took a moment to remember, a moment even to exhale at the realisation that they'd made it through a year. A full cycle of Christmases, birthdays, anniversaries and shifting seasons had passed and they'd survived. And now they were in a place where they could remember but still move forward. That was what a year was supposed to be, wasn't it?

'I thought I might spend some of the day in the garden,' Adam added.

Darcy nodded. That made sense. The castle's walled garden had been Alexander's pride and joy, and Adam had inherited his dad's green fingers. 'That sounds nice. I might come out and sit with you for a while.'

She could manage that. She could sit in the garden and smile and nod. She could do that for Adam, at least.

-

Nate lay in bed. It was barely ten at night. He couldn't remember the last time he'd been in bed before midnight. Normally service finished, and then there was clear-up, and then a drink or two to wind down, and then back across London to Ilford and finally to bed, where typically he'd scroll his phone until it was almost light and then grab desperately for a few hours' sleep before it was time to start again.

Thanks to the Owl's interventions he could enumerate very clearly all the reasons that this was unhealthy, and he had agreed to the suggestion that this temporary move to the Highlands would be a chance to form some better sleep habits. So here he was. In bed. At five past ten.

No reason not to go to sleep. No reason at all. The bed wasn't amazing, but it was a lot more comfortable than the lumpy single in the rented room in his shared house in London. The room was cool, but, despite Adam's apologies about draughts and chilliness, not too cold. And it was quiet.

Maybe that was the problem.

Nate couldn't remember ever having a quiet place to sleep. He'd been in shared flats and houses in the capital since he was seventeen, and before that group homes and foster care. There was always someone shouting, or moving around, or cars racing past outside. There were footsteps stomping down hallways, and lights flicking on and off beyond his door.

This should be better. Quiet, dark and still. The perfect conditions to just drift off into serene sleep. Nate rolled onto his side, and then back onto his other side. It wasn't right. The quiet wasn't restful. It was heavy. It was unknown and unknowable.

He sat up, flicked on the lamp next to the bed, and picked up his phone. He scrolled to a podcast app and set an episode playing. And finally, with light and voices around him, Nate Turner fell asleep.

Chapter 4

Cake decorating for parents and kids was, if anything, even more chaotic than Nate had imagined. Somehow his brain had allowed him to picture sweetly turned out, prettily pigtailed young girls who looked to have stepped right off the pages of an Enid Blyton boarding-school story, who would pipe neat little roses onto cupcakes. That seemed appropriate for a castle that might as well have been lifted from a children's book. The reality was rather more disordered. Any pretence that being sent here was not a punishment was rapidly abandoned in the face of his first cookery school class. It was as far from Michelin star kitchen territory as Nate could imagine being. He could be cooking over an open fire in the middle of a jungle and it would look more like the sort of cooking he understood than anything happening in front of him right now.

Firstly, the 'parents and kids' brief had been interpreted fairly loosely. Two of the 'parents' were, Nate assumed, grandparents, but it turned out were actually babysitters for children from the village or surrounding area. Both those ladies barged into his 'getting to know you' chat with Fiona, the castle's manager, and introduced themselves to him vigorously and rather forcefully.

'I'm Anna,' the older one started. 'I do the shop. Bella says you're a cook.'

Nate nodded, as Fiona made her excuses, or abandoned him to his fate, depending on your point of view.

She looked him up and down. 'You're a lad though.'

'Yeah.'

She glanced at the other lady. 'Well, I suppose you have to let them have a go.'

The other lady visibly suppressed a giggle. 'I'm Nina. I sometimes help out at the cookery school – just basic stuff, but I do a lot of the cooking for the village pub so I know my way around a roast and a pie dish.'

'Great.'

Nina pointed at two very small, bespectacled children. 'I've brought Albert and Hippolyta.'

'Hippolyta?' Nate queried.

Nina nodded. 'They did a module on Greek myths at primary school. Her mum liked the name.'

'OK. You don't meet many Hippolytas.'

'Thank goodness,' Anna muttered. 'I'm with Evie. She's my great-niece. Staying with us for the school holidays.'

Evie was, by looks, the oldest child here. Slightly too old, really, for baking with her great-aunt. She sat herself down on a stool at the island and sighed loudly.

Anna narrowed her eyes and looked at Nate. 'So you're the new boy?'

'I am.'

'Well, we'll see how that goes, won't we?' Anna nodded stiffly and took a seat next to Evie.

Bella beckoned Nate over. 'Don't worry about Anna.'

He hadn't been. Why would he care what some random woman thought of him?

'She just likes people to know who's really in charge around here,' Bella continued.

'I thought you were in charge.' That was a half-truth. From his first evening in Lowbridge, Nate had the strong impression that Veronica and Flinty were in charge.

'Well, yeah. Of the cookery school.' Bella shrugged. 'But the village is more of... well, not a democracy. More...' She shook her head. 'You'll see. You met Nina too?' she asked.

'Yeah.'

Bella looked away for a second, but Nate still noticed the grin she was trying to hide. 'Good. Good to get to know the local movers and shakers. Nina's going to be covering our regular absolute beginners' classes. They all love her, anyway. It's like having their mum or their nan teach them to cook, which most people don't have any more, do they?'

Did they ever? 'I guess not.'

'My nan loved to bake,' Bella continued. 'None of what she'd call "that cheffy nonsense", but cakes and pastry. Bread sometimes.'

Nate tried to keep his irritation at the phrase 'cheffy nonsense' off his face.

'She taught me the basics, really,' Bella continued. 'How about you?'

What about him? He was here to work, not to become bosom buddies. He shrugged.

'Did you cook much at home?'

'Not so much.' Nate was well practised in keeping things vague when people asked about his childhood. He wanted to be judged on the chef he was now, not the kid he'd left behind. 'I learned when I started work, really.'

'Fair enough. Anyway, so I don't need you to do much today, just hang out, chat to people, see how it works. This is a bit of a weird session – we mostly have adults, but you'll see that when we go through the schedule this afternoon, and this'll give you a taster.'

The class itself was chaotic and loud. Fun, for sure, but Nate wasn't convinced anybody's culinary skills were actually being improved. Nina was stepping in here and there to help out, which would not happen when Nate was teaching. It was going to be his kitchen, and his rules.

Hippolyta was clapping excitedly at her latest creation. Nate watched as Bella leaned towards her. 'A ladybird? Great job.'

'I want to make a ladybird,' Albert immediately decided, followed by a chorus of other new ladybird devotees.

Bella checked the fondant icing she'd already prepared. 'Nate, mate, could you colour half of this red and roll it out again? There's a board in the scullery.'

She pointed towards the corridor leading to what Nate thought of as the two prep kitchens, at least one of which was apparently a scullery.

He could, of course, colour half the fondant icing red. There was no job too small in the kitchen. No jobs you were above if you were part of the brigade. That was Guy's motto. Everyone started out on the basics, and everyone was expected to clean up, and could be sent to wash pots if things were busy. No airs, no graces.

Even so. As he dripped red food colour into the fondant and kneaded it in, before rolling it out to a perfect pound-coin thickness, Nate had to admit that some jobs did feel out of step with his status. His food had been written about in *The Observer*. He'd been on *MasterChef*, admittedly in the background while Guy took centre stage, but he was there, stepping in when a woman from *Made in Chelsea* couldn't keep up with the number of orders for lamb cutlets during lunchtime service. Rolling out fondant for six-year-olds to make ladybird cupcakes wasn't part of his career plan.

He carried the perfect red fondant sheet back to the main kitchen on a board and handed it over the heads of their charges to Bella. 'OK,' she called. 'Ladybird time.'

'I don't want to do a ladybird.' Albert folded his arms across his chest.

Bella beamed. Nate resisted the urge to force fondant icing down the kid's throat.

'OK. Well, how about a post box? Or a fire engine?' Bella suggested.

'Or a poppy?' Nina added.

'Or Father Christmas.'

Soon the group were settled to modelling a range of red-themed cupcake toppers, and one entirely miscoloured Elphaba.

—

Nate slipped out into the courtyard. He knew he was supposed to be observing, but he'd already seen quite enough. He couldn't stay here and teach toddlers how to use a cookie cutter. He pulled his phone from his pocket and rang the office number for La Mer. The voice at the other end confirmed that Guy was in. Nate waited to be connected.

'Hello, Nate. What can I do for you?'

'You can let me come back.'

No response.

'I'm sorry. I know I messed up and this is punishment, but I've learned my lesson.'

'You've only been gone twenty-four hours.'

'But I get it. You don't have to make me do time in kiddy baking classes. I can work on my style in London.'

'Nate…' Guy's voice was weary. 'I'm not in charge of you. If you want to come back to London then do, but you're on sabbatical from La Mer until the end of Bella's maternity leave.'

'What? No.' Nate was desperate. He belonged at La Mer. 'I'll keep it together. You can make Jules head chef. I don't care.'

'Don't you?'

Of course he cared. 'I don't mean that I don't care.'

'I understand that working up there is different.' Guy's tone was softer now. 'But I really think you should take this opportunity to show what you can do.'

'I can do that in London.'

'No doubt, and if you want to come back down, I'll write you an excellent reference.'

Horror sat hard in Nate's gut. 'You're firing me?'

'No. I'm just observing the sabbatical you agreed to.'

So he'd be job hunting. That wasn't an option. Nate couldn't be unemployed. He'd worked since he was fifteen years old. He didn't have rich parents to run back to if the money stopped coming in.

'And you made a commitment to Bella. As did I.'

'Fine.' What else could he say? 'You're right.'

'I'm glad to hear it.'

Nate hung up the phone.

'Who you all sad-faced at?' He turned towards the voice behind him. Evie, Anna's great-niece, was slumped on a bench behind him, phone in hand. 'Girlfriend? Boyfriend?'

'No.'

'Sure.' She didn't sound like she believed him at all.

Nate took a seat next to Evie. 'Not enjoying the class?'

'It's, like, fine.'

'It's ridiculous.'

She pulled a face. 'S'not ridiculous. It's fun for the little kids, innit?'

Fun for little kids wasn't part of Nate's culinary repertoire, or ambitions. 'You're staying with your great-aunt for the school holidays?'

'Not for the holidays,' she explained. 'Homeschooled.'

Nate frowned. 'Oh right. Is that cool?'

She shrugged. 'S'boring. But school was… meh. My mum took me out.'

'Right.' Nate let the silence sit, just like the Owl did to him in their sessions.

'But then she didn't have time to deal with me being round all the time so she sent me up here.'

Nate nodded. 'Mums can be shit.'

Evie looked at him. 'That's not what you say.'

'What?'

'That's not what adults say. They say she's probably very busy, and this will be like a lovely holiday, and they're sure she's missing me.'

Yeah. That was what people said. Nate shook his head. 'Well, they might be right, but I don't know that, do I?'

Evie looked wary. 'She is very busy.'

'What about your great-aunt?'

'She just doesn't know what to do with me.'

'But she wants to do stuff with you,' Nate pointed out.

'Is this the bit where you tell me I ought to come back in and embrace cake decorating?'

Nate bit back a laugh. Evie was a lot more aware than he'd been at her age. 'If I have to, I don't see why you should get out of it.'

Evie pulled another face. 'That's like super-negative energy to be going in with. You've gotta, like, put out into the world what you want to get back, you know.'

Nate wanted to be head chef at La Mer. He still didn't see how putting out layers of terrifyingly scarlet fondant icing got him nearer to that goal.

Evie shook her head. 'Millennials,' she muttered.

'I'm not a millennial. I'm basically gen Z.'

She laughed. 'No way.'

'I'm twenty-four.'

'Shit, mate. You gotta moisturise. You look old.'

Great. He was stuck here. He had no idea what Guy expected him to do to prove himself and he looked decrepit.

'I can probably count this as a food and nutrition lesson, can't I?' Evie got up and headed back towards the kitchen.

Nate didn't have much choice but to follow her.

'Nathan!' Fiona's voice from across the courtyard stopped him in his tracks. He waited for her to jog over to him and thrust her phone screen into his face. 'What does this picture say to you?'

The picture on the screen was of Fiona – head and shoulders, dressed in a purple work blouse, perfectly made-up, hair neat. 'I don't know.'

'Would it make you want to slide into my DMs?'

'I'm not…'

'Or ask me out?'

Nate tensed. *You don't shit where you eat.* That was one of Guy Fforde's immutable workplace rules. People did, of course. With the hours they worked it wasn't like you really met anybody else, but Nate had to be on his best behaviour here. Getting sent back to London because he'd got jiggy with a colleague wasn't the vibe he needed. 'I don't know if that would be appropriate.'

Fiona shook her head. 'No. Of course not. We work together and when Bella goes off I'll basically be your boss.'

Nate added another name to his mental list of people who thought they were in charge around here.

'That would be way out of line. And you're what? Nineteen?'

Great. So in two minutes of conversation he'd been dismissed as past it and then way too young. 'Twenty-four.'

'Even so. My bottom range is twenty-seven. And people who don't work here. But you're still a man.' She looked him up and down. 'And I can't find Adam.'

Nate looked at the picture. 'What's it for?'

She stared at her shoes. 'I'm signing up for some dating apps.'

Right. Finally, parts of the conversation were making sense. Nate wasn't generally on the apps, but he'd had enough break-room chats with colleagues who were to understand the basics. 'It's a bit formal, maybe.'

Her face fell.

'I mean, you look great. Just, do you have anything more Instagram and less LinkedIn?'

Fiona stared at the image. 'The last person I was with liked me to be presented a certain way.'

'OK.' Nate wasn't sure he wanted to pull on that thread.

'And until Bella makes her mind up, I don't even know what to put for my job. Is it "business manager"? "Business and marketing"? "Events and marketing"? Nobody will decide.'

'I'm not sure that matters that much for dating apps.'

Fiona sighed. 'Maybe you're not the right person to ask.'

'I just mean do you really wanna date someone who's mostly interested in your marketing expertise?'

'Well, I certainly don't want to date someone who's slapdash about details.'

'OK.'

Fiona stared again at the picture. 'Too formal,' she muttered. 'Right. I'll add that to the spreadsheet.'

There was a spreadsheet? 'It's not a bad picture, but maybe think about how *you* want to present yourself?'

Fiona nodded curtly. 'I need to do some more research. I wonder if there's a way of identifying the most successful accounts and creating a diagram of common features in how they come across.'

'Or you could just be yourself?' Nate suggested.

Fiona patted his shoulder in a way that felt like she was consoling him. 'Well, maybe. If the research plan doesn't work out.'

—

Darcy walked along the side of the castle towards the walled garden. Adam would be in the garden and would be expecting her to come by, at the very least, to share a hug and a quiet word about Alexander and what he'd meant to them both. And that ought to be what she wanted too. A year as a widow. A year since everything fractured. She should want to mark that. She should want to take a moment to reminisce and look back and shed a tear.

She didn't want it. She feared it. The uncontrollable stab of pain she'd felt constantly when Alexander first passed had gone now, but she knew it could still come back at any time. For months she'd found herself going through her day quite normally and then suddenly in tears at the slightest thing. The first daffodils coming up and the realisation that Alexander wouldn't see them. Bella putting more chilli than usual in a recipe and Darcy catching herself wondering if it would be too hot for Alexander's conservative taste buds. If tiny things like that could set her off then she knew she'd be a mess actually sitting down with Alexander's son and marking the year since he left them. And knowing that shot of pain was coming felt like voluntarily stepping into the path of an oncoming train.

It didn't matter what she wanted though. This was Adam's loss too, and he wanted to remember his dad. The least she could do was support him in that. Alexander would expect her to support his son.

She stopped at the entry to the walled garden. There were quiet voices inside. Of course. Alexander wasn't only someone's husband and someone's father. He was someone's son.

She pushed the worn wooden door open. Veronica Lowbridge was sitting on the bench nearest to her. Adam was squatting alongside a vegetable bed a few feet away, his back to Darcy as she came in. 'I've replanted this from seeds he'd saved,' Adam explained.

She knew that mattered to him. For Adam, the garden was a continuation of his father's work, a continuation, really, of his father. He was creating life from plants his dad had grown and planted, and using seeds he'd harvested and saved. 'He'd love that,' Darcy replied.

He truly would. Alexander understood that this garden was a living, moving thing – the idea of it continuing after he'd gone would have delighted him. She knew he would have been proud to see what Adam had done. Of course he would. She waited for the pang of anguish and the tears to come. Not yet.

Adam looked round as she spoke. 'Darcy! OK. So now we're all here, I thought we could raise a glass. I found some sloe gin in his tool shed. Still sealed.'

'Why not?' They would raise a glass. They would share memories, and the pain would come. Darcy could manage that.

Veronica nodded quietly, and they let Adam pour an inch of the sloe gin into mugs, which they chinked together. 'To Dad!'

'To Alexander,' Veronica replied.

Darcy just nodded and took a silent sip. Adam and Veronica needed this. She could bear another wave of the awful sadness to give them that.

'Did he always love gardening?' Adam asked.

Veronica nodded. 'Oh yes. Well, even as a child he loved having his hands in the soil. Mostly he seemed to pull up worms. Flinty and I introduced him to planting things in the hope of distracting him from popping worms in his father's slippers. Your grandfather did not find that amusing.'

Darcy could picture Alexander as a little boy, covered in dirt, running around Lowbridge causing havoc. That mischievous side of him had always been there, even if he kept it hidden under layers of lairdly responsibility. She waited, again, for the tears to come.

'I'm going to plant sweet peas against that wall.' Adam gestured to the wall behind Darcy, which got the best of the sun. 'They're almost ready to go out. You remember he always had sweet peas there when I was little?'

Darcy did remember. 'They were still there until, I don't know, recently.'

'I think last year,' Adam confirmed. 'But they're annuals and I didn't get new ones in last time round.'

'Annuals are the ones you plant new every year?' Darcy guessed.

'Yeah.'

She shook her head. 'Alexander said I was useless in the garden. Couldn't even remember the basics.'

She recalled the evenings they'd spent right here, with Alexander explaining what was what for the hundredth time and rolling his eyes at Darcy asking the same questions again and again. She loved those evenings. The realisation that there would be no more should set her off. Still nothing.

Sitting across from her, Veronica dabbed a tear away from her eye, and for a second Darcy envied her. She'd been in terror of the pain she knew this conversation would inflict on her, but now she felt robbed. There was no comfort in being beyond the searing anguish of Alexander's death. It wasn't better. It wasn't anything.

—

Afterwards, well, not actually afterwards – Veronica and Adam were still talking and sipping on the sloe gin – but as soon as Darcy thought was decent, she fled the garden and stopped, leaning back against the wall bathed in the morning sun. The bricks were warm against her skin, and she pressed herself against them to feel some sensation, but the idea of turning away from the castle and marching off along the cliff beckoned her – in those strange weeks after the funeral she'd walked up there a lot. None of the family knew what she did. None of them asked, and she'd have lied if they had. She hadn't been up there for a long time though.

She could have sworn she'd decided she wasn't going there today but her legs took over from her brain and walked her past the walled garden, away from the buildings and onto the cliff path, all the way up to the highest point, above the castle, looking out across the loch towards Raasay. No one could see her here, and no one could hear her.

When she'd come up here after Alexander's death, she'd had a sort of a ritual. She would open her mouth and she would scream. The noise would push up from her guts and fling out across the bay to be carried away on the wind. Somewhere inside her there had been a great well of emotion that she was balancing on the surface of. Screaming into the sky let out just a little bit – just enough for her to push the lid back down on the rest. And that was how she managed the boiling, rolling pain inside, when the hole in the heart of her was too deep and too heavy to be curated into words.

Darcy took a deep breath in, opened her mouth wide and... nothing. The scream she had expected to produce wasn't there. The tears she needed to shed weren't there. She kneeled down on the dry grass and just stared out to sea. She was supposed to be full of grief, or full of memories, or full of love searching for a place to land, but actually Darcy was just empty. Empty wasn't pain. And she was so tired of being so deep in pain. Empty must be better, mustn't it?

Nate wasn't used to having free time in the middle of the day. He wasn't really used to having free time at all. Nate worked. Nate slept. Nate worked again. At the end of the cake-decorating session, Bella told him to take a break. He could see that she was tired, and so he accepted her suggestion that they come back together later in the day to run through plans for the upcoming cookery school events, and nodded politely at her further suggestion that he take some time to have a walk and explore the estate.

Nate couldn't remember the last time he'd been for a walk without the express purpose of reaching a destination. He walked to the Tube. He walked to the bus stop. He walked back from the bus stop to his house share in Ilford. He didn't just walk for walking's sake. It was probably just the sort of thing Guy would approve of. Guy ran. Somehow, despite running multiple restaurants and appearing regularly on TV and bringing out a new cookery book every year, Guy still found time to run five K three mornings a week. Maybe Nate should try running. Maybe that would show the sort of commitment and motivation and focus that would impress his boss.

Nate was walking alongside a high wall that seemed to lead towards a path along the cliffs. What better place to kick off his new healthy habit? He picked up the pace to a jog, which he maintained for a good forty or fifty yards before bending over double. Obviously he wasn't wearing the right shoes. And he had jeans on. You couldn't run in jeans. As soon as he got back to his room he'd get online and order some running shoes, and one of those weird water things you carried on your back. And some shorts and... what else? Whatever else the internet thought you needed to be a runner, he guessed. For now perhaps walking was a sufficient challenge.

He continued along the cliff path. It was a weird place to walk. Sea on one side of him, hills on the other, castle behind him, and nothing but clifftop in front of him. It was a still, warm day, but a hint of chill fluttered around him in the breeze. He registered that you didn't quite get that in London. The buildings either sheltered you or funnelled the wind between them to knock you off your feet. Here the air danced around him like they all had all the time and space in the world.

What did people do in a place like this? People needed buildings and entertainments and offices and roads. Here there was nothing. Bella had suggested that if he took a walk along the clifftop he could look at the view. Was that a thing people did? Walk somewhere, look at the sea and the hills from a slightly different angle and then walk back. Why? They could at least have put a bar, or a cafe or something at the top to create some sense of purpose.

He had nothing else to do though, so he continued towards the higher point in front of him. As he got closer he could see that he wasn't alone. A woman was already sitting on the ground on the top of the headland, staring out across the bay. Nate started towards her, intending to walk on past and pretend that had always been his intention, but as he approached, she opened her mouth wide in the expression of a scream. Nate stopped.

The woman wasn't making a sound. It was eerie, more dreadful in a way than if she had been shouting at the top of her lungs. It felt as though he was witnessing some vast, unspeakable pain. Nate froze. A better man would offer something – some care, some wisdom to take away that agony. Nate had nothing. He recognised anguish but this wasn't Evie skiving out of cupcake decorating, or

Fiona faffing over a dating profile. This was something else entirely and he had no words to ease it.

He turned back and walked away towards the castle grounds. He couldn't just be in his room doing nothing. He'd tried going for a walk. Even without the woman on the clifftop, he wasn't sure he quite saw the point of walking when you didn't have a specific place you needed to get to. He'd been telling himself Lowbridge would give him a chance to rest. It was a slight shock to realise he didn't really know how.

Fortunately his new boss seemed to have the same weakness, because he found her sitting at the kitchen island with her laptop open.

'You were quick.' The tone was approving rather than accusatory. 'I was just going through the plan for tomorrow.' She turned her screen towards him. 'I've emailed you all this too, but basically it's a day of Scottish cookery.'

Nate scanned through Bella's impressively detailed notes. It was basic stuff. 'Fine. No problem.'

'We can do this one together, if you want,' she suggested.

For goodness' sake, nothing on Bella's schedule would challenge Nate further than boiling an egg. 'I think I can manage,' he said.

—

Darcy pulled herself together as she always did. It was good that she couldn't scream. It must mean she was moving on, progressing from the depth of grief that had consumed her. Maybe feeling nothing was just how things were now – like she'd had an allocation of feelings for life and she'd spent them all in fifteen wonderful years and a few unimaginably awful months. Perhaps that was supposed to be enough. Perhaps it was enough.

And she had things to do. She kept busy. That was the best thing, surely? Be useful. Be needed. Just keep on going every single day. She'd been acting as the estate's bookkeeper and admin person for nearly ten months now – years of temping in New York when she was trying to scrape together a living as a model had finally paid off and she actually had skills that were useful. Fiona was installed at the one desk in the office. Darcy stopped in the doorway.

'Oh. I was going to sort out the invoice round this morning. I know you did Kenny's for last week but he's booked again and there's the room bookings for community groups.'

'Oh, yeah.' Fiona nodded. 'Only, I was going to talk to you about that.'

'About what?'

'I've been setting this up. We used something similar for meeting-room bookings at the Other Place.'

The Other Place was the McKenzie estate – a much bigger and flashier venture on the other side of the hill, run by Fiona's slimy ex – from where they'd liberated Fiona a few months earlier.

Fiona spun her monitor so Darcy could see. 'So it's an online portal and they log in and book their space and it generates a payment page right there and then.'

'Right.'

'I mean, I'm just trying it out. I'm starting with Nina, cos she organises most things, but if it works for her we can give everyone who books regularly a login.'

'Great. That's great.'

'Yeah. So you won't need to spend so much time sending out invoices for every session.'

'That's really great.' Darcy had said 'great' too many times.

'And yeah, I did the outstanding invoices as I was setting it up. I was going through the groups we had in regularly anyway so I thought I might as well get things up to date.'

'Great.' Seriously, there were other words.

'Lightens your load a bit, doesn't it?'

'Yeah. I guess I'll get on with something else then.'

'Oh actually...' Fiona sounded uncharacteristically nervous.

'Yeah?'

'You took the photos for the website and leaflets and stuff, didn't you?'

Darcy nodded. She'd picked up a bit about photography when she was modelling. She was no David Bailey but she'd enjoyed feeling like she was helping.

'I wondered if you could take some of me?'

'For the website?' They had a staff profile section on the site.

'No. For my Tinder profile.' Fiona was back into business mode. 'I need at least three. At least one outdoors, and one more dressed up – like I'm going out out.'

'Do you go out out?'

'To the pub sometimes for curry night. Or with my dad to the quiz in Lochcarron.'

Darcy wasn't sure either of those really counted as big nights. 'OK.'

'I need to look approachable. Pretty but natural. Some skin but not too much.' She frowned. 'I mean, I think you get a lot of matches if it's all bikini pictures but it's quality as much as quantity, I think?'

'I'm not really an expert.'

'Do you have a tennis racket?' Fiona asked.

'What?'

'For the outdoor photo. Looking sporty and into physical exercise is a common factor in profile pictures.'

'Right. I'm not sure.'

'That's OK. We can take one in running gear.'

'Do you run?'

'I could run.' Fiona nodded. 'Fantastic. I'll put some looks together and we can do a shoot later in the week.'

A shoot? That was good. She wanted to keep busy. Photographing Fiona was a sort of busy. Darcy left Fiona to her portal and her dating app takeover plans, and headed to the kitchen instead. Bella was alone wiping down the island. Darcy checked the clock. The morning cake decorating must have finished. 'Good morning?' she asked.

'Yeah. There was icing sugar literally everywhere but people seemed to enjoy it, and some of them ended up with vaguely edible-looking cakes.' Bella paused. 'The new guy's a bit...'

New guy? New guy. Of course. She still hadn't actually met Bella's maternity cover. 'Nathan?'

'Nate, apparently. He's nice, I think. Bit cheffy. I'm not sure how he's going to get on with the sorts of groups we have here.'

'He didn't stay to help clean up though?'

Bella shook her head. 'Oh no. That's all done. He was just here actually. I knocked my mug over after he went.'

Darcy took the cleaning cloth off her. 'You're still supposed to be resting.'

'I'm not on bed rest or anything. And I'm not even officially on maternity leave for another couple of weeks. This is more of a handover period.'

Darcy smiled as sweetly as she was able. 'You know that will involve you actually handing things over?'

'We've been through the schedule for tomorrow. He's raring to go.' Bella winced slightly and lowered herself onto a stool. 'I'm just not sure. I mean he's never really done any teaching.'

'Well, neither had you before you started.'

Bella did not look reassured. 'I did offer to sit in.'

Darcy could picture exactly how Bella attempting to sit in would go. She'd be all good intentions to sit quietly at the back and let Nate do his thing but within ten minutes she'd have taken over and be working just as hard as she was at the moment, presumably pausing only to actually give birth before getting back to thickening her hollandaise. 'I thought you were planning to use the handover time to get on top of admin stuff.'

'Fiona's plenty on top of that.'

She certainly was.

'She is waiting on me to approve her marketing plan though. And the redecoration plans for the Dower House. And she wants to get quotes for renovating the north wing.' Bella rubbed her eyes. 'I do need to look at all of that.'

'Or Adam could.'

'He's going to be over in Edinburgh a lot the next few weeks.' Adam was a garden designer by trade and had kept his business in Edinburgh even after he moved back to Lowbridge to take over the estate. It was largely his income from that business that had kept them afloat for the last year. 'Trying to get ahead so he can take some paternity leave.'

'So you don't have time to babysit the new chef as well?'

'You're right.' Bella looked temporarily defeated. But only temporarily. 'But you could?'

Darcy shook her head. 'I don't know anything about cooking.'

'I'm well aware, but you know Lowbridge. And you know how we want the lessons to feel. You could, like, check out the vibe?'

Fiona didn't need her in the office. Molly was on top of the cleaning. Bella was the driving force, and now Nate was taking over the kitchen. And doing this would be useful. It would mean Darcy was still useful. 'OK then.' She nodded. 'And I can report back without making him feel like his boss doesn't trust him not to hold a kitchen knife by the pointy end.'

Bella frowned. 'It's not that I don't trust him. It's just that…'

'I get it. It's fine,' Darcy reassured her. 'You've built something special here. Of course you want to keep an eye on it.'

'So maybe I ought to be here…'

'The doctor said you should be avoiding stress,' Darcy pointed out. Now she'd found a purpose, she didn't want to give it up. 'Can you imagine anything more stressful than sitting here while someone else teaches cookery and not being allowed to chip in?'

Bella's frown deepened. 'I mean, I could chip in a tiny bit. Just if he wasn't doing it right…'

Darcy shook her head. 'Imagine how you'd feel if someone did that to you?'

'Fine.' Bella sighed. 'But you report back to me the second the sessions finish. Every detail.'

'Every detail,' Darcy agreed.

Chapter 5

Bella had told Nate three times now that she wasn't going to come to his first session. She didn't want him to feel she was checking up on him. Because she wasn't. Of course she wasn't. She was sure he'd do brilliantly. She absolutely trusted him. Wasn't worried at all. By the fourth time she told him, Nate did start to suspect that she was absolutely spinning out at the idea of handing over her kitchen to a virtual stranger. Her casual comment that Darcy, Adam's stepmother, might sit in 'just in case you need anything' confirmed that. It was sweet really, that she imagined he might need anything. Obviously he could cook this stuff in his sleep, so Nate was more than confident that he would knock this Darcy's socks off, so she would report back to Bella, and Bella would report back to Guy, and Guy would accept that Nate was ready to step up to head chef. All he had to do was impress this stuffy old castle lady and he'd be golden.

Today was the first day of a two-day Highland cookery masterclass for a tour group who'd stayed the previous night on Skye and then would have two nights with them before moving further north on their Scottish tour. Bella had already produced a plan for the two days and the larder was stocked with everything he would need, including what even Nate had to concede was an incredible-looking seafood delivery that had arrived this morning. The students had checked into their rooms. The first lesson was imminent, and then lunch, more lessons in the afternoon, more cooking the next morning, and then whisky tasting with Veronica Lowbridge in the afternoon. All rounded off with a grand Highland banquet, cooked for the attendees by Nate. Bella would be happy to help with that, she insisted. Bella wouldn't be able to bear not being in the kitchen to keep an eye on that, was what Nate heard. Fiona had greeted their guests and allocated their bedrooms with impressive efficiency, and absolutely no discussion about Plenty of Fish profiles. The only person he'd yet to be introduced to was his minder for the day.

And Nate was ready. Of course he was ready. Cooking a single portion demonstration for a group of novices was hardly a full Saturday night service at La Mer. He'd dressed in his chef's whites. He knew from the session yesterday that Bella kept things casual, but for Nate putting on his whites was like putting on armour. He wasn't Nathan the angry kid or Nathan the screw-up when he had his whites on. He was the chef. He had a role and a purpose. People treated him with respect. As a chef, at least, he'd earned that.

'Nate!' Fiona called through from the hallway. 'I thought you'd want to meet before you started.'

Meet who? He strolled to the door. Fiona was bearing down on him, followed by another woman. Model thin, cropped dark hair, wide blue eyes, and then she turned slightly and Nate caught her profile. It was the woman from the clifftop, the woman screaming silently into the abyss.

'This is Darcy. She's going to be sitting in.'

No. That couldn't be right. He'd been picturing a comfortably built, motherly sort, who'd be blown away by his culinary skills. 'I thought Adam's stepmum was sitting in.'

She nodded.

'But you're...'

'I'm what?'

Her voice rescued him from whatever he'd been about to say. 'American.'

She laughed. 'Well, some people are.'

Of course they were. And people moved around, and step-parents could be any age, really, when you thought it through. 'Great. Well, great. I'd better...' He turned back to the kitchen and walked away with what he hoped looked like purpose. He didn't need to do anything. He was entirely prepared already. He picked a spatula up, caught sight of Darcy staring at him from the doorway and put it down again.

'Hi?' A man stuck his head through the kitchen door. 'You must be Nate. I'm Kenny. I'm with the tour company.'

Nate grabbed the man's hand and shook it with vigour and relief at finding something to do. 'Good to meet you.'

'Fi says it's your first day.'

'Pretty much.'

'They're a nice enough group. Mostly Americans...'

'Well, some people are.' Nate echoed Darcy's comment and heard a definite sigh behind him.

'Just be prepared to have them tell you about their Scottish heritage,' Kenny continued. 'One older couple from somewhere in the Midlands as well. All very keen.' He checked his watch. 'You OK for me to bring them over now?'

Of course he was. Absolutely focused. 'Let's get started,' he said.

Darcy perched on a stool in the back corner of the kitchen and watched Nate Turner start his lesson. He was young, younger than she'd been imagining. Early twenties at most. At least he looked that young, unless Darcy had simply reached the age where everyone looked young. Thirty-nine was shortly going to tip over to forty. Maybe she was into her era of policemen looking like babies and shop assistants calling her 'madam'.

The lesson started with oatcakes. Nate moved quickly through the stages. The group crowded around him, watching him demonstrate a technique for them. He tipped the bowl in front of him towards the group. 'So that's the consistency we're aiming for. Breadcrumbs? OK. Then we just add a splash of water, enough to bring it together enough to roll it out and cut out our oatcakes. Everyone clear?'

The response wasn't overwhelmingly positive but Nate seemed happy they knew what to do. 'Great. Your turn then.'

The group dispersed to stations around the room, and the new guy pointed two pairs in the direction of the smaller prep kitchens that they used as overspill and then stopped in front of Darcy. 'You my minder?'

'No.' She shook her head. 'It's not like that.'

He smiled. 'It's exactly like that. And it's fine. If this was my kitchen, I wouldn't let some randomer take over without keeping an eye on things.'

Darcy found herself bristling at his reasonableness. Of course Bella wanted to keep an eye on things. Lowbridge wasn't just any kitchen. It was their home as well as their business.

'Look, I'm used to cooking a hundred covers a night at Michelin level. I think I can manage oat cakes with eight beginners.'

Now she was definitely bristling. 'Well, I'm sorry we're not up to your usual standards.'

'That's not what I meant.'

'I think we both know exactly what you meant.' He meant that this was beneath him – this kitchen that was Bella's pride and joy. This place that Bella, and Adam, and her Alexander, had dedicated their lives to wasn't up to Mr Fancy London Chef's standards.

'Well, come on. It's not exactly challenging, is it?'

Darcy went on the defensive on Bella's behalf. 'Actually, the cookery school has become very popular over quite a short time because Bella's teaching is excellent, so I'd hope you'd want to maintain the same standards.'

'Of course I—'

Whatever he was going to say next was interrupted by the sound of a huge crash from the scullery. Nate was already halfway there before Darcy was off her stool, but she caught up just in time to see him lifting a metal baking tray from the floor. The pieces of mixing bowl around his feet were going to be trickier to salvage. 'What happened here?'

It was the couple from the Midlands. The wife shrugged. 'I'm sorry, pet. I knocked the bowl and that knocked the tray and here we are.'

'Well, you'll have to start again.' There was an edge of irritation in Nate's tone. 'I'll get you fresh ingredients if you clear this up.'

'Oh no. I'll do that for you.' Darcy bent down to start picking up the shards. 'You're here to have fun,' she added a little more pointedly, but Nate Turner had already stalked out of the room.

The next part of the lesson was clafoutis batter. 'This isn't really Scottish,' Nate explained. 'But we're going to use a whole lot of berries that grow locally and it's a great way to use those up. And it's a bit different from just doing a pavlova or a crumble.'

Nate mixed his own batter in a matter of seconds, and set the group to do the same.

The first question came within a minute. 'Am I supposed to put all the milk in?'

For goodness' sake. 'What milk?' Nate asked.

The student held up the mini bottle that was on their station.

'No. That's for later. The double cream's for the clafoutis.'

'I think I put that in the oatcakes.'

Nate's jaw dropped open. 'How?' He shook his head. 'It doesn't matter. I'll get you some more.'

The next problem came before he'd finished dealing with that. 'Mine's all lumpy.'

He glanced into the bowl being thrust under his nose. It was indeed all lumpy.

'I think I put too much salt in.'

'My mixer won't work.'

'I used all the spoons for the oatcakes. Can I have another spoon?'

This was worse than cake decorating with children. The children, he now realised, had all come with a supervising adult to wipe their noses and clean up their spills. Now it appeared Nate was responsible for all of that. He was a long way from La Mer.

'Right. Shall we just go through this batter one more time?'

He struggled through to lunchtime, for which Bella had pre-prepared enough food to manage if the group hadn't produced anything edible. 'They will though,' she'd reassured him. 'They always do.'

Not this time. All of Bella's emergency food stock was brought into play, and Nate excused himself as soon as the group were settled at the dining table to try to clear the kitchen into a state where he could start the afternoon session.

By the time he got back there, Bella was already wiping down the island. She looked up as he came in. 'Busy morning?'

'Yeah. You know, par for the course, I guess.' Presumably this was just what happened when you let amateurs into the kitchen.

She was quiet for a second. An itch started in Nate's brain. 'Just that Darcy mentioned you'd had a couple of issues.'

The itch spread across the skin. 'I wouldn't say that.'

'A broken bowl?'

Breakages happened. 'That wasn't anything.'

'No. I'm sure. People drop stuff.' She finished wiping the bench. 'Just checking things are OK?'

'Sure.'

'Darcy also mentioned that...' She wasn't meeting his eye. 'Just remember that they're guests, right? Not juniors in a pro kitchen. They're here to have fun.'

The itch was turning into a burn. He tried to walk through the Owl's steps in his head. *Step away from the situation.* Tricky. He was trapped in the middle of nowhere with these people. *Wait until you're calm to express your concerns.* Again, not ideal when the students would be back from lunch in forty minutes. *Use 'I' statements to avoid aggression.* Fine. 'I feel that things went well.'

'Right.'

'I would prefer to be able to get on with things.'

He was 'I' statementing the shit out of this.

'I really don't feel there's a problem.'

Bella's face suddenly broke into a huge grin. 'Did Guy send you to that therapy bloke?'

'What?'

'Massive glasses, big office in Pimlico? Had a whole thing about expressing your feelings in "I" statements.'

'Yes!' Nate shook his head. 'Not you too?'

'Sort of. I only went twice. I told Guy I was fixed.'

'I tried that.' Nate felt the burning sensation receding. 'He didn't believe me.'

'Well, you're a terrible liar.' She gestured at the general detritus around the kitchen. 'I mean, you told me this had all gone fine.'

'It wasn't that bad.' Was it?

'I don't know, but I am going to step in this afternoon.' Her voice was calm but definite.

The itch roared back across his body. 'I can manage.'

She shrugged. 'Maybe, but my kitchen, my rules.' She patted her belly. 'For another few weeks at least.'

Darcy couldn't miss the glare Nate gave her as she came back into the kitchen. And she also couldn't miss the fact that Bella was front and centre again leading the lesson, with Nate acting as her spectacularly grumpy sous chef.

He was in front of her the moment there was a break in the demonstration. 'You told Bella I was shit.'

Wow. 'I didn't say "shit".' Although it would have been completely fair if she had. He'd been rude to the students, demo'd far too quickly and got annoyed when they couldn't keep up.

'You could have said something to me,' he pointed out.

'I said something to Bella.' She didn't have to sit here while he had a go at her.

Darcy looked right past Nathan and focused on the guest behind him. 'Is that a New York accent?'

The guy looked up and grinned. 'Was about to ask you the same thing. How long are you over here?'

Darcy shook her head. 'I live here.'

'Did you hear that, Pamela? This girl lives all the way out here.'

His wife looked up. 'Well, what brought you all this way, sweetie?'

'Oh, my husband. He's from, was from, here.'

Nate stepped in. 'This was his house.'

'His son's now,' Darcy corrected. 'He passed away.'

Pamela tipped her head to one side. People did that, Darcy found, like her grief was weighing them down by one ear. 'Oh I am sorry, sweetie. I lost my first husband too, Duanne. And my second husband.' She paused. 'He didn't die. He just ran off with a car park attendant. So not so much lost as mislaid.' She patted Darcy's arm. 'You're young. Still plenty of time for you.'

Darcy's whole body tensed. *First husband... plenty of time...* How dare she. Alexander wasn't her first husband. He was her husband. There wasn't plenty of time for anything without him. There was simply time, too much time, acres and acres of time that she was required to trudge her way through.

'I think maybe it's time to add the water now.' Nate directed the students back to their station.

Darcy slipped out of the kitchen door, along the corridor and out to the courtyard. This was when the pain would come. She couldn't summon it with memories any more, but the thought of moving on was different. It was unthinkable. She walked over to the bench at the furthest corner of the courtyard and waited for the tears to overwhelm her. Again, nothing.

And now someone was coming towards her. She looked up at the sound of footsteps, expecting to see Bella, but it was Nate who'd followed her out. Of course he had. He had no respect for anything here. No respect for the cookery school, for Bella, and certainly none for her pain.

'You OK?'

'I'm fine.' She must be fine, mustn't she? She wasn't a weeping mess. She wasn't dancing on tables. She was just sort of somewhere in the nothingness in between.

'Just, like, I thought maybe you weren't cos I saw you on…'

'Saw me where?'

He paused. 'On the cliff. Yesterday.'

Her whole body stiffened even further. 'Yes. Well, that wasn't anything.'

What had he seen? Darcy prostrate on the ground failing to scream. He must think she was insane. 'I just wanted to check…'

'Well, don't. I'm fine and I don't need some kid from London with an attitude problem fussing over me.' She stood up and marched away into the castle.

Darcy knew she ought to go back into the class. It would look odd if she dipped out now, but there was no way she could. Screaming on clifftops was not something normal people did, and failing to scream on a clifftop was a whole other level of crazy. It wasn't how Darcy wanted anyone to think of her, and especially not young, cocky little blow-ins from London, who didn't know her at all. If only he thought she was mad, but it was worse than that. She'd seen it in his eyes. He pitied her.

—

She made her way round the outside of the castle, checked that Nate had gone back inside and then headed back through the courtyard and out to the stables. Liberty and Larry didn't pity her. They did, she always thought, know when something was wrong though. Horses were sensitive, intelligent animals, and you had to form a bond with them. It would be more surprising if they didn't have a sense of how she was feeling.

'Darcy!'

She was stopped before she'd made it to the solace of the stables, by the shout from further along the path.

Flinty was bearing down on her, closely followed by Nina, Anna and Anna's bored great-niece who was staying with her for the summer.

'Darcy! We were looking for Bella but you're here and you'll do,' Flinty told her.

'I think Bella's in the kitchen.'

Anna nodded. 'Well, that's not right. She's got that new lad, hasn't she? Why isn't he in the kitchen?'

'I think they're both in the kitchen.'

'I should think so.' Flinty nodded. 'He's supposed to be helping. I hope he's not tiring her out.'

Nina sniggered.

'Have you seen him?' Anna asked Darcy.

'Yes.'

'And did you like what you saw?'

Darcy was aware that normally she joked along with conversations like this, but not today. Not him. 'He thinks he's far too good for Lowbridge.'

Flinty, Anna and Nina's faces all turned to thunder.

'I liked him,' Anna's niece offered.

The older women shook their heads. 'She'll learn,' Anna muttered.

'Anyway.' Nina seemed intent on pulling them back to the point. Darcy would be grateful if she did. 'We were talking in the shop – not officially talking, you see. It's not a group day.'

That was true. Ladies' Group wasn't until… Darcy ran through it in her head – Bella had a midwife appointment on Wednesday, green bins went out today, fish delivery came on Monday, so… tomorrow.

'But we were talking in the shop about the community hall.'

The community hall in the village had been unused for years. 'What about it?'

'Well, just with this place getting busier, now you've got Fiona…' Nina started.

'Not that that's a bad thing,' Flinty chipped in.

'No,' Nina agreed. 'It's good. Lots more people coming into the pub.'

'And the shop,' Anna added. 'And they spend as well. We've had to get more whiskies in.'

'Anything decent?' Flinty asked.

Anna shook her head. 'I mean, we keep your Veronica's behind the counter, but everyone else just buys the middle-priced one of whatever we've got.'

Darcy was reeling already from the silly woman in the cookery class, and the pitying look from fancy Chef Nate. She wasn't sure she could cope with the amount of mental gymnastics required to keep up with a conversation with Anna and Nina. 'What about the community hall?' she asked.

'Well, you remember before we started doing everything here? We were trying to raise funds to re-open it?'

Darcy did remember. Alexander had been a deeply private man, and when he was the laird the village hadn't been welcomed into the castle with quite the same enthusiasm as Bella and Adam offered, but the community hall in the village had been home to the local Scouts and Brownies and available for private parties and meetings.

'Well,' Nina continued, 'it's so busy here now that it's getting hard to book things in, and I know it's stopping Bella expanding the cookery school as much as she'd like – having things like parents and tots in the courtyard twice a week, so we thought maybe it was time to restart the fundraising?'

'We'd have a much better chance now, I reckon,' Flinty added. 'With all these new folk coming through with money to spend.'

'So anyway, special Ladies' Group tomorrow to plan the fundraising. We want everyone's ideas,' Nina explained.

'Well, not everyone's,' Anna muttered. 'Not daft ideas.'

'There are no bad ideas,' Nina shot back.

'Yes. There are. Like when Old Man Strachan wanted to do a bath of beans. Terrible idea. Waste of beans too.'

'That wasn't Old Man Strachan. That was his father,' Flinty objected.

'Well, he was Old Man Strachan then. Present Old Man Strachan was Young Strachan.'

'Then who was Young Strachan?'

'He was Young Strachan too.'

Darcy normally enjoyed these conversations. The way they meandered further and further from the point was restful in its own strange way, but today it was like something happening far away. It didn't concern her at all, and yet the noise of the voices felt like scratches across her brain. 'I'll think about it,' she promised. 'I have to go and...' She gestured towards the stables. Honestly, there was nothing that needed doing. Even Younger Strachan came in and mucked out five days a week now, so Darcy only had to do it on his days off. '...see to Larry,' she muttered as she walked away.

Larry, as ever, was just outside his stable door on the edge of the pasture, chewing contentedly. He was an old man, but he was her old man and she was determined to help him keep as fit as possible for as long as she could. She could make herself busy adding fresh bedding to his stall. At least Larry still needed her to look after him.

—

Nate sucked up his pride, let Bella lead the afternoon session and was therefore in a position to serve the students' own food back to them for dinner. Bella was a good teacher. And despite being very clear that he had messed up, she didn't seem angry with him. She ought to be angry with him. Nate was angry with himself. The Owl would have a field day with that fact. *Who are you really angry with, Nathan?* was one of his favourite questions.

Darcy hadn't come back to the cookery lesson after she'd walked out and she hadn't joined them for dinner. She'd need something to eat. Nate wasn't just angry with himself. He was angry with her as well. She'd run to Bella and told her Nate wasn't up to it. She thought he was a cocky little kid from London who knew nothing. Well, he'd show her exactly what he knew.

He checked through the ingredients for tomorrow's lesson and established that he could spare a couple of scallops. There was a thick chorizo in the fridge, and half a cauliflower left over in the larder. He jogged over to where his bike was parked outside the coach house and rescued a siphon flask from one of his panniers. Seared scallops with chorizo and a cauliflower foam. It wasn't as satisfying as putting his foot through the greenhouse glass like he'd done at a foster home when he was eleven, or as throwing a punch, as he'd done too often in his teens, but rage cooking also didn't leave him with the same flush of instant regret and shame.

Guy told all his chefs to put their passion into the food. He wasn't sure that saying 'fuck you' through scallops was quite what he had in mind, but it was what Nate was doing. Nate plated up his creation with care. Food should look as beautiful as it tasted, especially food that was going to show someone exactly who Nate was and what he was capable of. He carried the plate upstairs. Adam had told him that he, Bella and Darcy lived in the main house, so presumably Darcy's room was here somewhere. 'Darcy?'

No reply.

He knocked on a door. Nothing.

'Darcy?'

A door at the far end of the hallway inched open. Darcy Lowbridge peered out. She was wearing pyjamas, face clean of make-up, bare feet. 'Are you looking for me?'

'Yeah. I brought you some dinner.' He thrust the plate towards her. 'Just scallops with chorizo and a cauliflower foam.'

She shook her head. 'I wasn't going to bother.'

'You've got to eat,' Nate objected. He didn't add that there was a circle of hell for people who were capable of not bothering with food. He held the plate towards her. 'It's good.'

'Well, thanks.' She took it from him and stepped back into the room. 'Do you want to…' She looked behind her. 'Why don't I bring this down to the kitchen?'

'OK.' Nate followed her back downstairs and set about cleaning up his workspace. He didn't need to be staring at her to gauge her reaction. He'd hear the gasp of delight.

'Thank you. I like scallops.' She said it absently though, like she was remembering a fact rather than relaying a real enthusiasm.

Nate nodded. 'Are they local?'

'Probably. Bella tries to get everything locally if she can.'

'It must be a good area for produce.' Nate had never really considered the culinary delights of the Highlands, but thinking about the rural landscape and the expanse of sea and lochs around them, he could imagine it was a whole living larder of ingredients.

'Yeah. Beef, venison, all the seafood you could ever want.' Darcy took another mouthful of her meal and chewed silently.

'What?' Nate asked her.

'What do you mean "what"?'

What did he mean? He couldn't have a go at her for being insufficiently delighted. Actually, he could. 'You don't look like you're enjoying it.'

'No.' Darcy shook her head. 'It's lovely.'

Nate wasn't having that. He could spot an unhappy customer a mile away. Often you could spot the ones who were going to be miserable long before they sat down to eat. The ones who turned up twenty minutes late and fumed at the suggestion that their table might have been given to someone else. The ones who booked for four and turned up with six and told the front of house team they could easily fit them in. The ones that sent detailed instructions back to the kitchen as to how the dish should be cooked. Some people were geared up to hate everything you did for them. Darcy wasn't one of those. Was she?

'It's just...' She took another bite. 'It's great. Why does it need all these whistles and bells though?' She slid her fork through the cloud of cauliflower foam. 'What even is this?'

'It's cauliflower.'

'It's got bubbles. Is cauliflower supposed to bubble?'

Nate folded his arms. 'It's a foam. It adds flavour and moisture to a dish without adding bulk.'

Darcy wrinkled her perfect nose again. 'I'm sure it's very nice,' she murmured.

No. That wasn't good enough. It was clear that however good and fresh the ingredients were, what Nate had done with them wasn't making Darcy's heart sing. She still thought he wasn't good for anything. Crappy teacher was one thing, but he wasn't standing for her thinking he was a mediocre chef. 'So what do you love to eat?'

She shrugged. 'I'm not really fussy.'

'Too fussy for cauliflower foam.'

Darcy took another forkful of scallop and chorizo. However annoying and out of place Nate might be, he was clearly an excellent cook. Intellectually she knew that the things she was putting in her mouth tasted good, and she loved scallops. She ordered them a lot when they went out somewhere nice. She knew she liked them. Eating this plate should bring her joy but maybe since Alexander died, food didn't do that any more. She thought again. She'd got her appetite back after he died. She knew that. She remembered eating Bella's cakes and pasta, and Nina's pies, and them tasting wonderful and comforting. When had she last felt like that? She wasn't sure.

'Seriously, what do you love?'

Nothing any more. The answer dropped full and clear into her head. She shook it away. 'Anything's fine.'

'I'm aiming for slightly better than "fine".'

'I'll eat whatever. Mostly whatever Bella makes.'

'Bella's going on maternity leave, so you're stuck with me.' He leaned onto his elbows. 'OK. What was your favourite food when you were a kid?'

When she was a kid felt like a very long time ago and a very long way away. Because it was. 'That was a different life.'

Nate's tone was increasingly exasperated. 'I'm sure but, given that you're still alive now, you must have eaten.'

'Sure, but we weren't…' She waved her hand at their surroundings. 'We weren't rich, you know. Dinner was whatever we could scrape together.' She tried to think back. Cheap cuts of meat that had to be cooked and cooked. Whatever her mom could pick up at the end of the day before it got thrown in the trash. Apart from the days when... She smiled. 'Leftovers.'

'Your favourite meal was leftovers?' Nate pointed to her half-eaten plate. 'So if I take that away you'll love it tomorrow?'

Darcy bristled. 'Obviously not. Leftovers from my dad's work. He was a short order cook for a bit, and then he worked in a deli.' Another memory. 'He told me when I was little that it was the place where Meg Ryan faked her orgasm.'

'Katz's Deli?'

'You're too young to remember that.'

'My nan loved a romcom,' he said quickly, looking at the floor as he spoke.

His nan? Oh for goodness' sake.

'Carry on.' Nate turned his gaze back to her.

'I think he made the *When Harry Met Sally* thing up anyway. But it was kinda like that. If they messed up an order or made too many of something, sometimes they got to bring stuff home.' She could suddenly remember the thick sandwiches filled with deli meats, pickles and mayo. 'I think they messed orders up on purpose.'

'I can believe it.'

'He'd bring these sandwiches home and cut them up so we all got a bit.'

'OK.' Nate nodded. 'Challenge accepted.'

'No. I wasn't... you don't have to.' The last thing Darcy wanted was a fuss, and the absolute last thing was this arrogant, annoying twenty-something making a fuss.

'Too late.' He leaned back. 'I'm going to make you something that blows your mind while I'm here. I will show you how good I am.'

'You don't have to…'

'Oh, you don't know me at all, do you?'

Well, no. Obviously.

Nate's tone was dead serious. 'I cannot leave you unhappy with your food. It'll scratch at my brain and keep me awake at night. I'm going to cook something that you have no choice but to agree is fantastic, whether you want to or not.'

Darcy nodded weakly. There didn't seem to be a lot of point arguing with him, but honestly nothing excited or delighted her any more. Her horses comforted her. Spending time busy in the village and around the estate kept her going, but joy was a long way out of her reach.

Chapter 6

Ladies' Group had been a bit of a fixture in Darcy's life ever since she'd moved to Lowbridge. When she first arrived it had mostly been marked by endless cakes based on the need to feed her up. Apparently model thin was desirable when you were working as, well, a model, but not de rigueur at all in Highland villages. Then they'd grown a little wary of her as lady of the manor. There'd been mutterings, she thought, about Darcy swanning in and changing things. Not that she'd ever really tried to change anything. She loved Lowbridge – she always had – just precisely the way it was. And she'd pulled back to the castle, putting herself out there less and focusing on Alexander and her horses and life on the estate.

And now Adam and Bella had thrown down the drawbridge between the castle and the village, and Darcy had thrown herself, just as positively, back into village life. And all life was here. Who needed New York City when you could do spiritual drumming with Mrs Timberley from the pub every second Thursday? Mrs Timberley was at least eighty and didn't own any drums but was happy to let participants bash pots and pans until they felt at one with the universe.

Today's Ladies' Group was officially tai chi with Nina in Anna's back garden, but any sessions that were advertised as having an element of movement to them usually ended up with tea drinking, biscuit nibbling and discussions of how it was too late to get started now and maybe they'd put off tai chi, or samba for beginners, or getting started with Nordic walking, until next week.

Darcy and Fiona strolled over the bridge, matching Bella's increasingly slow pregnancy waddle. 'I was surprised you left Nate on his own,' Fiona said.

Darcy agreed. She'd been sure Bella would cry off Ladies' Group to babysit her new employee.

'He'll be fine. He knows yesterday didn't go very well.'

'Does he?' Darcy wasn't convinced about that. She hadn't seen anything close to contrition.

'I think so.' Bella laughed. 'And actually the students loved him. They thought he had a whole shouty Gordon Ramsay vibe. I think they thought he was playing the part of a highly strung chef.'

Fiona's eyes widened. 'Could we market that? Like "get your food criticised by a top chef" or something?'

Bella nodded. 'Could be an angle.'

Darcy didn't think that sounded like an angle. Shouty London chefs weren't what Lowbridge was about at all.

'I can't believe this thing doesn't come out for another two months,' Bella muttered, rubbing her back as she walked. 'I'm not gonna fit through doors.'

'You will.'

'Easy for you to say.'

Fiona grinned. 'You live in a castle. You have really big doors.'

'Fuck off.'

Fiona turned to Darcy. 'We should take a picture on the bridge. For my outdoorsy look.'

'What?'

'For her dating profile,' Bella reminded her.

Fiona thrust her phone into Darcy's hand. 'Take one now.' She looked up and down the bridge and across the bay. 'This way, so the sun isn't behind me.'

Darcy took a couple of photographs of Fiona standing by the railing, and checked her handiwork. She showed the screen to Bella, who pulled a face.

'What?'

'Just do you think you could look a little bit more relaxed?'

'I'm relaxed.'

'OK.'

Fiona was standing bolt upright, hands still at her sides, face fixed in a rictus grin. How to put this? Darcy bit the bullet. 'It just looks a bit more like a mug shot. I thought you were going for breezy and casual.'

'Breezy?' Fiona nodded. 'I can be breezy.' She shifted her body so she had one arm on the railing and half turned back towards the camera. It looked... uncomfortable. 'It would be easier if you'd found me a tennis racket to hold.'

Darcy found herself apologising for her failure to travel with sporting equipment about her person.

'How's that?' Fiona asked.

Darcy and Bella exchanged a look. 'Better,' Darcy conceded. 'Definitely better.'

After the impromptu photo shoot, they made their way to the far end of the village, where Anna and Hugh ran the Lowbridge shop from their garage, and shed, and a good part of their driveway on sunny days. They picked their way past the overflowing displays in the garage and through the side door into the garden. Anna was laying out tea things on the garden table. 'I thought we'd have a cuppa before this tai whatnot.'

'Tai chi,' Darcy supplied. 'It's supposed to be very calming. Gets you in touch with your body's energy flows.'

'I don't know if I want to touch my energy flows. Not out here with all you lot standing around watching.'

Darcy opened her mouth to explain but was cut off by the arrival of the rest of the group. First Flinty and Veronica – who seemed to have come around to village activities since she moved out of the castle and into Flinty's cottage on the main street – and then Nina and Netty, both stalwarts of village life. Nina in particular seemed to be in a constant state of polite warfare with Anna for Queen Bee status.

'Is the reverend joining us?' Nina asked.

'She said she was, but you know how she is. Never where she says she'll be.'

'That's not fair,' Darcy objected. The reverend was their local minister, Jill, who Darcy had always found to be entirely reliable.

'Well, she was supposed to come to walking group last week and she never turned up.'

'That was cos Old Man Strachan fell into that pit. She was out with the mountain rescue.'

'Yes. Well.' Anna shook her head. 'It meant Hugh had to walk with the slow coaches at the back. He was grumpy about that all day. And Old Man Strachan was fine. He had a sandwich.'

The other women nodded. 'I think he was more embarrassed than anything else. It wasn't like it was a new pit that had just appeared,' Nina explained.

'Should he still be out and about like that? He must be eighty at least,' Darcy pointed out.

The other women stared at her. 'Fit as a fiddle, Old Man Strachan,' Anna countered.

'Eighty's barely any age at all,' Flinty agreed.

Veronica frowned. 'Well, I'm sure we don't feel old in many ways, but Darcy has a point. None of us are getting younger.'

There was a brief silence while the group absorbed the twin glitches in the matrix of Veronica agreeing with Darcy, and the suggestion that she might be in any way affected by the ageing process.

'Tai chi is very good for maintaining mobility,' Nina announced brightly.

'I thought maybe tea first,' Anna said. 'I've done a Battenburg.'

Everyone nodded enthusiastically. No tai chi was being undertaken today.

Once tea was poured and cake was handed out, Veronica cleared her throat. 'So I understand you're keen to restart the community hall fundraising, Nina?'

Finally, the real point of the meeting.

'It's getting so busy at the castle. Not that we don't feel welcome,' she hastily added, glancing to Bella and Darcy, squashed together on a garden bench. 'But you've got more and more visitors coming; it would be wonderful to have some more facilities for them and the village.'

'So what would you want to use it for?' Bella asked.

'Well, community groups could go back to meeting there so it would be easier for you to open the castle up to visitors more days. And really anything else. We could have exhibitions, start a little museum about the village history.'

'Is anyone interested in village history?' Veronica asked.

'I don't see why they wouldn't be,' Anna harrumphed. 'We have fascinating history.'

Fiona broke the silence. 'Do we?'

'Of course. There was...' Anna faltered. 'Well, there was... the blizzard.'

'Which blizzard?' Lowbridge definitely had snow. Some of the snowstorms would fairly be described as big, but Darcy had never heard of one particular blizzard that stood out in village folklore.

'I don't know.' Anna folded her arms. 'I'm sure there was one though.'

'There was snow last week,' Flinty announced.

Darcy frowned. It was May and they'd had an unusually warm and mild spring so far. 'I don't think there was.'

Flinty peered at her. 'Was what?'

'Snow last week.'

'No. Of course not.' Flinty nodded to the flowers blooming in Anna's patio containers alongside them. 'It's practically summer.'

Darcy ran the conversation back through her mind. Like so many conversations at Ladies' Group, it made no sense at all. The best thing to do was just move on. 'Right. So, fundraising?' She addressed the question to Nina in a bid to get them back on track.

'Yes. Well, we have about fifteen hundred in the account already, from donations in the tin in the shop and at the pub.'

'Wow. That's a lot.' Bella raised an eyebrow.

'Thanks to you we have a lot more people coming through,' Nina explained. 'And Anna is quite...' She glanced at her frenemy. 'Quite efficient at getting people to donate.'

'I just encourage them.'

'I'm not sure refusing to hand over their shopping until they've donated is really encouraging,' Veronica observed.

'I don't refuse. I just don't rush myself.'

'Anyway, we already know we're going to need a lot more than that to do a full job, but I had a talk to Pavel last night,' Nina continued. Pavel was Nina's son – usually resident in Lowbridge as their local builder but currently off travelling around Europe with his girlfriend.

The women all beamed. Pavel was a sweetheart. 'Oh, how is he?' Darcy asked.

'And how's Jodie?' Bella added.

'They're both fine. Doing really well. They're thinking about going to America next. You know my dad had a cousin who moved over there, so they were talking about looking them up. And...' Nina smiled. 'He even joked about eloping to Vegas. I told him if they get wed without me there'll be hell to pay.'

'Quite right too.' Flinty nodded. 'We could all go to Vegas though. Like a girls' trip.'

'What happens in Vegas stays in Vegas.' Bella giggled.

'We could play blackjack and poker and...' Anna paused and stared at Darcy. 'What's the one with the spinny wheel?'

'Roulette?'

'Right. You'll know about that.'

Darcy tried to fathom for a second how or why she would be considered the group's roulette expert. 'Not really...' she ventured.

Anna shook her head. 'Being American though. They're into all that casino business, aren't they?'

'I guess.' Darcy had been to a casino precisely twice in her life. Once in Rome during her short-lived modelling career when she'd narrowly avoided getting sent straight home by her agency for turning up late to her fittings the next morning. And once in Edinburgh with Alexander not long after they first met, when she'd come back to

Scotland with him in a whirlwind of romance and excitement. They'd been staying in the capital for a few nights before coming back to Lowbridge, and they'd gone to a casino and played poker badly, and then put all their remaining chips on red and lost the lot. She remembered Alexander's wry shrug and his explanation that the odds in roulette weren't 50:50 at all. Because of that one green zero, the house ultimately always won. He'd looked a tiny bit wistful when he said that.

Of course casinos weren't his thing any more than they were hers. She'd thought him worldly and sophisticated, when in reality he'd been out of his comfort zone trying to impress a woman he'd seen as more exciting and dynamic than him. How strange to fall in love with such an erroneous idea of someone, and then fall in love all over again with their reality.

'Darcy!' Bella nudged her in the ribs. She hadn't been listening. She'd been desperately trying to think her way back to that hotel corridor with Alexander years ago, giggling on their way back to their still separate rooms. That was the real him. Cautious, respectful, patient, but romantic. He was, of course, out of her reach. 'Darcy!'

'Sorry?'

'Anna was asking if doing a casino night as a fundraiser was a good idea.'

'Erm, I don't know.' How would she know?

'Wouldn't there be a lot of rules about gambling and suchlike?' Veronica asked.

'If it's not commercial you don't need a licence, I don't think,' Fiona replied. 'But there are still rules about prize value and things. I could find out.'

Nina sucked the air through her teeth. 'You'd need a lot of playing cards. And them little token thingies. And waistcoats.'

Everyone nodded in agreement. Darcy didn't ask about the waistcoats.

'So what other ideas do we have?' Veronica calmly but very definitely kept the group on track.

Half an hour later they were staring at an unrolled sheet of wallpaper onto which they had, in Anna's words, 'done a braincloud'.

Fiona and Bella's suggestions that it was actually a brainstorm, or possibly a word cloud, did not gain much traction with the group. The braincloud included such gems as 'dye all the sheep pink' – pretty but not at all clear how it would raise money – and 'auction Pavel's gym stuff while he's away' – very quickly vetoed by Nina.

None of these ideas were good enough. They needed to do something bigger and bolder, something that would shake away the inertia that was pressing Darcy down. 'We could do a bungee jump.'

Nina wrote it on the sheet, in smaller letters, Darcy noticed, than she'd written the pink sheep thing. But it was a good idea. It felt good. The idea of falling, hurtling down towards the ground. That would be a rush, surely? 'Or a sky dive. Or...' What else? There must be something that would make her feel, well, something.

Veronica narrowed her eyes. 'Are you quite all right, Darcy?'

'Yeah.' She was fine. Absolutely unexcitingly fine.

'Very well. I'm not sure whether sponsoring someone for this sort of thing will bring in enough support.'

Fiona nodded. 'They can be really expensive to set up. We need something that doesn't cost the earth to do.'

Great. The first time Ladies' Group had ever been governed by good sense was when Darcy wanted to do something crazy.

Anna stared at the sheet. 'I mean, we could definitely put a bigger collecting tin in the shop,' she murmured.

'That's not going to get us very far very fast though, is it?' Nina pointed out.

They fell silent. They had a whole sheet full of ideas and nothing that was both practically possible and likely to raise more than fifty or sixty quid. That was a long way short of a new roof for the community hall.

The quiet was broken by the sound of a newcomer bustling through the garage door and into the garden. Reverend Jill arrived, as she arrived everywhere, in a flurry of curls and smiles and tote bags. She dropped her things onto the patio. 'Sorry I'm late. I forgot I was doing assembly at Lochcarron infants. Hadn't planned a thing. Just made them sing "All Things Bright and Beautiful" three times and then had them pretend to be creatures great and small. The headteacher was giving me right daggers by the end. Josie Logan was refusing to stop being a snail. And then Kenny rang just as I was getting in the car, and…'

All the ears in the group pricked up. 'Kenny rang?' Nina asked.

'Yes.' Jill was not forthcoming.

'So are you and he…' Anna leaned forward. 'Stepping out?'

'They don't say "stepping out" any more,' Nina replied.

'I'm not sure they ever did,' Veronica agreed.

'All right then.' Anna folded her arms. 'Courting then. Wooing. Is he wooing you?'

'I think she's already wooed,' Flinty pitched in. 'Just tell them he's your boyfriend and they'll stop going on.'

Telling them that seemed unlikely to discourage the women of Lowbridge from going on about it at all.

'He's not my boyfriend. He's a boy who is a friend.'

'What's the difference?' Anna asked.

'It means she's not doing you-know-what with him,' Nina explained.

'Well, I should think not. She's a vicar.'

'Vicars are allowed to do you-know-what.'

'I don't think they are.'

The group fell silent and turned as one to Jill, as if awaiting clarification on the vexed theological issue of whether vicars were allowed to do you-know-what. She sighed. 'It's fine. We just have to get a note from the moderator.'

'I don't think that's...' Anna started to object.

Jill ignored her and peered instead at the wallpaper. 'What are we doing here?'

'Fundraising ideas for the community hall.'

Jill nodded. 'Pink sheep?' she asked.

'We might have been a bit past our best by then.' Bella laughed. 'You got anything better?'

Jill paused. 'What about a talent auction?' she asked.

–

The morning at Lowbridge felt very different to the day before. Then he'd been confident. No. That wasn't right. He'd been complacent. He'd broken one of Guy Fforde's cardinal rules and thought he was too good for the dishes he was cooking. That wasn't OK. In Guy's kitchen you might be spreading jam on toast for a pre-service snack, you still spread it with care. You respected your ingredients, even if your ingredients cost pennies. Nate hadn't done that, and he hadn't respected Bella or her business either. Today he was going to do better.

Maybe that was it. Maybe that was the lesson Guy wanted him to learn. Should he message him now and tell him he was respecting the shit out of everything? Would that be his ticket home? It was a nice thought, but Nate knew, in his heart, that there was no fast track back to La Mer. He was stuck in the slow lane. All he could do was convince Guy that he'd made the most of it.

That was what he'd told himself when he'd sat up into the early hours of the morning watching YouTube videos of cookery demos, noting how the most effective ones took their time and broke things down into far more steps than Nate would ever have thought of. By four a.m., when he'd finally switched to a podcast to take the edge off the quiet while he tried to get to sleep, he had pages of notes breaking down every part of today's lesson. Messing up once was forgivable. If he messed up again he didn't know what would happen, but he knew that if he lost the job here there wasn't one automatically waiting for him back home.

He'd also noticed that Bella never took her eyes off the students. When they were working independently she was there, pulling tea towels out of the way of gas flames, and switching out sugar for salt before disasters occurred. So that was the second part of his plan. Observe everything. Check on everything. He wasn't a teacher, but he could cook and he understood how a kitchen should run. He would do the very best he could.

The lesson was still chaos, but perhaps it was a slightly more orderly chaos than the day before. Questions still came thick and fast but they were questions that suggested people had grasped the basics. By late morning Nate was almost enjoying himself. Everyone's venison was in the oven. Veg was roasting, and sauces were in progress.

He caught Jenny, the wife from the couple from the Midlands, looking anxious over her pan. 'What's up?'

'I don't think it tastes right.'

That was good. That meant she'd tasted it. *Taste everything* had been Nate's clear instruction, which he had then hastily had to row back to clarify not tasting raw things that ought to really only be eaten cooked.

He grabbed a clean spoon and checked the sauce. Not bad. A smidge more salt and a whole lot more blackberries. He opened his mouth to tell her what to do, and then stopped. 'What do you think it needs?'

'I don't know.'

'Well, what do you think? It's supposed to be savoury but fruity at the same time, cos the venison's rich so it can handle a bit of oomph in the sauce.'

She took another tentative sip from the tip of her spoon. 'More blackberries?' she asked.

Nate nodded.

'I don't think I put enough in. It looked like a lot.' She shrugged. 'It just tastes like regular gravy now though.'

That was exactly right. Nate felt something like pride in his chest. 'Great. So put the rest in.'

'Will that work? They were supposed to go in at the start.'

'It's better at the start but you've got time. It'll be fine. Just go for it.' Nate moved on to the next station.

Bob the Brooklyn grill chef. 'What are you grinning at?'

Nate hadn't realised he was. 'Nothing. How are you getting on?'

By the end of the session, despite Nate's novice teaching skills, the group had stirred, chopped, roasted and sauteed themselves an entirely edible lunch. He was just clearing that away and calming himself by restoring order on the kitchen when Veronica Lowbridge arrived, with – from what he could glean – her partner, Flinty, in tow to lead the afternoon whisky tasting.

'Good afternoon, Mr Thomas.' Veronica greeted him formally. Nate had spent enough time in very fancy places to be comfortable with that.

'Nice to see you again.'

'And you're settling in well?'

He nodded. 'I've set everything for the whisky tasting out in the...' He frowned. 'Not the dining hall...'

'The dining room?'

'Is that the one next to the stairs?'

Veronica and Flinty exchanged a look. 'That's the small dining room.'

'Right. Then maybe the dining room.'

'Before the ballroom. After the Yellow Room?' Veronica asked.

Nate had learned this part. 'The Yellow Room's the green one, right?'

'You might say that,' Veronica conceded.

'Then yes. It's in the dining room.'

'Thank you.' She glanced up at the clock. 'And they're due back at half past?'

'Yeah.' Nate grinned. 'I rationed the wine at lunchtime a bit so hopefully they're not half-cut already.'

'Very sensible. I do always try to encourage them to simply taste the whisky but people do get carried away.'

'Well, you've got to get your money's worth, haven't you?' Flinty nodded. 'And they're on their holidays.'

'I'd like them with it enough to enjoy the dinner tonight though,' Nate pointed out.

Veronica smiled very slightly. 'I make no promises.'

Nate thought of something else as the two women started to make their way out of the kitchen. 'Wait. Sorry. Darcy…'

'What about her?'

'She grew up in New York?'

Veronica nodded. 'Indeed. Not her fault I suppose, but still.'

Nate stifled a laugh.

'Course it's not. I mean, this one's English.' Flinty nodded in his direction. 'You can't hold him responsible for that either.'

'No. Erm… Thanks?' Nate tried. 'Anyway, Darcy's dad worked in a deli or diner or something?'

Flinty nodded.

'I just wondered if she'd ever talked about a particular sandwich he made that was her favourite.'

Veronica looked entirely blank. 'A sandwich?'

'Yeah.'

'Pastrami on rye,' Flinty supplied. 'With extra corned beef.'

'How on earth do you know that?' Veronica asked.

Flinty shrugged. 'She goes on about missing it all the time. The things she gave up for your Alexander.'

'I've never heard her mention that at all.' Veronica paused. 'Was this recent?'

Flinty hesitated, just for a second. 'I don't know. The days all merge, don't they?' She turned back to Nate. 'Pastrami on rye though. Extra corned beef. Why do you want to know?'

'Oh just thought, you know, if I'm taking over some of the cooking around here from Bella it would be nice to make people things they really love.'

'People?' Flinty asked. 'Or person?'

'No. It's not like that.' Quite the opposite. Darcy hated him for starters.

Veronica shook her head. 'Leave the young man alone, Margaret.'

He let them head off to get ready for the whisky tasting and sat down with his notebook. Pastrami on rye bread with extra corned beef. Straight away he was pretty sure there was only one of those ingredients that Lowbridge was going to be able to offer him. Maybe this was a stupid idea. Maybe he could just make her a massive chocolate cake and be done. Everyone loved chocolate cake, didn't they?

But that might not do it. He had to win Darcy Lowbridge around. She was Bella's eyes and ears in his kitchen. And Bella was Guy Fforde's eyes and ears at the castle. Which meant that Darcy was his path out, not just of this purgatory, but all the way to the top job at La Mer, leapfrogging his rivals to the place he desperately wanted to be – the place where he was no longer Nate whose talent was always mentioned in the same breath as a caveat about his temperament, or his reliability, or his self-control.

That was the reason he was telling himself. But there was something else. She hadn't been impressed with the first meal he cooked her, and now he needed her to be impressed. He needed her to concede that she'd been wrong and he was a great cook. He didn't know why that mattered. He suspected the Owl would have plenty of thoughts about it, but that was the way things were.

So pastrami on rye it had to be. He tapped his pen against his notepad.

'What are you planning?'

He'd been too caught up in his thoughts to notice Bella come in.

'Just thinking about recipes.'

She grinned. 'For tonight?'

'No, actually. I thought you had that covered.' More than covered. Bella had handed him a folder full of detailed recipes and timings for the preparation of tonight's meal.

She wrinkled her nose. 'Sorry. Am I being too controlling?'

After yesterday he'd have had no right to be cross even if she was. He would have to just suck up the urge to tell her he could manage. 'Just controlling enough,' he said.

She lowered herself awkwardly onto the stool next to him. 'So what recipes?'

He glanced behind her. 'Darcy's not with you?'

Bella shook her head. 'She stayed at Ladies' Group to carry on the fundraising plans. I pleaded pregnancy tiredness.'

'Or maybe you wanted to check I hadn't burned the place down?' Nate suggested.

'No. We'd have been able to see the smoke from the village if you had.' She nodded at his notebook. 'So what are you working on?'

'Would you believe New York deli sandwiches?'

'Ooh, I love a Reuben. People get weird about sauerkraut though.'

'I'm thinking pastrami on rye.'

She nodded. 'With spicy brown mustard.'

Of course. He added that to the list of things you almost certainly couldn't buy within a hundred miles of his current location. 'I'm not going to be able to get half the ingredients, am I?'

'There's a decent deli in Portree. You might get pastrami there.' She paused. 'You could probably substitute Dijon for the mustard.'

'Or make it from scratch?'

She pulled her phone out and searched. 'Yeah. Not impossible.'

He thought it through. He'd have to soak the mustard seeds overnight, and then let the finished mustard rest a day or two before he could use it. That would mean no sandwich for Darcy before the weekend.

'Anna and Hugh are surprisingly good at knowing where to order stuff in though,' Bella added.

He'd met Anna at the cake decorating. 'They have a shop in the village?' he asked.

'They have *the* shop in the village. Dinner's not until seven. Where are you up to with the prep?'

'Most of the advance stuff's done. I woke up early.'

'Great. So you're free until five maybe? You could walk down and see what they've got.'

'I might do that. You're not curious why I suddenly want to make a pastrami on rye?'

Bella shrugged. 'I know what it's like.'

'What what's like?'

'When you've got an idea in your head and you just need to make it and make it until it's perfect, you know.'

Nate did know. He remembered that feeling, of tasting something and knowing it was good but it was just a pinch of something away from being great, and knowing you wouldn't rest properly until you'd worked out what that something was. He hadn't felt like that recently though. Recently it had all been about his place in the kitchen, about moving up and moving on, and getting to where he needed to be. He nodded. 'Yeah. It's something like that.'

Darcy should have pretended she was helping with whisky tasting and made her escape when Flinty and Veronica left after the third cup of tea. Or at the very least insisted on seeing Bella home safe when she'd snuck out before the second round of sandwiches. But she hadn't. And now she was stuck here with Reverend Jill, Fiona, Nina, Netty and Anna – the crack fundraising team, as Anna insisted on calling them.

'So explain it again, Reverend,' Anna suggested.

Darcy felt her stomach sink a little lower. This was the fourth time, at least, that Jill had explained the idea of the talent auction. Or, more accurately, the fourth time she'd started to explain it. Somewhere along the way they did keep finding themselves distracted.

'Right. So the idea is everyone volunteers a talent.'

'Like that thing with the balloons that Mrs Timberley used to do for stag parties.'

This was, Darcy had to concede, a new distraction. 'What thing?'

'Well, she'd pin them to her...' Nina gestured to her cleavage. 'And all around, really, and then she'd pop them. Oh, the lads loved that.'

'And some of the girls,' added Netty.

'Our Margaret,' Anna agreed.

Darcy watched Jill's mouth open and close a few times while she tried to form a response. 'Like a burlesque sort of a thing?'

'A burl-what? No. It was stripping. Talents like that?'

Anna shook her head. 'You'll not get Irene Timberley doing her balloon dance these days. She's waiting for a new hip.'

'She could do it sitting down.' Nina pouted.

'You can't do it sitting down. Nobody'd be able to see her derrière. She had a lovely derrière, did Irene.'

'We could hold up pictures of it,' Darcy suggested. Fiona shot her a look. A 'you're not helping, Darcy' look.

'I don't think we need pictures of anyone's derrière,' Jill insisted.

'And her Derek used to play the accordion for it,' Nina added. 'Could your Hugh do the accordion part?'

There was an uncharacteristic silence from Anna. Apparently even a loving wife couldn't find anything positive to say about Hugh's skills with his accordion.

'It doesn't have to be a performance anyway.' Jill grabbed the chance to get the conversation back onto some sort of track. 'It's not a talent show. It's an auction. The idea is people volunteer their talent or skill and people bid for it and then they do whatever it is for the winner.'

'Like a private dance? Would she have to still bring her own balloons?' Anna asked.

'No.' Jill closed her eyes for a moment. 'No balloon dances. I'm going to say no stripping at all. Things like, I don't know, Netty will design a logo for your business, or Nina will make you a cake a month for a year or something. Whatever people are good at that other people might appreciate.'

'Lots of people appreciated Irene's balloon dance.'

'I'm not saying they didn't. I'm just saying we can think beyond the balloon dance.'

Nina nodded seriously. 'So the one where she covered herself in foam?'

'I don't think even Mr Timberley would want a repeat of that.'

'Well, of course not. He's dead.'

'I know he's dead. It was his heart, wasn't it? Wouldn't be at all surprised if it was the foam that brought it on.'

'OK.' Jill steepled her hands together. 'No stripping. Nothing with balloons. Nothing with foam.'

'What if someone's talent is cleaning?' Netty had been quiet throughout the meeting, and this was the question she'd chosen to ask.

'What if it is?'

'Well, that'll involve foam.' Netty's expression was absolutely neutral. As ever with the quietest of that trio, Darcy could never be 100 per cent sure if Netty was serious or if she was absolutely winding them up.

'Offering to clean for people will be fine.'

Nina opened her mouth.

Jill held up her hand before she could start. 'Fully clothed cleaning. We're not going through all that again.'

Slowly but surely Jill marshalled the group back onto topic and handed over the floor to Fiona, who navigated her way, as efficiently as anyone ever could, to a rough plan for putting flyers around the village, and to the farms around and about, and over to Lochcarron, asking people to volunteer their talents. She also checked the castle calendar on her phone and confirmed that the event itself could take place in the ballroom. Thanks to her they did seem to have the beginnings of a relatively coherent-sounding fundraising event.

'How much is this actually going to raise though?' Darcy asked.

Jill shrugged. 'Depends on the talents, and who comes along to bid.'

'You should ask your Kenny if he can bring some of his fancy Americans.'

Jill didn't meet anyone's gaze. 'He's not my Kenny,' she muttered.

'Well, why on earth not? Anyone can see that—'

'We're just friends,' Jill insisted.

Anna rolled her eyes. 'Well can you ask your *friend who happens to be a boy* to bring some of his fancy guests?'

'I can help with that,' Fiona chipped in. 'My dad still knows all the local great and good.'

'So does Darcy,' Anna pointed out. 'The old laird used to go to all those posh fellow things, didn't he?'

It was true. They had socialised with other lairds and landowners. Some of them had even tried to keep in touch after Alexander had gone. Darcy had let them slip away. 'I'm sure Fiona can manage.'

'Could we charge for tickets as well?' Netty asked.

'We'd have to have more than the auction going on,' Jill pointed out. 'We can't charge people just to come and give us money. Could Bella do a fancy meal for them?'

Darcy shook her head. 'She's supposed to be resting.'

'You've got your lad in to help though, haven't you? Could he do it?' Nina asked.

Nate. Darcy bristled slightly at the idea of Nate Thomas swanning in and showing them all how a proper fancy London chef did a banquet.

'Oh he's great,' Fiona replied. 'I'm sure he'll help.'

'We could ask him,' Darcy conceded.

'I heard he's had two of those Michelin stars,' Anna said.

'His boss does,' was all Darcy would allow.

'But still. He must know his way around the kitchen.'

'He's pretty young though.' Nina shook her head at this clear failing of character. 'People are these days, don't you think? Very young.'

'You don't think maybe you're just...' Jill was halfway into the sentence before Darcy saw her expression change. *Don't say it. Don't say it.* 'Just...' Jill stumbled.

'Just what?'

'Just noticing it more...' She was still struggling. 'For some reason? I don't know.'

'I wouldn't have thought so. No.' Nina's tone was ice.

'So about asking Kenny to bring people?' Jill fell on her sword to distract Nina from the new offence. 'Maybe I could do that. I do see him quite often.'

—

Nate walked from the castle, out past the coach house and onto the footbridge towards the village. Any worries about finding the way were dealt with by Dipper, the castle's resident chocolate Labrador, pulling him along by her lead. Nate had never really had a pet. His nan had a little terrier of some sort when he was tiny, but Nate remembered the dog as old and slow and entirely uninterested in playing with a toddler. Dipper was a different proposition. Nate's uncertainty about taking her with him on the walk to the village had been obvious enough for Bella to offer reassurance, promising that Dipper would happily go with anyone she thought might be able to offer walks or biscuits. And, so far, this did appear to be the case as she alternated between contentedly ambling along at Nate's side, and dashing forward in great fervour at some, apparently imaginary, excitement ahead. Nate was finding her unexpectedly cheering company. If he was struggling to work out how to unwind, Dipper appeared to have it down to a fine art.

Right now, she was darting forward towards a familiar figure walking the other way. Darcy Lowbridge. Nate took a deep breath in and pressed on. Bella knew where he was going, so there was no need for the voice in his head that said she'd be judging him for skiving off work. He was officially off duty until dinnertime, and he had as much right as anyone to be going about his business in the village.

She bent down to pet Dipper as they drew close.

Nate hung back, standing to one side to let Darcy pass. 'Just going to check out the village shop. Bella says it has to be seen to be believed.'

Darcy nodded. 'Sounds about right.'

'I'm not needed until dinner so…'

Another nod. Silent this time, and she walked away.

Nate continued quickly along the shore, pausing only for Dipper to take a sniff of whatever delights were hidden beneath the shingle. Across the street a row of houses lined the narrow strip of flatter land before the steep hill rose up behind them. Nate wasn't sure how he felt about the countryside. He'd never really spent enough time in it to have to find out. There had been one weekend when he was maybe fourteen, when the council had a grant from somewhere to provide what they termed 'developmental experiences' for young people in care. They'd spent two nights in an Outward Bound centre somewhere near

Dartmoor and it had rained and the social worker who'd been supposed to be leading the thing had broken her wrist on the first afternoon. Nate's experience of the great outdoors was feeling sick after his first vape and trying to play Boggle with two of the letter cubes missing while rain streamed down the windows outside.

There was something deeply disquieting about being out in scenery like this though. Lowbridge village was stretched along the coastline of the sea inlet that led up to the castle headland. Bella had told him it was a sea loch. She'd even told him its name but that hadn't stuck. Across the loch he could see islands and, turning inland, steep hills rose up behind the village. And the sky. The sky was so much bigger than he was used to in London. There should be buildings, nice solid hunks of concrete and stone hemming the sky in and stopping it from overwhelming a person.

How did anyone find their way around out here? Where were the street signs and the Tube stations and the landmarks you anchored yourself to? This felt like somewhere you could walk for hours and still be in basically the same place. Nate was used to walking for a few minutes and being bombarded with five different languages and the cooking smells from eight different countries. All of those sensations were what made him feel alive. He was used to there being stuff around him, not just all this space.

Bella had told him the shop was at the end of the village. When he'd asked for more specifics, she just said he wouldn't be able to miss it. Without something to navigate by Nate didn't see how that could be true, but as he approached the last row of houses, before the road turned slightly inland, he saw what she meant. Lowbridge Village Store was barely a shop at all. It was a garage, with goods and produce spilling out onto the driveway and a sign proclaiming, 'Lots more to buy through the door at the rear'.

Even with that confident prediction there was no way a shop this size was going to have half of what he needed. He crossed over the road, picked his way past the displays of barbecue charcoal and potted herbs and made his way into the shop itself. An older gentleman was standing behind the till, shouting towards the back of the shop. 'Come out of there!' The man frowned, entirely unaware of Nate's presence. 'Stop that!' He sighed. 'Queen Latifah, you stop that this minute.'

Nate peered along the line of the display stand and saw a tiny white dog sniffing happily at a shelf full of breakfast cereal. Dipper pulled on her lead at the sight of the other dog.

The man turned back and started slightly at Nate's presence. 'I'm sorry. Queen Latifah hasn't had her walk yet. So she's all full of beans.'

He wasn't going to ask. He wasn't going to ask. 'Queen Latifah?' he asked.

'In honour of the seminal remake of *The Equalizer*. Have you watched it?'

Nate shook his head.

'After Edward Woofwoof died I wasn't sure about getting another dog but Anna thought I should and I haven't regretted it for a moment.' He looked Nate up and down. 'You're from the castle?'

News spread fast around here. 'What makes you say that?'

'Well, Anna said she'd met the new chap. Said you were young and sounded very London.' There was no hiding the hint of not disapproval exactly, more pity, Nate thought, in the man he assumed was Hugh's tone. He nodded down at Dipper. 'And if you're not him, then you're a dognapper. And there's no way you'd take that big dopey thing when Queen Latifah's right here.'

Dipper rubbed herself against Nate's leg. 'Right. Yeah. Bella reckons she doesn't get enough good walks with her bloke being away and Bella being supposed to rest.'

'She's probably right. Labs need a lot of exercise. Cos they don't stop eating.' Hugh seemed to suddenly become aware of their surroundings. 'Sorry. What can I do for you?'

Nate looked around. 'It doesn't matter. You're not going to have it.'

'Oh, won't we?'

Of course they wouldn't. It was a tiny village shop in the middle of nowhere. They'd probably never heard of rye bread.

'Why don't you let me know what you're looking for and we'll find out.'

It was a waste of both their time. 'Fine. Pastrami, rye bread and...' This last one was definitely a lost cause. 'Spicy brown mustard.'

'We've got salami, I think. Not pastrami or rye bread.' Nate bit back the thought that he had told him so.

'Can get them both though if tomorrow's OK.'

Oh. 'Yeah. That would be great.'

Hugh sucked the air through his teeth. 'Spicy brown... hold on.'

Nate browsed the shelves while Hugh disappeared through a door at the back of the garage. The range of produce for such a tiny space was actually mind-boggling. He was bent over a display of fresh herbs when he heard voices heading back in his direction.

'Of course we can sell him it.'

'I'm not sure.' That was Hugh.

A second later Anna appeared in Nate's eyeline. 'He's being all soppy but it's fine.' She placed a jar on the counter next to the till. 'Spicy brown mustard?'

'Yeah. Wow. Why do you have this?'

The couple exchanged a look.

'Well, to be honest, it was a special order.'

'Who for?' Before he'd finished the question he knew the answer. Who around here would try to order spicy brown mustard – a New York staple?

'It was for Darcy,' Hugh muttered.

'But it was her husband who asked us to get it.' Anna pursed her lips. 'Just before he...' Her voice trailed away.

'I think she'd mentioned missing it and he thought it would be nice for her to have a taste of home, so he asked if we could source some.'

'We've got a whole case in the back fridge,' Anna added. 'It's still in date and it's not open. We just... we should have given it to her, but it came in after he passed and it never really seemed like the right moment.'

'It's a strange gift to bring to a wake,' Hugh agreed.

Nate could see that. *Very sorry for your loss. It's £15.99 plus shipping for your condiments.* It wasn't the most empathetic approach.

'Apparently this was her favourite one though. Alexander, the late laird, wrote it all down. I told him he could probably order it himself online but he wasn't really one for all that.'

Nate looked at the jar in front of him – bought for Darcy by someone who loved her and about to be repurposed for his bid to impress her. No. That was the wrong way of thinking about it. He was trying to make her a dish she would love, and this was an ingredient he knew she loved. 'I'll take it. If that's OK?'

Anna nodded briskly. 'No point getting sentimental over mustard,' she muttered. 'What else did you want?'

'Pastrami and rye bread.'

She nodded. 'We can get pastrami in from Cooper's. They cure all their own meats, you know. Small farm back towards Strathcarron. Rye bread?' She looked at her husband. 'Does Nell do rye?'

'To order, I think. I'll ring her. Hold on.'

Nate stayed by the counter while Hugh wandered into the driveway with his mobile held to his ear.

'The signal in here isn't very good,' Anna explained.

'No problem.'

She tapped a fingernail on the pot of mustard sitting on the counter between them. 'You're an American mustard lover?'

'Not really.'

'No. I didn't think so. It's for… someone then?'

'Just for a dish I want to try.'

Anna nodded. 'A dish for someone who does love American mustard?'

'Yeah. Darcy.' Obviously. What was the big deal about that?

Anna nodded. There was a smile pulling at her lips.

'Nell over in Portree has rye bread in today if you can get over there or she'll be making more tonight for tomorrow if you'd rather pick it up here,' said Hugh as he returned.

'Where's Portree?'

Hugh smiled. 'On Skye. The bigger island over the loch.'

The rye bread was over the sea?

He glanced at his watch. 'Young Strachan will be heading over there about now. Last taxi boat of the day. If you run down now you'll just catch him. He'll be twenty minutes or so in the harbour over there. Plenty of time to run up to Nell's, collect your bread and make it back.'

Anna nodded.

'Boat goes from the little jetty down this way.' Hugh turned back to Nate. 'You can leave Dipper with me and Queen Latifah. She's not good on boats.'

'OK.' Nate hesitated. Dipper wasn't his dog. Was leaving her with someone he'd only just met better or worse than taking her to a different land mass? 'Do dogs get seasick?'

'That one does.' Anna's tone was definite. 'Pavel reckoned the boat never smelled right since. And it used to be a fishing boat so it never smelled great.'

'Dipper'll be fine. She can play in the garden with Queen Latifah and I'll bring her back over when we go for our evening work.'

'If you're sure?' Nate let himself be hustled down the driveway and along the shingle beach to a short jetty, where a middle-aged bloke with weather-worn skin was sitting on a small open boat with an outboard motor fixed to the back.

'This is the new chef from the castle. He needs to pick some bread up from Nell.'

The man nodded. 'And come back over?'

'Aye,' Anna said, 'so don't go leaving him stranded.'

'Hop in. You might be the only one. Not many going over at this time.' The bloke held out a hand. 'I'm Young Strachan.'

'Hi. Nate.'

The trip across the bay to Skye didn't take long, but it was long enough for Nate to decide that, while he was on the fence about countryside, he really, really liked the sea. If anything, it was more featureless than the countryside, but you knew you were somewhere on the sea. You could feel it in your body, and on your face. You could taste the salt on your lips. The water was still, and the wind was light, but he felt a shiver of cool sea breeze against his face. The boat picked up speed as they came out of the bay at Lowbridge and into more open water. Just ahead of them something broke the surface of the water. 'What was that?'

'What?'

'Was that a dolphin?' Surely you didn't get dolphins in the UK. You got dolphins at theme parks and on nature documentaries.

'Whereabouts?'

Nate pointed to the now calm patch of water. Young Strachan killed the engine for a moment. 'Just one or a pod?'

Nate must have looked blank.

'A group?'

'Just one.'

'More likely a porpoise then. Harbour porpoise. Usually see them on their own or just two or three. Dolphins tend to be in bigger groups.'

'Wow.'

'We'll give him a minute, shall we?'

'Don't you have people to pick up?'

Young Strachan shrugged. 'A few minutes won't hurt them. They're gonna have to wait for you to fetch your bread when we get there anyway.'

They sat on the calm waters and looked out to where Nate had seen the flash of something in the water. And there it was again. Closer this time, the distinctive curved shape of the back of the porpoise rising about the waves. Young Strachan nodded. 'Harbour porpoise. Pretty common but never gets dull.'

Nate believed him. He watched the porpoise bob its way even closer and right by their little boat. 'That's amazing. I thought dolphins and stuff were just like…' What had he thought? 'I don't know. Like in the Caribbean and stuff.'

'Nope. Dolphins, porpoises, seals. Lots of seals. Minke whales. Orca – you don't see them very often though, and everything else clears off when they're around. Angry buggers, they are.'

'Wow. How do you get anything done? If I lived here I'd be out looking for whales every day.'

Young Strachan was looking at him oddly.

'What?'

'Anna said you were the new chef at the castle.'

'Yeah.'

'So you do live here.'

'Well…' Nate shook his head. He lived in London. His life was in London. Well, his work was in London and his work was his life. 'Only temporarily.'

'So temporarily take some time to look for whales, mate.'

Bella was leaning on the kitchen island when Darcy came back into the castle. Her notebook was open in front of her with what looked like plans for tonight's dinner.

'I thought Nate was dealing with that.'

'We're doing it together. I'd already written the menu before he got here, and it's a lot for one person.'

'You usually manage,' Darcy pointed out.

'Yeah, but it's an unfamiliar kitchen and it's not his menu. He's done most of the prep already.'

'And then swanned off goodness knows where.'

'He's gone to the shop. I said it was fine.' Bella put her pen down. 'Why are you pissed off with him?'

'I'm not.'

'OK.'

'He's fine.'

'Are you pissed off with him about yesterday?'

Of course she was. He'd seen her up on the clifftop. It felt like an intrusion. And then he'd been all faux sympathy, and he was… she shuddered. He wasn't right for Lowbridge. 'I'm just not sure he fits in. He's very London.'

Bella gave her a very pointed look. 'Didn't they used to say you were very New York?'

'That's different. He's all cheffy.'

'I'm all cheffy.'

'Not like him.'

Bella put down her pen. 'I worked in professional kitchens longer than Nate has.'

'Yeah but you're…' Darcy didn't know what she wanted to say. 'You don't want to make us all different.'

She didn't even need Bella to point out that she'd changed loads of things when she came to Lowbridge. The whole cookery school that Darcy was feeling so protective of was less than a year old.

'I just think someone should keep sitting in with him.'

'He was fine this morning. The students were all delighted with the session.'

'I don't mind sitting in.' And, if she didn't do that, what would she do? Without an activity to keep her going, she feared she would simply stop altogether.

'You don't have to. You could spend some more time riding,' Bella added.

That seemed to be all she ever heard. Darcy pushed down the growing feeling that Lowbridge didn't need her any more. Sitting in with Nate's lessons was useful. Someone needed to keep tabs on him. It was just annoying that she was the only one who could see how much everything was changing. 'You don't think he's too young?'

'Not if he's got the skills. He's been working since he was fifteen.' Bella shrugged. 'Why are you so wound up about him?'

'Why are you not?' Bella was a control freak and the cookery school was her life. 'Three days ago you wanted to sit in with him yourself.'

'I know but actually it's a relief. I did not want to let go, but now he's here, it's a relief.' Bella tapped the side of her head. 'There's just so much going on in here. Plans for the castle and the rest of the estate, and the baby's coming. Letting something go, at least a little bit, actually feels really good.'

Darcy envied her. She felt like she had nothing going on. 'Well, I'm happy to keep sitting in. Just to keep an eye on things.'

'OK then,' Bella acquiesced. 'He's an excellent cook though and he'll get used to the teaching.'

'He's a baby,' Darcy muttered. 'And so cheffy.'

'What else are you up to today?' Bella asked.

Nothing. There was nothing else for her to do. 'I don't know. Fiona still wants me to take some more pictures of her.'

'For her perfectly planned dating profile?'

Darcy nodded.

'Have you ever thought of...' Bella's voice fell quiet. 'I mean not now necessarily, but sometime, you know, trying to meet someone new?'

She shook her head. 'I'll go see if Fi's free now.'

Fiona wasn't free. She was on the telephone, berating a supplier of – Darcy could not tell what – over an incorrect invoice. 'Well, you might be sorry, but you were sorry yesterday and the new invoice is still wrong, so what if nobody had to be sorry and the thing was done correctly?'

Fiona frowned for a second and then smiled. 'Yes. I think a discount off our next order by way of apology would be perfect. Lovely to talk to you.'

She hung up the phone, beaming. Darcy snapped her picture.

'What are you doing?'

'For your profile. You had such a lovely smile.' A smile of victory at grinding a small business owner into the dust, but a great smile nonetheless.

'No. No.' Fiona shook her head. 'The interior shot was supposed to be businesslike but approachable. Like I'm successful but not a threat.'

'Who'd be threatened by your success?'

Fiona shook her head like a nanny dealing with an unexpectedly dense child. 'Well, men.'

'Don't you want one who isn't threatened?'

Fiona sighed. 'Clearly that's the ideal but this is a percentages game. I need matches before I can apply a filtering system.'

'Whatever you say.'

'It's a really good filtering system. I put all their info into my spreadsheet and it scores them on a prioritised list of desirable attributes and creates a score out of one hundred, so I can compare matches from different apps.'

Darcy had only been in one serious relationship in her life and it had happened entirely by accident, so she was really in no position to advise. But. 'You don't worry that you might have lost some spontaneity? You know, that romantic spark?'

Fiona shook her head. 'Better to be organised about things, I think. You can't trust a spark.'

'OK. I do think you should use this picture though.' Darcy held her phone out so Fiona could see the picture she'd taken. 'It is a really pretty smile.'

'My chin looks too long.'

Darcy checked the picture again. Fiona's chin looked entirely normally proportioned.

'Let me pose for it.' Fiona put her elbow on the desk and rested her regular-sized chin on her hand. The effect was more CEO on the company brochure than potential romantic partner. Darcy took the photo anyway.

—

Two hours later, Nate was at the kitchen island laying out plates for the grand dinner starters, while Bella checked on the dishes in the oven. 'How did your ingredient search go?'

'Much better than I expected.'

'That's the village shop. I do actually think they sell everything.'

'Not quite, but Anna says they can get pastrami in from some place that cures their own meat?'

'Cooper's! Of course. I should have thought of that. They're incredible.'

'And she sent me to Skye by boat to get rye bread.'

'From Nell?'

Nate nodded. 'And we saw a porpoise on the way.' He could still barely believe that.

'Yeah.' Bella was smiling. 'Sometimes you see dolphins from the cliff path.'

'The seafood here is amazing.'

'And the beef. And you did venison this morning. Lamb, obviously. We're really lucky.'

'I can see that. And Anna and Guy had spicy brown mustard in stock.'

'It's getting to you, isn't it?'

'What?'

She smiled. 'Lowbridge. The scenery. The wildlife. The food. The mad shop. There's always something that just gets people.'

Nate shook his head. 'I'm just passing through.'

'Course you are.'

'And the scenery is weird.'

She laughed out loud at that.

'It is. Places shouldn't have this much sky. You people need to build some more stuff.'

'I can't see Nina or Anna approving a skyscraper.' She checked the clock. 'Our waiters should be here by now. Ten minutes to service?'

'Yes, Chef.' Nate caught himself smiling back at her. It was dinner for thirteen people, but having staff in to serve and the two of them working together in the kitchen was giving him a little bit of the adrenalin he used to feel in the early days at La Mer. There was that sense of a performance about to start, the knowledge that you'd done everything you could to prepare and now things were just going to happen. Anything that went wrong would just have to be dealt with and moved on from. There were no do-overs, no chances to go back and start again. They were on a moving train now, and there was no stopping until the last person in the dining room had drained their after-dinner coffee and headed off to bed.

He arranged salad garnish on the starter plates as two more bodies shuffled into the room. Bella smiled at them. 'Waiters. Excellent.'

The first person Nate recognised. 'Evie?'

She nodded. 'Auntie Anna says it counts as life skills. And she said to check my pay and that'll be maths.'

'Homeschooling going well then,' Nate agreed.

Evie rolled her eyes. 'I did, like, online stuff all afternoon. So boring.'

'Have you waitressed before?'

'Yeah. My dad had a cafe.'

Nate noticed the past tense but didn't comment on it. 'Great. Well, we're not doing anything fancy and silver service or anything tonight. The idea is that it's a home-cooked dinner but elevated.'

'That's right,' Bella confirmed. 'So don't try to carry plates up your arm or anything unless you're super confident. Two at a time is fine. Me and Nate can help if you need us.' She turned to Nate. 'That's all right, isn't it? They've been cooking with you the last two days. It'd be nice for them to see you tonight as well.'

'Sure.'

'And Fiona's around if we need an extra pair of hands. I've got her on drinks when they arrive at the moment.' Bella checked her notes. 'So it's eight guests, plus Kenny, who runs the tours, and Veronica, Flinty and Darcy to make them feel like they're dining with the family, not just in a faceless restaurant.'

'And Jill.' The young man who'd come into the room with Evie piped up. 'She was pulling up when I got here.'

Nate looked up. 'Who's Jill?'

'Shit,' Bella muttered. 'Kenny asked if he could bring her. I completely forgot.'

'That's OK. We've got enough. No panic.'

'Sorry. Jill's the local vicar, and Kenny's sort of...' Bella shrugged and turned to their second waiter. 'What do you say, Young Strachan? She says she's not his girlfriend but...?'

'Course she is. She gets a right hump on if you say that though.'

Nate's brain caught up with the conversation. 'Sorry. She called you Young Strachan?'

'Aye.'

'I got a boat with Young Strachan earlier.'

The lad nodded. 'My dad.'

'But you can't both be...' Nate shook his head. 'Shouldn't he be Old Strachan?'

'My grand-da's Old Strachan,' new Young Strachan explained. 'And only since his dad died. So some of the old folk still call him Young Strachan too.' He shrugged. 'People seem to know who they mean.'

Nate had no idea how that could possibly be true. 'Don't you have a first name?'

'Alfie.'

Bella giggled. 'I didn't know that.'

'Don't really use it. Doesn't help anyway. I was named after my dad.'

'Of course you were.'

'And he was named after his dad. Who was named after his dad and... yeah. It's Alfs, Alfreds and Alfies all the way back.'

'OK then. Young Strachan, you've waited tables before?'

'Yeah. I've done a few of Bella's fancy dinners since she got here.'

'Young Strachan's grand. If you can turn up and get paid for it, you can bet he's a dab hand.'

The lad nodded. 'Mostly we're farmers, but, apart from Bella, it's hard to get anyone to give you a fair price for meat, or wool, these days, so I do whatever needs doing.'

'And your dad runs a water taxi?'

'We both do.' He shrugged. 'Just whoever's available.'

'Just try to avoid the days Flinty's driving the boat,' Bella added.

Young Strachan laughed. 'Yeah. Bit of a speed demon. Bad enough on the road. Worse on the water. I mean, she'll get you there. You just might not still have your lunch inside you by the end of the trip.'

'OK.' Nate checked the time. 'We probably need to get down to it. Service in five minutes.'

—

Darcy took her seat halfway down one side of the large dining table in the small dining hall. Veronica was at the head of the table. That used to be Alexander's place, of course. Not a place he ever felt that comfortable. Alexander had loved the land. He'd loved his garden. He'd loved the wildlife, and the farm. He'd never been a natural at the more public elements of being the laird. Darcy had helped him though, she thought. She'd been good at the hostessing. She could be all American and effusive and chat and smile and giggle.

'Are you all right there, honey?' Pamela, from the cookery class, was leaning towards her from the other side of the table.

'I'm fine.' Why wouldn't she be?

'Just you were laughing to yourself.'

Was she? Darcy didn't feel like laughing. She'd been thinking about the times before when she'd smiled and laughed with guests. She tried a little experimental laugh. It sounded strange and tinny and far away. She shook her head. 'I don't think I was.'

Pamela was looking at her quite strangely now. Darcy turned away and tried to focus on the rest of the table. Flinty was next to Veronica in the first seat on the left-hand side. Darcy was about halfway down the right-hand side and Kenny and Jill were opposite one another towards the bottom end of the table. They tried to spread themselves out for guest dinners so visitors wouldn't feel that it was the family at one end and the visitors excluded. Part of what they were paying for was dinner with the family from the castle – a real taste of authentic Highland life, putting aside the fact that the only reason the small dining hall wasn't covered in dust sheets was the people paid to come and eat in it. Struggling to make ends meet, and constantly looking for a bucket to pop under the nearest leak, had been a more authentic representation of Highland life for most of Darcy's time at Lowbridge.

But things were changing. Everything was changing. Money was flowing in now, with Bella's inspiration and hard work, and Fiona's efficiency and attention to detail. In the last few months bits of roof had been patched and the stock of buckets was more commonly found neatly put away in the cleaning cupboard than in the middle of floors across the building.

Pamela leaned forward again. 'Are you feeling better, dear?'

All she'd done was giggle. 'Sorry?'

'Nathan said you weren't feeling well yesterday.'

'Right. Yeah.' Well, he'd have had to say something, wouldn't he? 'Much better. Thank you.'

'It's just…' Pamela looked a little sheepish. 'Bob did wonder if I'd spoken out of turn. I do that sometimes. Just shoot off without thinking.'

'No. It's fine.' A plate was put in front of Darcy with whole langoustines and a sweet chilli dip. You had to snap the langoustine and pull out the flesh. She knew that. She could do that. She stared at the plate.

Pamela was still talking. 'You don't have to move on until you're good and ready. There's no time limit on grief. Not when you've found the right one. I was cut up when Duanne passed but now I look back and honestly we wouldn't have stayed together…'

Langoustine. Langoustine. What a strange word. Was it French? Lots of words were French. Aperitif. Soufflé. Pâté. Food words. Lots of food was French, maybe.

Pamela's voice was a long way away now. 'We were young. We only even thought of getting married because I was pregnant. I'm sad that he's not out there somewhere living his life, and it breaks my heart that Susie – that's my daughter – didn't really get a chance to get to know him, but I know that if he was still with us, he wouldn't be with me. You know?'

Or maybe the British just liked to call their food French things because it sounded fancier. 'Pâté' rather than 'meat paste'. 'Soufflé' rather than 'eggy pudding'. Darcy caught herself before she giggled again.

'But that was just me. If I lost my Bob now…' Pamela reached across the table and grabbed Darcy's hand. 'Well, I don't know if I could ever move on from that.'

Was that how Darcy felt? She'd felt sick at the idea of moving on and finding someone new. But the thought of this soul-defining grief that seemed to be the alternative didn't make her feel anything. The only thing she felt right now was hot. Hot on her skin where Pamela was gripping her hand. Darcy pulled away. She was supposed to say something, wasn't she? '"Langoustines" is a funny word,' she offered. 'French, I think.'

'I would say so,' Pamela agreed, before turning to her neighbour across the table. Darcy sat back. What a strange woman.

–

The main course was generous sharing platters of local beef, alongside fat juicy lamb lollipops, with perfectly crisp chips, and wilted greens as a nod to health. Darcy was sure it was all delicious. Her fellow diners clearly thought so from the exclamations of appreciation and delight. Darcy ate politely, focusing on chewing every bite until it was a flavourless mush. If she chewed and swallowed and chewed and swallowed and thought only of that then the meal would eventually be over. If she held tight to her attention and didn't think about why chefs had suddenly started putting meatballs on sticks and calling them lollipops then she wouldn't laugh without knowing and get another round of sympathy and advice from her companion across the table.

'Lollipops' though. That wasn't French. Was it English? Maybe it was one of those strange words imported from across the empire? Like 'pyjamas'. 'Pyjamas' was Indian, she thought. 'Where do lollipops come from?' Darcy heard her own voice outside her head, before she'd realised she was speaking. How curious.

Bob, Pamela's big, cheery third husband, shrugged. 'The candy store, I guess.'

That made sense. Darcy nodded. Not meat lollipops, of course. They would come from the butcher. So probably not Indian at all. Although butchers could be Indian. Or any nationality, she supposed.

'Are you doing OK there?' Now Bob was looking at her with that strange concerned face Darcy had got used to in the weeks after Alexander died.

She shook her head. 'I don't really know. Maybe I'll just…' She pushed her chair back from the table. 'Maybe I'll just have an early night.'

Darcy wandered out of the small dining hall and through the corridors of the castle. She stopped in the entrance way and bowed to Colin, the suit of armour who stood on permanent guard at the bottom of the stairs. 'Good evening, Colin.'

He didn't reply.

She wandered upstairs, and sat on the edge of her bed in the Gardenia Room. She'd moved here after Alexander died after a battle of wills with her mother-in-law about the proper place for a spare dowager to live. Initially, she'd fought to stay in the rooms she'd shared with her husband, but really this was better. Here she could tell herself that she didn't feel Alexander close to her because they'd never shared this space. She could imagine that if she went back to his old room, she'd be able to feel him. That was how it was supposed to be, wasn't it? That was what Pamela had been thinking of when she said she couldn't imagine moving on if she lost Bob.

Instead she kept catching herself in moments like this, moments where she'd paused and somehow got stuck. Most commonly it happened right here, sitting on the edge of the bed, not doing anything, but it wasn't only here. She would find herself sitting in the Land Rover, having arrived home, not moving, not opening the door, not doing anything. Or standing in front of a window, looking, she imagined, to all the world like she was admiring the view, when really she was quite absent, not seeing what was in front of her at all.

And this evening the ties that rooted her in the real world felt looser than ever. For months she'd been able to distract herself from the emptiness with busyness, with socialising, with being perky, sparky, outgoing Darcy. She'd been able to tell herself that she was doing well, that she was moving on and making a new life. But recently the fog that descended when she was alone, that seemed to create a barrier between her and life itself, came more and more often, and the numbness was harder and harder to shift. She had to keep busy. Busyness was like an anchor keeping her in place. She needed to do things. Any sort of thing would do.

Right now, she needed to brush her teeth and get ready for bed, and climb under the covers and turn out the light but right in the moment that all seemed difficult and far, far out of reach. So she continued to just sit on the edge of the bed, letting time flow on.

Chapter 7

The next morning Nate set about preparing the perfect pastrami on rye. How hard could it be to make a sandwich? Nate was a professional. He had made sandwiches before. Delicate little cucumber sandwiches for afternoon tea. Hearty gastropub steak sandwiches. He had never, he now realised, eaten, let alone made, pastrami on rye. He had, in the last twenty-four hours, read a huge amount about pastrami on rye. He'd watched YouTube clips on a highly niche channel with only twenty subscribers discussing the minutiae of how much mustard was too much, and he only just managed to stop himself getting into quite an involved argument about Dijon as a substitute in the comments thread. He had a deep theoretical understanding of the role the extra corned beef played in elevating the whole. But he'd never actually tasted one.

What he had in front of him, he thought, tasted pretty damn good. The rye bread adding a bit more flavour and oomph than a regular dough, the kick from the mustard hit just enough but didn't overpower the cured meats. The addition of the corned beef was the real genius though. Nate wanted to find out who'd first come up with that and shake them by the hand. It didn't just deepen the meaty notes. It gave the sandwich a whole new layer of moisture and warmth that the pastrami alone didn't quite deliver.

Short of finding a tame New Yorker to taste and critique, Nate concluded that it was as good a pastrami on rye as he was going to manage. Was that enough though? Darcy's utterly joyless reaction to the last dish he'd offered her was replaying in his mind. And she hadn't enjoyed last night's dinner enough to stay for dessert. This carefully honed Darcy-specific treat was going to prove her wrong.

He carried his creation up the stairs and knocked gently on the door to Darcy's bedroom. When she didn't answer, he set it on the floor outside and knocked again. 'I've just made you some lunch. I could leave it out here but I don't want Dipper to get it.'

A sound on the other side of the door confirmed that Darcy was in there. The face that peeked around the door wasn't the put-together woman he was used to seeing. She was still wearing the clothes she'd had on last night and her face looked drawn and tired. It felt as though she stared at him for a second before her mind caught up with his presence. 'I slept in.'

'That's OK.' He held the plate towards her. 'I just thought you might want something to eat.'

'I'm fine.' She made to close the door.

Nate hesitated. Saying he'd made it especially for her sounded weird. 'It's just... I'd really love a New Yorker's opinion. It's pastrami on rye. First time I've made it. Would be good to get an expert take on it.'

Her expression softened a touch. 'My dad used to bring me pastrami on rye. It was my favourite.'

'Really?' Nate feigned surprise. 'I put extra corned beef in it. Some of the recipes online suggested that.'

Darcy nodded. 'Definitely. Makes it so much better.'

She took the plate from him and started to open the door a little further. 'Actually... erm...' There was a side table against the wall in the hallway with two stiff-backed old chairs. 'I'll try it out here.'

Nate watched Darcy carefully place the plate on the side table and take a seat, before lifting the sandwich to her mouth. She was quiet for a second after the first bite. He watched as she chewed and quickly took another. This time she closed her eyes.

Nate turned away. He loved seeing customers enjoying his food. At least he remembered that he used to love it. He rarely got time to visit the dining room any more, but watching Darcy felt like he was intruding on a private moment.

—

Mustard sharp, deep spice from the meat, a softness from the corned beef, the sound of her dad's laughing voice telling her not to eat it all at once, the smell of the air in their New York apartment, the feeling of the cheap velour on the couch against her legs. The taste of pastrami and rye bread wasn't just good. It was transporting. 'This is incredible,' she murmured.

'Really?' She became aware of Nate pacing the hallway in front of her.

'Really.'

He exhaled and took the seat at the other side of the table. 'I'm glad. You said about deli sandwiches and your dad and it got me thinking it would be the right thing to make.'

'It's perfect. Almost as good as my dad's.'

'Almost?'

Darcy smiled. 'That's pretty damn good. It tastes like being back home.'

He grinned. 'So you acknowledge I can cook.'

Darcy frowned. She'd never thought otherwise. 'Sure.'

'Sure?'

She looked up at him. 'Sure.'

He let out a deep sigh. 'Right.'

She took another bite – a smaller one this time, lest the sensation overwhelm her. It tasted of excitement and rebellion, of not eating the planned meal that they were supposed to have according to the list that was always on the front of the fridge, but instead illicit, unexpected treats. It tasted of family, and everyone together. It tasted of a life before she'd ever come here. 'Oh.'

'What?'

'Nothing.' Not nothing, but nothing she could explain. 'It made me think of New York.'

'You've never thought about going back?'

'No.' She hadn't. Not even for a moment. She missed it, especially when she first moved here, but she'd made the decision to make Lowbridge her home when she fell in love with Alexander, and that was what she'd done. 'This is home.'

She took another bite of her sandwich. That tasted like home too. 'What about you?' Darcy asked the question quickly before he could ask her anything else.

'What about me?'

'Where's home?'

'London.'

Darcy shook her head. 'Whereabouts? Nobody's just a Londoner, are they? I used to model with a girl from Chelsea. She'd never say just "London".'

'Well, I'm not from Chelsea.' Nate sighed. 'When I was born we lived in Hounslow, but my mum couldn't look after me and my nan wasn't very well, so I got moved around a lot. Different foster homes, temporary places, all that. They don't have enough foster carers so you end up in different boroughs.'

'Oh.' Nate had come to Lowbridge with a sense of confidence that Darcy had mistaken as the result of the sort of upbringing that never causes someone to doubt themselves. 'I'm sorry.'

'Don't be. Everyone starts out somewhere. And I found the thing I was meant to be doing, so it worked out all right.'

'Where's home now?'

He frowned. 'La Mer.'

'Where's that?'

'Sorry. The restaurant I usually work in. I was living in a shared house, but they'll have sublet my room about twenty minutes after I set off here. Wherever I lay my hat is good enough for me. Work's home.'

Darcy took another bite of her sandwich. 'My dad used to cut these up and then we'd fight for the bit in the middle, cos that's where you get the most filling. When we were older he'd make one of us cut it and then the others got to choose their piece. You know, to stop the cutter from dividing it unfairly.'

Nate nodded.

'The first time I had enough money to go to a diner on my own and order a whole pastrami on rye I felt like I'd won the lottery.'

'How old were you then?'

'Seventeen, maybe. I want to say that's when I got scouted by the model agency, but I don't think it was. Same diner, maybe. Not the same day.'

'You were scouted?'

'Yeah.' It felt like remembering a different life, but with the taste of New York on her tongue she could imagine herself back there. 'I nearly told her where to go. I thought it was a scam. It kinda was. They weren't ripping me off or anything, but it's all "We love you. You're going to be a star," when what they mean is "You'll do. You might scrape together just enough to get by." I did a lot of temping and waitressing while I was officially a model.' She laughed.

'I've only ever had one job.'

'You always wanted to be a chef.'

'Nah. I wanted to play for Arsenal. But only because everyone else did. My nan bought me an Arsenal scarf when I was…' He frowned. 'Four, maybe. Could never afford to go to a match though. First month working for Guy he took all the apprentices there. Corporate box, meet and greet with the players afterwards. Should have blown my mind but all I could think about was what I'd do to improve the catering.'

'So you found your calling?'

'Yeah.' He fell quiet for a second. 'Seemed like it.' He checked his watch. 'Sorry. I've got students at two. I'd better go set up.' He paused at the top of the stairs. 'Are you sitting in again?'

Darcy hadn't woken up intending to. She'd woken up intending to stay right where she was and tell herself that she was fine. She knew that 'sitting in with Nate' was a made-up job. She didn't need to be doing it, but now she was feeling alive again, the thought of retreating back to her room felt like a horror. She'd been right before. She needed to keep busy. She needed to keep going. 'Yeah,' she replied. 'I'll be there.'

The afternoon cookery group was the session normally led by Nina – the castle's ongoing basic cookery class. Nate introduced himself to the students at the start of the session. 'Unfortunately Nina has been called away today to…' He checked a handwritten note that he pulled half scrunched from his pocket. 'To take Mrs Timberley to the chiropodist and Queen Latifah's stool sample to the vet.'

Darcy stifled an unexpected giggle. The rest of the group nodded, like that was the most normal reason for missing class in the world.

'And Nina and Bella thought it would be good for you all to work on some knife skills.'

Darcy looked around the group. There were three graduates, including Youngest Strachan, from Bella's short men-only cookery course, one eighteen-year-old from Lochcarron who was away to university in the autumn and had been given driving lessons and cookery lessons for her birthday, Anna's great-niece, Evie, and, rushing in after they'd officially started, Reverend Jill.

'Sorry. Sorry. Was meeting a family about a funeral and you can't really cut that short because you're late for Five Fun Ways with Fennel.' She pushed her curls out of her eyes and pulled her hair into a ponytail, peering at Nate. 'You're not Nina.'

'No. Nate.'

Jill nodded. 'I know who you are. You're just not who I was expecting.' She frowned for a moment. 'Mrs Timberley's chiropody appointment?'

'Yeah.'

'And Queen Latifah's poo,' Evie added. 'They tried to make me take that.' She shuddered.

Jill winced. 'Is it still very loose?'

'Right. OK. Less dog bowel chat, more cooking,' Nate called the group to order. 'We're going to spend some time on knife skills. Bella told me that in her very first lesson someone cut themselves and it turned into a whole big horror show?'

All the eyes in the room turned towards Jill. 'It was just a little nick. My friend I was with fainted at the blood. That was what caused all the bother.'

'Oh, I didn't realise that was you. Well, that's fine because the point of learning good knife skills is to avoid accidents. You want to be able to cut things precisely, efficiently and without losing the end of your finger in the process.' Nate unrolled his set of chef's knives on the bench in front of him. Bella had bought in some more basic sets for her students to use. They weren't particularly expensive, but neither were Nate's – the best he could afford at the time – and really it wasn't so much the quality of the knife as how well you looked after it. He talked quickly through how a sharp knife was much safer than a blunt one, because it gave you more control of the cutting motion, and then he pulled a huge bag of tomatoes onto the kitchen worktop. 'Right. By the end of the afternoon I am afraid you are going to be sick of the sight of tomatoes, and I'm going to be left having to make my own body weight in soup and pasta sauce to use up all the practices you're going to do, but you will also be – I hope – much more confident chopping, dicing and slicing in your own kitchens.'

—

Darcy perched on her stool at the back of the room as Nate started his first demonstration – simply slicing a tomato.

He talked about even slices and he talked about how the firmness of the skin and the softness of the fruit inside made the tomato a particular challenge – and therefore particularly good for practice – and a good test of how sharp your knife was. And then he started to slice, holding the tomato against the board with his fingertips slightly curled in away from the blade. His knife slid through the fruit with a rhythmic flow. He was talking about being consistent and concentrating and not rushing. 'Everyone sees chefs chopping things and thinks it's all about speed. Speed will come. Be safe and consistent first.'

He pulled another tomato from the bag and cut this one in smaller slices still. Darcy was mesmerised. The motion of the knife. The calm authority with which he talked on a subject he was sure about. The attention to detail. The precision. The absolute competence. 'Oh.'

Nate looked up in her direction. 'Are you OK?'

'Fine.' Why on earth was he asking?

'Just, you said "oh".'

Had she? Darcy shook her head.

'You did.' That was Jill.

Young Strachan nodded in agreement. 'Oooh,' he confirmed.

'I thought it was more "ow",' Evie offered.

Jill shook her head. 'That would be if she'd hurt herself. This was definitely "oh".'

All eyes were on Darcy. 'Just clearing my throat.'

Nobody in the room looked convinced.

'All right then.' Nate set his students up with knives and tomatoes and a simple instruction. 'All you need to do is cut your tomato into five-millimetre-wide slices. Off you go.'

Darcy continued to watch him, moving from student to student, helping them tweak their technique. Had she said 'oh'? She must have. Was it like when she'd giggled last night? It didn't feel the same. That had felt like she was floating somewhere far away from the room she was physically in. This was all about what was happening right in front of her. Somehow the bubble of unfamiliar emotion that was growing inside her must have burst out. She shouldn't have let it. She shouldn't even have felt it. She wasn't really sure what it was that she had felt.

That was a lie she was telling herself. She knew exactly what she'd been feeling watching Nathan Thomas chop tomatoes. It wasn't a feeling she associated with kitchen work benches. She'd felt it before. Of course she had. She was a married woman. That thought caught in her mind. She was a widowed woman. And widowed meant that part of her life was over. She was supposed to be grieving. Or was she supposed to be recovering by now? She was sure she wasn't supposed to be having inappropriate thoughts about young – how young even was he? – men in her kitchen.

'Do you want to have a go, Darcy?' The young man interrupted her thoughts.

'How old are you?'

'What?'

'How old are you?'

Nate frowned. 'Twenty-four. Why?'

Twenty-four. Darcy was forty in a few weeks. Twenty-four. And an employee at the castle. Even if Darcy was ready for someone new, he would never be that someone. 'Just wondered. You're very good. Seem very, you know, competent. I wondered if you were older.'

'Been cooking since before I officially left school so yeah. You get experienced fast.' He nodded towards the chopping board he'd been using for his demo. 'Do you want to have a go?'

'OK. I guess.'

She took the knife he offered her and grabbed a tomato. At first she pressed too hard, the tomato squashing under the pressure.

'The knife's sharp. Let the knife do the work. You just need to guide it.'

She tried again, and grinned as the knife did simply slide through the tomato.

'Can I?' Nate gestured towards the hand holding the knife.

Darcy nodded.

He moved to her side and his hand covered hers. 'Just relax your grip a fraction. Still holding firmly, but no need to try to squeeze the life out of the handle.'

Darcy opened her hand just a tiny bit, feeling the back of her fingers brush minutely against his touch.

He pulled his hand away and stepped back like he'd been stung. 'Better. Er...' He swallowed hard. 'That was better.'

Darcy could feel her cheeks starting to colour red. She'd been thinking scurrilous inappropriate things about a man who recoiled at the slightest touch.

'You just need to hold it more gently,' he stuttered.

'You said that already.'

'Yeah. Right. Well, good.'

Darcy was supposed to reply. That was how conversation worked. There was nothing to say. She had nothing to say. She opened her mouth.

'Can I borrow Young Strachan?' Fiona's voice at the kitchen door saved her.

Strach looked up. 'What for?'

'I want a man's opinion.'

The poor lad looked terrified. 'What on?'

Fiona consulted the tablet in front of her. 'Number one, first-date conversational openers; number two, suitable first-date attire; and number three, appropriate levels of casual touching for flirting without seeming overeager.'

Nate was swallowing back laughter. 'Sure. You can skip out for a while.'

'I don't know.' Strach's face was bordering on desperation. 'Weren't you about to go on to something new? Something important?'

Nate shook his head. 'You're fine.'

Darcy told herself she was taking pity on Young Strachan, rather than just running away. 'Why don't I come too? I mean, I'm not a man, but I've been on dates.' A very long time ago.

Fiona shrugged. 'The more the merrier.'

'Brilliant.' Jill jumped off her chair. 'That sounds like an invitation.'

'Wait,' Nate started.

Evie put down her knife. 'We should all help. I mean, dating is, like, so last century but whatever. I've seen *Pride and Prejudice*. I get it.'

'We're in the middle of...' Nate sounded distinctly unamused at the idea of his whole class disappearing.

Fiona ignored him. 'Excellent. We'll start with clothes. I have pictures for four outfits and two first-date scenarios. Either a walk in the countryside followed by a casual drink, or a more formal dinner at a restaurant.' She set her tablet down on the island unit. 'Wait here. I'll print out some more questionnaires.'

'There are questionnaires?' Nate shouted after her.

'Just two sides of A4. It won't take more than ten minutes!'

It took more than ten minutes. Way more. Jill and Evie both turned out to have very strong – but rarely overlapping – opinions on questions of dating etiquette. Fiona's first two looks had either way too much, or possibly not enough, make-up for a nice meal out. Knife skills weren't getting a look in.

On conversation topics, politics was agreed to be 'like, way depressing', but Jill was, understandably, on side with discussion of religion. The weather was deemed safe but boring, and while talking about your career was fine, Jill did question whether Fiona would be able to stop talking about work once she'd started. Nate was supposed to be in control of this class. The last time things had got away from him, Bella had had to step in. That wasn't happening again. No chance.

Eventually his frazzled patience ran out. 'I'm supposed to be teaching these people knife skills.'

Fiona nodded. 'Sorry. I'll go. I shouldn't have interrupted.'

'I thought you were going to show us your flirting?' Evie wasn't going to get dragged back to the lesson that easily.

Fiona shook her head. 'I think Nate wants to get back to the class.'

'Nate doesn't mind,' Jill insisted.

Nate really did mind. The tension in his shoulders was rising. He tapped his fingers on the counter as a distraction.

'It's quicker to just let it happen.' That was Young Strachan.

'What?'

'Seriously. Sometimes you just have to give in to how things are done here.'

No. Nate had to be here. He had to make the best of it. He didn't have to embrace full-blown insanity. He shook his head. 'No flirting practice in my kitchen.'

'We're just having a laugh,' Evie protested.

Nate forced himself to breathe. The Owl would ask why the situation made him so tense. The Owl wasn't here. The feeling that the whole lesson was spinning out of control was, and Nate was trapped in the middle of it. 'I just feel the class might go better if we left the flirting for later.'

He saw the look that Darcy and Jill exchanged before Darcy nodded. 'Nate's right.'

'Good.' The students gravitated, with varying degrees of reluctance, back to their chopping boards. 'That's good,' he repeated, telling his own overwrought nervous system that everything was back under control.

Nate moved on from slicing to dicing, and continued the class. Darcy didn't participate, but retook her seat at the back of the room. Nate fancied he could feel her watching him.

Young Strachan held up his chopping board. 'How's that?'

Nate looked. It was good. Actually, it was great. Neat. Precise. Not a drop of blood to be seen. 'You've done this before?'

'Nah. Bella says I'm a danger to myself with a knife.'

'Clearly not.'

The young man gave the sort of shrug Nate recognised from his younger self. The sort of shrug that you gave when you were super happy with something but didn't want to show it. 'Just did what you told us.'

'You did really well. Shall we move on to something a bit more complicated then?' Nate continued demonstrating different ways to cut and chop, but Young Strachan's comment sat in his head. He'd just done what Nate told him. Nate had explained something, and someone else had watched and listened and now they could do that thing too. That was brilliant.

-

Nate finished the class. He saw the last student off and headed back into the kitchen. Darcy was collecting up chopping boards and piling tomatoes into the biggest pan around. 'I wasn't sure what to do with this,' she said.

'In there's fine. I'll take some out for dinner tonight and make the rest into stuff we can freeze.'

He went towards the pan as Darcy came the other way. Nate stopped. Darcy stopped. He started again. She did too. Now he was close to her. Too close. And yet not close enough. Neither of them stepped back.

Until she did.

Nate felt his body start to breathe again. 'So you enjoyed the sandwich?'

'Yes. I really did. Thank you. I felt...' She shook her head. 'Something.'

'Something is good?'

She didn't meet his eye. 'I don't know.'

She couldn't even look at him. Nate told himself he needed to let whatever this was go.

Darcy continued to wipe the kitchen worktops. She didn't need to be doing this. Nate was quite capable of clearing up. She was probably in the way, more than anything, but busy was good. Busy was the thing.

He brushed past her, reaching for the last board left on the counter. Darcy was definitely feeling things again. Unwelcome things.

'You're twenty-four?' she asked.

'Yep.'

'So you were born this century.'

'Yeah. Why?'

Born this century. That was ridiculous. Darcy shook her head. 'No reason.'

'Clearly some reason.'

'When was your mother born?'

Nate paused. For a second his face shut down and then she saw him breathe in deeply. 'I'm not sure.'

'What?'

'I lived with my dad's mum, so I don't really know.'

'I...' She had no idea what to say to that. 'I'm sorry.'

'Don't be. Why do you care?'

She couldn't answer that. 'Just nice having more younger people around the place.'

'You don't sound like it's nice. You sound like it's freaking you out.'

'No.' Well, yes. 'It's just odd. Like you'll have grown up on totally different things to me.'

'Yeah, but that's true anyway.' He pointed to her and then him. 'American. British.'

That was fair. 'But even global stuff. Like pop music and movies.'

'So what's your era?' he asked.

'NSYNC.'

'I'm sorry.'

This was her point. 'Justin Timberlake before he was solo famous.'

'I thought he was a Backstreet Boy.'

'You wash your mouth out.'

'What?'

'Seriously? BSB and NSYNC? It's like Oasis and Blur.' She glanced at Nate to see further confusion on his face. 'Really?'

'Maybe I'm just not that into music.'

'Taylor and Katy Perry?'

Nate grinned. 'Taylor Swift! I know her.'

'Yeah. Deaf octogenarians in the Arctic know Taylor Swift.'

'Why are you quizzing me about my knowledge of pop music history?'

'History?'

He shrugged, but there was the hint of a smile in his eyes. 'I didn't say "ancient history".'

'You'd better not.'

'So why are you quizzing me?'

Why was she? 'Just to...' To what? *To remind myself that you're off-limits.* But she didn't need to be reminded of that, did she? Everyone was off-limits. Darcy was off-limits to herself. She wasn't interested in anyone. 'Just feeling old, I guess.'

Nate stared at her for a moment. 'You're not old.'

'I'm older than you.'

'And younger than lots of other people.'

'Just let it go,' she muttered.

—

Nate didn't want to let it go. Nate wanted to keep pressing, keep searching for why his relative youth bugged her so much. It felt like she was trying to convince herself of something. He took a breath. Always wanting things sorted out right now was something he'd talked to the Owl about. He needed to get better at sitting in uncertainty, apparently. Sitting in uncertainty sucked.

'I'll leave you to it anyway.' Darcy moved towards the door.

'So what should I make for you next?' Nate blurted out the question.

'What do you mean?'

What did he mean? He'd asked something, anything really, to make her stay a minute longer. 'Well, you liked the sandwich. What's next?'

'You didn't make the sandwich just for me?'

'And if I had?' Another question was out of his mouth before he had a chance to filter.

'But you didn't…' she started.

'If you say so.' This was mad. But in for a penny. 'So what next?'

'Really, I'll eat anything.'

'Sure, but what will you love?'

She shook her head. 'I don't really feel that way about food.'

That wasn't true. He'd seen the moment when she closed her eyes and savoured the second bite of pastrami on rye. 'Come on. There must be something you've really enjoyed in the past.' What did he know about her past?

'What about when you were modelling or was that just celery sticks and slimming pills?'

Darcy shook her head. 'No. Well, yeah. A bit. It's fine.' She was at the door now. 'You don't have to make anything for me.'

He watched through the kitchen window as Darcy made her way across the castle courtyard towards the stables. He should let it go. He knew she'd liked the sandwich and he thought she was warming to him. The whole reason for trying to make the perfect Darcy dish was to get in her good books so she'd send back good reports. Acting on whatever fire was currently coursing through his body wouldn't help with that. At best she'd be politely appalled. At worst he'd be sent back to London under a seriously dark cloud. Nate had placed his fingers over hers to guide her knife an hour, or more, ago, but he would have sworn the skin still tingled. He squeezed his hand into a tight fist. He needed to do his job. He didn't need any complications.

Now was the time to stop.

Instead he pulled out his phone and searched for 'Darcy Lowbridge'. She was on Facebook, but she didn't post publicly other than to share promotion for the cookery school and the castle. She was on Instagram but her account was private. So no clues from social media. He scrolled down the list of results. *Highland Life*. He clicked on the link and read the article.

Meet the Highlands' Newest Baroness

It was a profile from not long after Darcy had moved to Lowbridge and married Alexander. The writer was clearly thrilled at the idea of a New York model turned Highland lady and there was lots of enthusiastic prose about her swapping catwalks for hill walks. As he scanned down, one paragraph caught his eye.

> The new baroness clearly has a sense of humour. She happily told me anecdotes of her life as a model, including the revelation that after her fortnightly weigh-in with her former agency she would hightail it across the street to the nearest diner and gorge herself on the pie of the day. 'Cherry, Key lime and good old apple were often on the menu, but banoffee was my favourite.'

Nate closed the article and put his phone down on the bench. He wasn't going to make her banoffee pie. He was going to teach the classes, and cook the meals. He was going to make a success of his time at Lowbridge and go back to London to be greeted like the returning hero. No complications. He squeezed his hand closed again.

—

Darcy had intended to take Larry out for a gentle walk this afternoon but as she neared the stables she was drawn to Liberty's stall. A slow walk along the shoreline wasn't what Darcy needed right now. She needed to feel something, something that wasn't going to make her guts swirl and her skin fizz.

They set out past the walled garden and up onto the clifftop. Here there was space to make Liberty pick up to a canter and then a gallop. The wind rushed past them, and Darcy felt the dry tingle of salt on her lips. Normally this feeling exhilarated her and grounded her all at the same time. She was so utterly in the moment that everything else faded from view.

Not today. Today it felt like she was trying to scratch a full-body itch with a single fingernail. She needed something more. She turned inland and galloped across the hillside towards the woodland. Up here the river flowed down into the loch at the foot of Lowbridge headland with a narrow gully. Liberty had jumped this gully before, but not for many months. Darcy hadn't ridden her this hard since... The end of the thought flew away from her. It was the same as so many of her thoughts. She hadn't ridden Liberty like this since Alexander died and Darcy's life ruptured into before and after.

Today she pressed on, pushing Liberty to go faster and harder and right at the brink of the gully to rise up and over and... no. Liberty refused. She turned sharply, jolting Darcy in the saddle and sending her crashing to the ground. Darcy threw out a hand to break her fall, but still hit the earth hard – knee, then hip, and then hand. 'Damn.'

Liberty ambled around in a comfortable circle and nuzzled her prone rider. Darcy couldn't help but feel that she was being looked at with confusion, an expression of *well, what on earth are you doing down there?*

It was a very good question. Darcy's urge for adrenalin had receded the second she felt her weight shift and her body recognised the start of a fall, long before her brain caught up. What had she been doing? Liberty was unused to being ridden so hard, and Darcy hadn't prepared her for the jump. Of course she'd refused.

She stood up cautiously. Her knee twinged but she could stand on the leg. She suspected she would have an impressive set of bruises down her side in the morning, but for now she was relieved nothing was broken, and she could walk. She took Liberty's reins in her hands and patted her long neck. 'I'm sorry. I don't know what came over me.'

The walked together, much more slowly and sedately, down the hill and onto the road, making their way down to the coach house and the entrance to the castle. Their slow progress made them sitting ducks for the ambush.

'Darcy! Darcy, love!' Flinty was marching up the path from the Low Bridge towards her, followed, more sedately but no less determinedly, by Veronica. 'Tell her you'll do it.'

Darcy let Liberty amble over to the grass verge and accepted her fate. 'Do what?'

'This whole talent thing. Adam's going to be in Edinburgh and they've got the idea it has to be someone from the castle. Well, Nina's got that idea. Anna is all very keen on doing it herself. And I said it should be Veronica but she got that look she gets…'

Veronica arrived at her partner's side. 'What look is that?'

'Oh, you know.'

'Imagine that I do not.'

'That look like you're chewing a wasp.'

'And when did I get that look?'

'Well, when Nina said…' Flinty frowned. 'This morning… when… Oh, it doesn't matter.'

Darcy caught a hint of fear in Veronica's eyes before she turned to Darcy. 'I'm sorry. I think what Margaret is trying to say is that they need someone to host the talent auction. Nina thinks it would be appropriate for someone from the family to do it.'

'Aye. That's what I said.'

'In a manner of speaking.'

Darcy had done things like this when she was first married to Alexander. He'd been relieved to let her. Recently that had changed though. People said it was because of the pandemic, but honestly Darcy thought her husband had been glad of the excuse to retreat inside his castle walls. She wasn't the lady any more though. 'Did they ask Adam?'

'He's in Edinburgh,' Veronica explained.

That made sense. Adam was away a lot at the moment, trying to get everything on track with his landscaping business before the baby came and he took some paternity leave to be with his family. 'Bella?'

'Is supposed to be resting,' Veronica pointed out.

'Yeah, but has anyone told her?'

'I said Veronica could do it,' Flinty added again.

'And Veronica disagreed,' Veronica disagreed.

'I don't know.' Darcy shook her head. Once she'd have jumped at the chance. She loved being up on stage. She loved playing the hostess with the mostest. It would have sounded fun. Even six months ago she'd have said yes without a hesitation. So it wasn't that Alexander's death had changed her. It was the months after that. She wasn't getting better from her grief. She was getting worse – not from the spiked pain of those first few days, but from something longer and bleaker and harder to see a way out of. She tried to tell herself, again, that it would be good to do it – that keeping busy was the key. But keeping busy wasn't helping her. Nothing was. Nothing cut through the fog that sat between her and the world. 'Maybe Jill?'

Flinty shook her head. 'Was a time when nothing happened in this village without a Lowbridge there to kick it off. Why isn't your Alexander doing it?' she asked.

Veronica and Darcy stopped. Veronica's gaze dropped to the floor.

'Alexander's passed on, Flinty.' Darcy spoke quickly and quietly as if everything was normal when nothing was normal at all.

Flinty froze. 'I know that. I meant... your...' She stopped again. 'The new laird.'

'Adam's in Edinburgh.'

'Aye. Right. So we'll tell them you'll do it then.'

Darcy was stuck. Veronica wouldn't meet her eye. 'Of course. I'll do it.'

'Good. Good.' Flinty nodded and then looked around for a second as if she wasn't quite sure what was happening. 'Anyway, best get on.' She turned and started to walk away. Veronica made to follow her. Darcy hadn't always had the best relationship with her husband's mother. She strongly suspected that she wasn't at all Veronica's idea of an appropriate wife for her son, but recently the older woman had softened towards her. And Flinty, who had been housekeeper at the castle for many years, had always been kind. Always.

'Veronica?' She called her back.

'Yes?'

'Is... is Flinty OK?'

Veronica Lowbridge didn't answer for a moment. 'Just a little tired,' she eventually replied. She nodded and for a moment Darcy thought she was going to say more. 'Thank you for hosting the auction. I shall let Nina know.' And she walked away after her partner.

Darcy continued her walk back to the castle, settled Liberty in the paddock after a good rub down, and walked back past the coach house. It still felt like there was a lot of day to fill and too much energy to spend it quietly.

She needed activity. She still needed something more to distract her mind and to punch through the fog.

Nate's motorbike was parked outside the coach house. She'd never ridden a motorbike. She imagined that would be thrilling. She ran a finger over the handlebar. Her eyes slid closed – the speed, the power, the adrenalin of riding over the narrow Highland roads. That would really be something.

'You'll need this.' She opened her eyes to see Nate's hand holding a crash helmet out to her.

'I didn't hear you…' She looked back towards the castle gate.

'Just saw you out here. You look like you want to go for a ride?'

'I don't know how to.'

He laughed. 'I wasn't suggesting you go on your own.' Nate, she realised, was already wearing a leather biker jacket, and gripping a second helmet in his other hand. He looked her up and down. She was wearing riding boots and her chest protector under a high-vis jacket already. Nate nodded towards the bike. 'You wanna?'

'Yeah. OK.'

—

Nate hadn't been out on his bike, just for the fun of it, for a long time. In fact, riding up to Lowbridge was the first long ride he'd done for years. He zipped about the capital a bit, when the Tube or the bus wasn't convenient, but actually letting go and just feeling the power and the joy of riding the bike was something he never did any more. For years it had been his day-off staple, to ride out of the city and clear his head on the open roads. Lately he just slept, and scrolled his phone, and wondered where the time had gone.

He swung his leg over the bike, and leaned it on its side stand to make it easier for Darcy to get on. 'OK. You need to hold on properly. Best option is the bar behind you.'

He felt Darcy wriggle behind him.

'That feels weird.' She laughed. 'I'm used to having my arms forward to hold the reins.'

'OK.' Nate swallowed hard. 'How about one hand on the bar, and the other arm around me?'

Darcy's right arm slid around his waist.

'How's that feel?'

This time she took a second to answer. The second stretched out for hours in Nate's mind. 'Good. Better. It feels better.'

'All right.' He twisted his head to make sure she would hear his last instructions. 'The most important thing is that you're not driving. I know you're used to riding a horse so you're used to being the one in control of things, but here you're not. So don't try to lean too much. Don't try to steer. You'll feel when I lean and you can go with me a little bit but no more than that. If you move unexpectedly I can lose the balance of the whole thing.'

'I understand.'

'One more thing. If you want to stop at any time, you squeeze my leg.'

'OK. What about if I want to go faster?'

He shook his head. 'That's up to me, I'm afraid. Safety first. You're OK going fast though?'

'Definitely.'

Nate revved the engine and pulled the bike away from the coach house. He took it cautiously at first, getting used to the weight of Darcy behind him, feeling the way she moved on the bike and changing his style to accommodate her. As they came out of the village, Nate picked up speed, and then dropped his gear to turn onto the pass that went up into the hills and over towards Lochcarron.

The roads twisted and turned in front of him, and he channelled all his focus into the ride. Nate's awareness focused down from worrying about La Mer, from thinking about the cookery school, from the fear that Guy had cast him out, from the gnawing sense of dislocation that had followed him from London, from the pressing silence of his room at night. There were only three things in his mind. The weight of the bike beneath him, the road in front of him and the press of Darcy's body behind.

He rode through the hills and back down to the shoreline, turning off the road and following a lane into Achintraid, where he pulled over at the edge of the water, tilting the bike on its stand to help Darcy dismount.

−

Darcy pulled her helmet off and ran her hand through her hair, which was stuck to her forehead with a sheen of sweat.

Nate followed her down the slim shingle beach. 'What did you think?'

'It was great.'

'Have you ridden before?'

She shook her head.

'I'm surprised. You were a good passenger.'

'Not much to it.'

'You'd be surprised. A lot of people try to lean too much into the turns and it's all you can do to keep things upright.'

'You told me not to do that.'

'Yeah, but it's a lot of trust in someone to just let them ride while you cling on.'

He was right. Darcy hadn't thought about it. From the second he'd turned on the engine, she'd felt safe. Excited, alive, but safe.

'Bit different to riding a horse?' he added.

'Yeah. You haven't quite converted me yet.'

'Maybe I'll have to try horse riding.'

'Have you ever?'

He shook his head. 'Happier with an engine. Horses are way less predictable. I'm glad you liked it though.'

'I did. I really enjoyed it.' She said it quietly, testing out the idea for size. She hadn't enjoyed very much recently. 'I think because it was new.'

'What do you mean?'

'I...' She couldn't say it. She stared out at the sea. 'I never did anything like that with Alexander.'

'So it's not full of memories?'

She nodded. There was something else though. Something else poking at her. 'But maybe I'm not supposed to enjoy new things. Like putting down new memories without him feels like I'm letting him go.'

'The old memories are still there,' Nate assured her.

'Are they though?' Darcy wasn't so sure. Sometimes they were, but other times they felt further and further away and that was like losing him all over again. 'I hate that I can't feel him any more, but I'm scared that if I could it would hurt too much.'

Nate didn't reply. He just walked over, put his arm around her shoulder and squeezed so gently. She let her head rest on his shoulder, just for a second. Only for a second, before she moved away. 'Come on. We should probably get back.'

Chapter 8

The cookery school session started at ten a.m. Darcy was ready at 9.45. Nate would be in the kitchen. She could go down and say hi. But then what? He'd mentioned the motorbike ride a couple of times over the intervening week. She feared he was building up to inviting her out for a second trip. So far she'd managed to change the subject, but what if he did ask? Would that be the start of something? It couldn't be the start of something. It simply couldn't.

Or he might not mention it at all. Darcy tried to convince herself that wouldn't be worse, that his indifference wouldn't cut like the sharpest chef's knife. She slipped in at the back of the lesson at quarter past ten, just as Nate was finishing up his welcome and introducing the first recipe of the day. Darcy had read Bella's notes for the session and knew exactly what to expect. The lesson was all about fabulous desserts. They were making apple pie, strawberry meringues and chocolate mousse with some sort of fancy sugar-work flourish. Bella had it all laid out.

'So our first recipe today is going to be banoffee pie,' Nate announced.

That wasn't on Bella's plan.

'We're going to start with this because there are lots of stages – the base, the caramel and then the banana and the cream – so we'll keep coming back to it through the day.

We are going to be working on the base first. It's super easy and you get to take out all your aggression on some poor innocent digestives.'

Nate organised the group into pairs, and set one person gently melting butter and the other bashing biscuits up with a rolling pin. Compared to his first lesson, Nate was a different man. The impatient arrogance was gone. Now he was a round peg in a perfectly fitting hole. He'd dispensed with the chef's whites and had a Highland Cookery School apron tied over a simple grey T-shirt and jeans, and was happily chatting to students, correcting mistakes and making jokes. The same calm Darcy had felt on the back of the bike was suffusing the kitchen.

That was, if anything, even more enraging. This wasn't his kitchen. Darcy slipped out of the room. She found Bella in the Yellow Room, laptop open on her knee.

'That doesn't look like resting.'

'I'm pregnant, not sick,' Bella shot back. 'What's up? I thought you were in with Nate today.'

'I was. That's the problem.'

Bella sat up. 'What's wrong?'

'He's doing banoffee pie.'

Bella nodded.

'Right now,' Darcy emphasised. 'With your students.'

'Yeah.'

'The schedule said apple pie.'

'He said he wanted to do something a bit different.' Bella shrugged. 'Most of them are doing the pub classics day tomorrow and there's a steak pie on that, so he thought it would be better to mix things up.'

Darcy shook her head. This wasn't right. The cookery school was Bella's baby. She was always all over every detail of what happened in her kitchen. 'Well, he shouldn't just come in and change things.'

Bella closed her laptop. 'Look. When he told me, my first instinct was to ask how he had the nerve to change a single thing, but then I took a breath. Take a breath, Darcy.'

'But it's your cookery school.'

'Which Nate has come all the way from London to run while I grow a human. He's not doing anything crazy. He hasn't got them mixing up nerve gas in the good saucepans. He's tweaking some of the lessons to focus on things he wants to cook and he's trying to do a good job.'

'But his first lesson was…'

'Better than mine. Nobody ended up in A & E.' Bella took a deep breath. 'Handing things over to someone else is horrid but I want the school to still be here, and to be thriving when I'm ready to come back to it. And Guy recommended him, and I just have to trust that he's doing a good job.'

'But…' Darcy didn't have an argument. Nate was here to look after the cookery school and that was what he was doing. Bella was happy. The students were happy. It was only Darcy that had a problem with him.

'I thought you were coming round to him. I saw you coming back with him on the bike.'

'We just went for a ride. I've never been on a motorbike.'

'Cool.' Bella looked for a second as if she was going to say something else. She shook her head. 'That's cool. Did you have fun?'

'It was fine.' It was wonderful. 'I should probably still keep an eye on him though.'

'You don't have…'

Darcy ignored her.

Nate had noticed that Darcy had slipped out while he was encouraging the students not to be shy about bashing their biscuits into smithereens. It was one of his favourite things to do in the kitchen. It was sad that most of the time food processors carried that load. There was really nothing better than properly whacking something with a rolling pin to work whatever was in your head, out of your system.

He noticed as well when she came back in. His back was to the door, but – and Nate realised this with a start – he recognised the scent of her. Sweet, almost toffee-like. Nate had never in his life recognised the scent of a woman. The scent of a hundred different fruits, the deep richness of a red wine, the punch of a beef stock, the warmth and welcome of a hot apple pie – those were the smells Nate lived his life by. He did not go weak at the knees over a nice perfume.

He looked around despite himself. 'You OK?' he asked.

She nodded and perched back on the stool in the corner. Nate continued the class. Biscuit crumbs were stirred into melted butter, and bases pressed into tins and refrigerated. The group gathered again for his demonstration of how to make the caramel layer – melting sugar into butter and adding condensed milk and heating and stirring for just the right amount of time. 'This is one where you need to keep an eye on things but also be patient,' Nate explained. 'If you take the caramel off the heat too soon it'll never set in the fridge.'

He spooned his own thickening caramel over the base of his demonstration pie and slid it into the fridge, before going to help the rest of the group.

'How's everything going here?' Fiona was standing in the doorway to the kitchen. Nate was relieved that his students responded with positive comments and appreciative smiles.

'All good, I think,' he added.

'Could I have a quick word?' She gestured towards the hallway.

'Sure. Just give me a yell if there's a problem. Darcy will look after you though.' Nate stuck that on slightly naughtily. He was pretty sure Darcy was no expert in the kitchen. With her in charge he imagined he'd be coming back to a room full of burned sugar.

Fiona stopped in the hallway. 'You've heard about the talent auction the village are planning?'

Nate shook his head.

'It's a fundraiser to renovate the old community hall. People volunteer skills or talents and people bid on them. Like Nina's offering a home-made pie once a month for a year. Young Strachan'll come round and do decorating. You know?'

'Which Young Strachan?'

'Baby Strachan I think.' She looked at her tablet. 'Old Young Strachan's offering water taxi services and odd-job stuff. Old Man Strachan tried to put "advice on how to avoid falling down a pit".'

'What?'

'Yeah. I mean, most of us manage that already, don't we?'

Nate certainly always had.

'Anyway, getting involved in stuff like this is excellent for our community engagement and relations.'

'Our what?'

'Our burning need for the village not to hate us.'

'Right.' That made more sense.

'Adam's offering some gardening time, and normally Bella would offer to cook a slap-up meal or something, but the baby's due a few weeks after the auction and she's supposed to be resting and…'

Nate saw where this was going. 'You'd like me to step in?'

'Exactly. Can I put you down for cooking a dinner of the winning bidder's choice?'

'Sure.' Nate answered automatically, and surprised himself with his answer. It made sense. Keeping the village happy would keep Bella happy and that would make Guy happy. And it was cooking. He was always happy to be cooking.

'How many people?'

He blew the air out. He'd be cooking on his own, possibly with prep at the castle and then final touches in an unfamiliar kitchen. 'Twelve? Is that OK?'

'Perfect. Most people don't have that many friends anyway. I'll say maximum of twelve, and I presume it's fine if it's less?'

Nate nodded.

Fiona touched his arm. 'Thank you so much for this. I really appreciate it.'

'No problem at all.'

'Good.' She stepped back. 'Can I ask you something else?'

'Yeah.' He glanced back towards the kitchen door. 'Just quickly, you know.'

'Of course.' She had her phone out and glanced down at the screen. 'I touched your arm a moment ago.'

'Yeah.' Oh shit. If getting tangled up with the laird's stepmum was bad, he couldn't imagine that bringing the estate business manager into the mix would make anything better.

Now she was definitely reading from her screen. 'Did you find that friendly, flirty or just inappropriate?'

'Erm…' What on earth? 'Friendly, I guess. I mean until you started with the follow-up questions. This that we're doing now – this is weird.'

'Right. Sorry. I'm just trying to hone my flirtation technique.'

'On me?' This was bad. This was definitely bad. 'It's just… I mean, you're really nice but we both work here, and I'm not sure…'

'Oh for goodness' sake, no.' Fiona frowned. 'I wasn't flirting with you. I was just looking for some feedback. Obviously age-wise you technically fall outside of my sample group, but there aren't that many people available to ask.'

'No. Right.' Nate was getting used to conversation at Lowbridge getting away from him, but he wasn't sure he'd ever been in sync with this one to start with.

'Well, you wouldn't let me do the flirtation part of the survey last week.'

Of course. 'Right. No. Sorry.' Why was he apologising?

'So at the moment I have no data at all on that.'

'Right. Isn't dating more of a going-with-how-you-feel-in-the-moment thing?'

Fiona stared at him for a second. 'I suppose you could try it that way, but it seems fraught with inefficiencies.' She stepped forward again. 'So...' She rested her hand on his shoulder. 'Two, three, four. Was that friendly, flirtatious or too much?'

'The counting made it weird.'

'I wouldn't do that on a real date, obviously. Studies show that touching someone on the upper arm for as little as one to two seconds builds rapport so I thought doubling that would really get the point across.'

'I don't know. Maybe that was a little bit long.'

Fiona tapped her screen. 'OK. Wait there.'

'I really need to get back...'

Fiona was already past him in the kitchen door. 'Darcy!'

'What's up?'

'Can you just stand here and touch Nate's arm?'

Darcy frowned. 'What for?'

'So I can see. He thinks I'm doing it too long.'

'I don't understand...'

'It's for her dating plan.'

'Right.' Darcy stomped over to him and clapped her hand onto his arm. It wasn't gentle or friendly or in any way flirtatious. It should have felt like being slapped on the back by a drunken punter. Instead it fizzed against his skin, sending a wave of unmistakeable heat up his arm and into his chest.

'One, two, three...' Fiona nodded. 'I see what you mean. It is a long time, isn't it?'

Nate nodded mutely. It was ages. It was a lifetime.

Darcy's hand was still resting just below his shoulder, her little finger just brushing the skin below the sleeve of his T-shirt.

'Thanks anyway. I'll let you get on.' Fiona's voice was far away. He was aware of her turning to leave. 'Oh. You can put your hand down now, Darcy.'

Only then did she move.

—

'Sorry.' Darcy pulled her hand back. 'Miles away.'

'Where?'

'What?'

'You said you were miles away. Where were you?'

That was the problem with lies, even little white ones. People asked questions, and then the lie got bigger. Of course she hadn't been miles away. She'd been right here, in this moment, aware of every nerve ending in her body, for the first time in months.

'Were you thinking about NSYNC?'

'No.'

He smiled. 'Whatever you say.' He glanced over his shoulder. 'I'd better get back. Unsupervised caramel isn't a great idea.'

'Of course.'

She didn't follow him back into the kitchen. She couldn't. She wanted to. She wanted to stay close, to keep drinking in whatever it was she was suddenly feeling, but at the same time she absolutely could not do that. The urge to follow him was the same urge that had pushed her to try to force Liberty to make that jump. It wasn't good for her.

She returned to her room and told herself she was surprised when the knock on the door came.

Nate was standing outside, holding a plate with a perfect wedge of banoffee pie. 'I made this especially for you and you ran away.'

'You didn't make it for me and I didn't run away.'

'Well, I know you're at least half wrong.'

Darcy didn't meet his gaze. 'Why did you make it for me?'

'I...' He stopped. 'Maybe I just like a challenge. But I did, so please take it. You have no idea how insecure chefs can be about the idea of someone not wanting to eat their food. It's like dissing someone's art or writing or, I don't know, first-born child.'

Darcy couldn't stop herself from smiling. 'Well, I wouldn't want to do that.' She glanced behind her. The bed was made. There was no underwear on the floor. 'Why don't you come in?'

Nate followed her into the room, leaving the door half open. 'Wow. This is an amazing room.'

Darcy looked around. 'I guess. The view's nice.'

Nate made his away over to the window that wrapped around the corner in a mini bay, with a seat built into it. 'It's incredible. You are so lucky to live here.'

'I know.' She felt herself bristle. 'I didn't always live here.'

He held his hand up. 'I know. I wasn't having a go. Just saying it's great. And you're right about the view.'

She stared past him. 'When I first came here, I couldn't imagine ever tiring of it.'

'You're tired of it now?'

'I'm...' Darcy brought her plate of pie over and sat down on the window seat. 'I think I'm tired of everything.'

Nate leaned on the wall, looking out beyond her towards the cliffs and the ocean. 'Try the pie.'

Darcy slid the fork through the cream and then the banana and the toffee into the biscuit base, and brought it to her lips. Butter, sweetness, fruity ripe banana, soft cream. 'Oh.'

'It's good?'

Darcy nodded silently. It was better than good. It was all-consuming. She closed her eyes and took another mouthful. The taste of the pie filled her senses. She could almost feel the pleasure tingling on her skin. She ate in silence, eyes closed, mind full of toffee and cream and banana and pure fleeting joy.

And then she looked up. Nate was still leaning against the stone wall, half smiling. The tingle on her skin intensified under his gaze. She looked away. 'I used to get banoffee pie all the time when I was a model. Straight after agency weigh-in, we'd go over the street and split a piece of pie between us.'

'I know.'

Darcy froze. 'How do you know?'

'I… erm… I read an article. I was…' He shook his head. 'This is going to sound creepy. I saw how much you enjoyed the sandwich and wanted to find something else you'd like, so I…' He winced. 'I searched online to see if you'd posted about favourite foods or anything and I found this interview where you talked about banoffee pie.'

'*Highland Life*?' She shook her head. 'That was a whole thing when I first came here. New York model becomes Scottish lady. I think one of the tabloids picked it up.' Darcy thought back. 'For a while there was a photographer who used to hang around waiting for me to do something exciting and scandalous.' She glanced out of the window. 'It's possible he's still waiting.'

'Living in the hills? Scavenging for food?'

Darcy laughed and then stopped herself. The sound felt alien, too far away somehow. 'Maybe you should leave a slice of pie out for him.'

He grinned. 'Oh damn.'

'What?'

'I forgot the second thing.' He pulled his phone from his pocket, tapped his thumbprint to the screen. 'Hold on.'

A second later the sound of 'I Want It That Way' filled the room.

Darcy shook her head. 'Seriously?'

'What?'

'Backstreet Boys? You come here to make your offering and you bring me Backstreet Boys?'

His face was all innocence. 'So that's not your Timberlake people?'

'It is not.'

He shrugged. 'Well, it's all the same, isn't it?'

'Absolutely not.'

He tapped and swiped again, and the music was replaced by 'Bye Bye Bye'.

'Thank you.' There was something else she wanted to say to Nate, something that had been sitting in her head after the pastrami on rye, and that was screaming at her even louder now. 'So you really are cooking things specifically for me?'

He nodded.

Something approaching anticipation bubbled up in Darcy's gut. She had a crazy idea why he was doing that. A crazy idea she wanted to be wrong about. Of course she wanted to be wrong. 'Why?' she asked.

'Because, well, I want you to like my food.'

'Right.'

'Because you're reporting back to Bella, aren't you? And she is to Guy, so yeah. It matters that you're happy.'

The anticipation thudded away, replaced by the safe, familiar emptiness Darcy had become accustomed to. He wasn't going to ask her to go out for another ride. He wasn't going to grin and suggest she give him a horse-riding lesson to balance the score. She was a work contact he needed to keep on side. That was all. 'Right. Of course. Well, all good reports on the banoffee pie. Thanks.'

Nate stopped, and for a second she thought he was going to say something more, but he just picked up her empty plate and nodded. 'Glad you liked it. That's... that's all I wanted.'

Chapter 9

'Are you sure you're OK with all this?' Nate asked again, as Bella heaved a roasting tray out of the main oven.

'I'm fine. I've done nothing but rest for weeks.'

Nate was dead sure that was a lie.

'One day of work isn't going to break me.'

'OK. It's just that if it does, then Adam and Darcy and...' Nate paused over the great horror that had now struck him. '...Veronica are going to blame me.'

'I won't break. I'm pregnant, not sick, and I'm bored. And we have pretty much all the village and half of Lochcarron and fuck knows who else arriving expecting a top-class buffet in less than an hour, so you really, really don't want me to go and lie down, do you?'

Obviously he didn't. 'Don't want you keeling over in my nice clean kitchen either though,' he muttered.

Bella waved her spatula at him slightly murderously. 'Whose nice clean kitchen?'

'This nice clean kitchen you are very kindly letting me squat in for a while.'

'That's better. Nina said you were being auctioned tonight.'

'Yeah. Well, my cooking skills,' Nate clarified. 'Nothing more.'

'So long as Anna knows that. If she thinks they'll raise more if you offer to cook naked, she'll have your whites off before you know what's happening.'

Nate's mind boggled. 'There's a lot to unpack there.'

'That's what she'll say,' Bella quipped.

'OK. I'm going to check the dining room set-up before this turns into a sexual harassment claim.'

Nate jogged from the kitchen through the main hallway and towards the ballroom. The plan was to set out the buffet in the dining hall that adjoined the ballroom. According to Bella, that was what they'd done for Hogmanay and it had worked well, so they were repeating the layout for the talent auction tonight. They were covering the cost of the buffet from selling tickets to the auction event, which meant that the money raised on the night would all go to the community hall appeal.

The set-up looked good. They had heat lamps for the hot food and ample space for salads and breads. Evie and Youngest Strachan were coming in to help marshal people serving themselves, and make sure empty trays were cleared away and replenished promptly.

They'd set out the tables in the ballroom last night, but he headed through to check nobody had come and 'helpfully' rearranged things. 'Oh. Sorry.'

Darcy was pacing on the small raised platform at the far end of the room, hastily installed by a pair of Strachans earlier in the week. She looked up. 'No. Sorry. I didn't know you were in here.'

'I wasn't. I just arrived. Are you OK?'

'Fine.'

He moved towards her. 'Really?'

'No.'

'Anything I can help with?'

'No.'

'Want to tell me anyway?'

'No.'

'OK.' Nate hesitated. He was needed back in the kitchen. He should be on his way back there now. He didn't move.

'I haven't done anything like this since…' She took a deep breath in. 'Since Alexander died. I used to like it – being the hostess, playing the lady of the manor.' She shook her head. 'I don't know. I don't know if I can be that Darcy any more.'

Nate really was needed back in the kitchen. Bella would be cursing him right now. 'What was she like?'

'Who?'

'That Darcy.'

'I don't know. I know people used to say I was fun. So I guess I must have been.'

'You don't remember it?'

She shook her head. 'Of course I do. I can tell you about events and places we went and stuff, but I can't…' She jabbed a hand into her own chest. 'I can't feel it here. You know?'

Nate nodded. 'That's what it's like when I lose my rag.'

'What?'

'I have – had…' He pushed it into the past tense. 'When I was younger, I had some issues with anger. And afterwards I knew I'd lost it and I could remember what I did but I couldn't feel it any more. The Owl reckoned…'

'Sorry? The Owl?'

Nate realised what he was saying. 'Yeah. So, like, I saw this therapist for a bit.' He told himself not to be embarrassed. Lots of people had therapy. There was no reason to be embarrassed.

'No reason to be embarrassed.' Darcy smiled. 'I'm American. Everyone's in therapy.'

'OK. Well, he said it was because I push emotion down and then it all erupts as anger but once that's passed, I push it down again.' Nate shrugged. 'Sorry. That sounds stupid.'

'No. It doesn't. Not at all.' Darcy jumped down from the stage. 'Thank you.'

'What for?'

'For the pie,' she whispered.

The pie. Of course the pie. 'I'm just really, really glad you liked it.' Without thinking he took a step towards her. That scent again. Warm and buttery and... 'What perfume do you wear?'

'I don't.' She frowned. 'Not recently.'

There was definitely something.

'Why do you ask?'

'Because you smell wonderful.' Shit. That wasn't something you could say to your employer, or even to a woman who was sort of employer adjacent. A widow who was sort of employer adjacent. A widow who was fifteen years older than you, and sort of employer adjacent. That would definitely score 'inappropriate' on Fiona's post-flirting feedback questionnaire. 'I'm sorry.' Nate stepped back, stumbling over his own feet and knocking awkwardly into the table behind him. 'I'm sorry. I have to go back to the kitchen.'

He turned, head down, and marched away. Darcy was important to his career. Her opinions would get back to Guy. That was why he was cooking for her. That was the only reason. It wasn't the thrill he felt as he watched her lips wrap around the fork. It wasn't the exhilaration he felt when she gasped in pleasure. It wasn't the pure joy of seeing her smile. It was for his career.

It wasn't for his career at all. Nate knew he had messed up at work before. Lots of times. So many times that he'd ended up here. But falling in love with your boss's stepmum. That would be his biggest screw-up yet.

—

Darcy watched him go. She should say something. She should tell him it was OK, that it was just a silly comment, that she knew he didn't mean anything by it. She didn't say any of that.

Standing in front of him had, just for a second, been like banoffee pie meets pastrami on rye turned up to eleven levels of sensation. Every nerve ending in her body had been alive. When he'd stepped towards her she'd felt – not just pictured, physically felt – how it would be if he took another step, and then another, and then reached a hand to her cheek, and pressed his lips softly to hers and…

Darcy waited for the feeling to subside, like the perfect joy of the pie, or the flood of home that came with pastrami on rye. The feeling wasn't going away. She felt… good? She climbed back onto the low stage and picked up the notes she'd made. She could do this. She could host the auction. She could be that Darcy – the Darcy who'd been shut away for the last year. That Darcy was still in her somewhere, waiting for her time to come again.

She gathered her notes together and went to get changed. By the time she came back down, in a red evening dress she hadn't so much as looked at since New Year 2020, the ballroom was filling up and Evie and Young Strachan were moving through the gathered crowd with trays of fizz and fruit juice. She grabbed a glass of champagne – just one to calm her nerves – and made her way into the fray.

'Have you got a gavel?' The first person to catch her attention was Anna, who didn't so much catch attention as hold it at gunpoint and insist it meet her demands.

'I think Jill found one, from when the amateur dramatics did *A Witness for the Prosecution*.'

Anna nodded. 'And you know when to bang it.'

'I think so.'

'Cos if you bang it too soon that's a contract, you know.' Anna stared at her seriously. 'And you don't want to go making contracts with all and sundry, do you?'

'It's just a local charity auction. I'm sure…'

'It's legal. When you bang your gavel. None of this "it's just local" business. The law's the law.'

Darcy nodded. 'Of course.'

She turned from Anna straight into the happily gavel-bearing Reverend Jill. 'I brought this for you.'

She accepted the gavel. 'Thank you.'

'Be careful with it though. Once you bang it down it's a done deal.'

'So I'm told.' Darcy looked around. 'Is Kenny with you?'

Jill's cheeks reddened slightly. 'I think he's here somewhere. He's got a group staying at' – she lowered her voice – 'the McKenzie estate, at the moment.'

The McKenzie estate was Lowbridge Castle's closest rival, although significantly less of a rival since they'd successfully poached Fiona from them to work her business management magic on the side of the – in Darcy's opinion – good guys.

'That's OK. He doesn't need our permission.' Jill's friend who was a boy, Kenny, was welcome to take his tour groups wherever he pleased.

'No. I know. It's just that I told him about the auction, and so he told his tour group and then...' Jill was looking at her feet.

'And then what?'

'Oh no!' Jill wasn't looking at Darcy. She was looking off behind her. Darcy turned. Fiona MacCellan, poised, professional, unflappable Fiona MacCellan, was standing in the doorway to the ballroom. Even from halfway across the room Darcy could see the horror in her face. She followed Fiona's gaze. John McKenzie was waltzing into the room, with a redhead Darcy didn't recognise on his arm.

'Do you know who the woman is?' Darcy asked Jill.

Jill winced again. 'I think that's his wife.'

'Oh for...' Darcy glanced at the minister to her side. 'For goodness' sake.'

Darcy marched over to Fiona. 'Are you OK?'

'I didn't know Mr McKenzie was coming.' She frowned. 'Nina gave me the list. I didn't see... I didn't think.' She shook her head. 'I should have seen his name. Silly Fiona. Another mistake.'

Darcy hadn't seen Fiona like this before. Fiona was competent, efficient, always on top of things – things that didn't involve flirtation, anyway. Annoyingly so. 'What do you mean? You're the least silly person I know.'

Fiona looked at her. 'Really?'

'Really.'

'Right. I just... seeing him, just gets me. Still.'

Even though Darcy knew that Fiona had been involved with her former boss, she still didn't have the full chapter and verse. She was aware that John had swooped in and bought the ailing MacCellan estate from Fiona's father on terms that favoured the buyer very strongly. He'd then rubbed salt into the wound by hiring Fiona to run his tourism businesses from the estate. And, Darcy understood, given Fiona to understand that he was free and available when their relationship tipped from the professional to the personal. On that note – Darcy cleared her throat. 'Jill said that the woman he's with is his wife? She thinks.'

Fiona paled further. 'Yes. Yes. That's her. Looking a lot less tragically deceased than he led me to believe.' She shook her head. 'I can't believe how stupid I was,' she added in a slightly more world-weary tone.

'Are you OK being here? You can duck out if you need to.' Darcy wasn't sure that was true. They'd done events at Lowbridge before Fiona came on board, but they had tended to run with a slightly thrown-together rustic charm, rather than the well-oiled seamless rhythm Fiona created.

'It's fine. I told Nina and Anna I'd be here to keep an eye on things.' She paused. 'Well, I told Nina I'd keep an eye on Anna to stop her taking over, and I told Anna the same about Nina. But still. I should be here. It's not like he's going to make a scene with his wife here, is it?'

Darcy hoped Fiona was right.

'Anyway, it's nearly time to start.' Fiona was back into business mode. 'One last pass of drinks service for latecomers and then time for you to welcome everyone, get them seated and into the auction.'

Darcy felt a tingle of adrenalin through her body. She had twenty-two lots to auction. She was starting with Nina's pies, because Jill and Hugh had both promised to bid on those to create a bit of early buzz, and then she was going to intermingle higher- and lower-value items. And hopefully keep things moving.

'And be careful with that gavel,' Fiona cautioned. 'It's legal once you tap it down, you know.'

'I know!'

Darcy set off back towards the stage. Nina and Netty intercepted her within a few steps. 'You've got the gavel,' Nina noted. 'That's good. But oh...'

'But don't bang it down too early. It's all legal once I do,' Darcy shot back.

'No. I was just going to say the tag's showing on your dress.'

Darcy stood in silence while Nina tucked the stray tag back in.

'She's right about the gavel though,' Netty murmured. 'Can't be too careful.'

Finally, Darcy made her way to the stage and leaned towards the microphone. She'd been a spokes-model for Downtown Auto Services back in the States. She'd recorded adverts and stood in front of displays of tyres for photos. This was just like that. Only not in a bikini and nothing to do with tyres. 'Good evening, everyone,' she started. 'If you could take your seats, we're just about ready to announce our first lot of the night.'

She waited for people to find their places and for the babble of chatter to quieten a little. 'First up we have the offer of a home-baked pie, sweet or savoury, once a month for the next year. So you can choose from a whole menu of flavours and fillings and mix it up every month. These will be prepared by Nina Stone. If you've been to the village pub recently you've probably already been lucky enough to eat one of her pies. So who will start the bidding for me at fifty pounds? That's less than five pounds a pie. Come on.'

As promised, Hugh offered £50, and Jill quickly took them up to £60. A flurry of bids took them up to £180, which felt like a very respectable start indeed. Darcy tapped down her gavel to confirm the first sale of the night.

—

Nate watched through the double doors that linked the dining hall to the ballroom. Darcy on stage was spectacular. Funny, confident, clearly in her element.

'What you staring at?' Evie came in behind him. 'Ooh.'

'What?' Nate turned away from the ballroom and surveyed the buffet table. 'Those plates need stacking up more. We haven't got space for four piles.'

'And that's totally what you were thinking about.' Evie sniggered.

'What do you mean?'

'You've got a crush on Mrs Lowbridge,' she half said, half sang at him.

'Don't be ridiculous.'

'Then why were you staring?'

'Everyone's staring. She's the one on the stage.'

'Everyone's *looking*,' Evie muttered. 'You were gawping.' She pulled a moonstruck face, jaw slack, eyes wide. 'You're in luuuurrrrve.'

'Plates,' Nate replied. 'Now.'

Evie skulked away. Nate turned back towards the stage. Not for the reasons she said. Just because that was where the action was.

'So the riding lesson is currently going to Anna at the front here.' Darcy's voice was, for the first time, slightly strained. This was her lot. She'd offered a riding lesson at the Lowbridge stables. Nate suspected she hadn't expected Anna to be the winning bidder. 'Any more bids? Anyone? Anyone at all?'

No one responded.

'OK then. Going once… any more bids?'

Nate almost bid himself to put her out of her misery.

'Going twice? Anyone?'

He shouldn't. He didn't even know how much the next bid was, and so far people seemed to be bidding generously. It could end up costing him hundreds of pounds.

'Going three times?'

Nate opened his mouth.

Darcy's gavel tapped down.

Too late. Too slow.

'Sold to Anna Flint.' Darcy's smile was back. 'And now our final lot. A dinner of your choosing for up to twelve people cooked by our very own Nathan Turner. Nathan is currently on loan to us from La Mer in London and before that he's worked in Michelin star kitchens in London, Paris, Nice and Barcelona.'

Technically that was true. Less technically he'd been chucked out of the place in Barcelona in less than a fortnight for telling a customer where they could stick their perfectly medium-rare steak after they sent it back for the second time.

'Who will open the bidding? Shall we start at one hundred pounds?'

Nate bristled slightly. You couldn't get a single course at La Mer for much less than that.

Veronica Lowbridge, sitting quietly at the right-hand side of the ballroom, raised her hand to open the bidding.

She was soon joined by Nina and Netty and, slightly unexpectedly, two different Strachans, who seemed entirely unconcerned that they were bidding against one another. The bidding raced up to £500. Nate smiled. And then £800. That was a lot of money. He suspected Veronica had a bit tucked away, but for the other villagers, this was serious spending. This wasn't cooking for suited city boys who were chucking it all on expenses. He felt himself tense slightly.

Bidding slowed but crept up to a slightly hesitant 'One thousand pounds' from Veronica.

That was the highest bid for anything all night. There was a ripple of nervous whispers around the room.

Darcy raised her gavel. 'Going once, going twice, any more bids? Going three…'

'Fifteen thousand pounds!'

What?

Nate strained to see where that bid had come from. A tall man in his forties had his hand raised at the front of the room.

'Fifteen *thousand* pounds?' Darcy queried.

'Fifteen grand, and I get to name part of the new community hall,' he called back. 'It's for a good cause.'

'Right. OK then.' Nate saw Darcy glance over to Veronica and saw the small but definite shake of the head in response. She wouldn't be bidding again. Of course she wouldn't. Fifteen grand for dinner was crazy. Darcy shot another look towards Nina, but Nate couldn't make out her reaction. 'Fifteen thousand pounds for dinner cooked by Nathan Thomas and part of the refurbished community hall named in his honour. Going three times.' She dropped her gavel. 'And sold to Mr McKenzie. A round of applause, I think, for that very generous bid?'

Nate would have expected the response to be ecstatic but it was decidedly muted. A polite ripple rather than a wholehearted ovation. He made his way over to Fiona, who was standing, rather stiffly, at the back of the room. 'Who's the big spender?'

'John McKenzie.' The name came out through gritted teeth.

'Generous guy,' Nate commented.

'Not the word I'd use,' she replied.

—

Darcy came down from the stage and was immediately accosted by Nina and Anna. 'Fifteen thousand?' Anna exclaimed.

'Yeah.'

'It's a lot of money,' Nina added.

'I know.'

'It took us over twenty thousand for the whole auction. I thought we'd do well to get into four figures.'

'People were generous,' Darcy agreed.

'People were drunk,' Anna pointed out.

'Well, so long as Fiona gets their money out of them before they sober up, that doesn't matter.'

Oh. Fiona was dealing with the payments, wasn't she? 'Maybe I should go and help.'

As she approached her colleague, she saw she was too late. McKenzie was bearing down on her. 'Fiona! Hope you're being a good girl over here.' He looked around. 'This place is probably more your speed anyway.'

Fiona was staring directly at her shoes. 'Fifteen thousand pounds. How will you be paying that?'

'Credit card OK?'

'That's fine.' Darcy could see Fiona's fingers shaking slightly as she input the amount on the card machine.

McKenzie entered his PIN number with a flourish and turned away from Fiona. 'And so is this the chap who's cooking my dinner?'

Nate nodded. 'A dinner of your choosing. Ingredients compliments of the Lowbridge Castle Estate.'

'Who have sponsored the whole auction,' Fiona added.

McKenzie looked around. 'It's great when these smaller enterprises try to do their bit, isn't it?'

Darcy bit her tongue. He'd just donated fifteen grand. It would have taken them years to raise that much.

'So I want the works.' McKenzie was focused on Nathan now. 'Truffle, lobster, langoustine.'

'Right. How many for?'

'Twelve was the deal, right?'

'Right.'

He clapped Nate on the shoulder. 'And maybe if you do a good job, we might have a little chat about some real opportunities.' He nodded towards the platters being laid out by Young Strachan and Evie. 'Not just making buffet food with some lass who teaches the locals how to make Victoria sponge.'

That was too much. Bella was just as experienced a chef as Nate was. And Victoria sponges were surprisingly tricky to get perfect. How dare he belittle her. Darcy opened her mouth.

Someone else was already talking. 'I don't know. You can learn a lot from making the perfect Victoria sponge.' Nate smiled. 'And I'm very happy where I am.'

McKenzie laughed and tapped his nose. 'Right you are.'

'Yes.' Nate stepped back. 'I'm sure you've got contact details for someone here, so get in touch with your menu ideas and preferred dates. I look forward to cooking for you.' He paused. 'As a one-off.'

He turned away. Darcy followed him to the buffet table. 'Well, he seems charming,' Nate whispered.

'Oh he is. Very charming. Nothing underneath the charm though.'

Nate shook his head. 'I got that.'

'You're not a fan?'

'I don't like snobs. That's all.'

Darcy left the crowd to fill their boots at the buffet and headed outside into the cool of the courtyard. She'd loved being on stage. She'd loved being at the centre of the night. She'd felt bright and excited and full of life.

She'd felt full of life.

Full of life.

Alive.

And that was awful. She was alive. Alexander wasn't. And then a new feeling came. Horror. Guilt. And there in a wave the thing she didn't know she'd been holding at bay. Grief.

It was unfair. It wasn't right. It wasn't OK that she was still here and he was gone. It wasn't right that she would never get to talk to him again, never get to tease him again for being a fuddy-duddy with his books and his nature. It wasn't right that she was expected to carry on and get through each and every day. It wasn't right that people told her it was all right to move on. None of it was right.

The absence of Alexander filled her whole body. She'd felt the edges of this despair in those first few weeks, but she'd got through them. She was better now. Everyone said she was better now. This feeling had passed.

The feeling disagreed. It clung to her, wrapped itself around her, stabbed at her as fresh and pointed as the very first day.

Darcy dropped to her knees, bent over double on the cold cobbles of the courtyard and wept.

Time passed, and she wept.

—

'Darcy?' Nate was tentative at first. He'd walked into something private. Part of him wanted to walk away, but she was in pain. 'Darcy.' He placed a hand very gently on her shoulder.

She looked up at him for the first time. Her face was blotched and stained with mascara down her cheeks. Her dress was dirty from the cobbles. 'What?' she asked.

'Are you OK?' Stupid question. Stupid.

'No.'

'What's wrong?'

'My husband died.'

'I know.'

'I'm supposed to be over it.'

'Who told you that?'

Darcy shook her head. 'Nobody. But it's been a year. "Get through the first year." They say that, don't they? A full round of birthdays and Christmas and Valentine's and whatever. Get through the first year and you'll be OK.'

Nate had no idea if they said that. He knew that if he had to put a plaster on his finger he still thought of his nan though, and he hadn't lived with her since he was five years old, and she'd died a decade ago. 'I don't think it's that simple.'

Darcy pulled herself to her feet. 'No. It was that simple. I wasn't feeling all this.'

'OK.'

'And now I am and...' She jabbed a finger into his chest. Nate stumbled backwards. 'This is your fault.'

'What?'

'You came here and you made me feel all this stuff.'

He made her feel stuff. Nate's mouth was suddenly dry. 'What stuff?'

'All the memories and the tastes. Your stupid cooking and your... your...' She stopped. 'The cooking.'

'What else were you going to say?'

She shook her head. 'Nothing. There's nothing else.' She took a huge gulp of breath and rubbed her hand across her cheeks to dry the tears. 'Before you came I wasn't feeling anything. I was numb.'

'You can't live like that,' Nate pointed out.

'I can't live like this.' Darcy was swaying in front of him. She put her hand on his shoulder. 'I can't feel all this. It's too much.' She staggered into him, her body now against his chest. 'Make me feel something else,' she whispered.

Nate stepped back. 'I don't think this is a good idea.'

Darcy shook her head. 'It's not. It's a terrible idea but I need to feel something else.'

'I could make you some dinner?'

'No.'

No.

She reached out and ran a finger down his cheek. That scent. Again. Sweet. Toffee. No. Cocoa. His hand raised to hers and caught it against his face. 'You smell incredible.'

'You said that before.'

'And you're beautiful.'

'I'm a mess.'

'A beautiful mess.' Nate's resolve was slipping away. 'You're upset.'

'Yeah.'

'I don't wanna take advantage of you.'

Darcy shook her head. 'You wouldn't be.'

'You're emotional.'

'Yeah.' Darcy hadn't stepped back. 'I'm feeling all this stuff and it's big and complicated and it's too much. I had so much fun tonight. Doing the auction.'

'You looked incredible up there.'

'But then I felt awful. Like it's wrong to be enjoying life this much.'

'That's ridiculous…'

'I don't know. I just…' Her hand was still on his cheek. 'I just want to feel something else. Just for tonight. Distract me.'

Nate knew he shouldn't. He knew that in the morning she'd be mortified and he'd be… what? He'd be in too deep to swim back to shore. But she was looking at him with those ridiculous big round eyes, and she was hurting and she was asking him to make the pain stop, even if it was just for a short while. 'Are you sure?' he whispered.

'He's out here!' The voice echoed across the courtyard Nate had been sure was empty. Darcy jumped back from him like there were rockets under her feet.

Anna bore down on them, closely followed by Nina, and then Flinty and at a slower, altogether more regal pace, Veronica.

Nate saw Darcy turn away, pressing her hand to her eyes.

'You'll cook for it, won't you?'

'For what?'

'The opening of the community hall,' Anna announced triumphantly. 'We've got plenty of money to get started now.'

'Sure.' Nate nodded. 'I'm sure I can.'

'Can he?' Flinty folded her arms. 'Building work takes forever. He's only here a few months.'

'I thought it was a year?' Nina chipped in.

'Up to a year. Bella'll not take the whole year though, will she?'

'Well, either way. One of us will cook for it, I'm sure.' Nate was aware that Darcy was still standing a few metres away from them, sinking back into the darkness. 'Why don't you head back in now, and we'll talk about it another time?'

'They might be right,' Anna continued. 'About it taking ages.'

'Maybe we could have a ground-breaking party when the works start?' Nina suggested.

'Won't that just cost money we need for the building?'

'Well, any sort of opening event will cost money,' Flinty pointed out.

'We have to do something,' Anna insisted.

Nate needed them to go. He needed to go back to Darcy. He needed to find the thing that would make everything all right.

Veronica was looking over towards Darcy too. And then back to Nate. And then back to Darcy again. 'Why don't we discuss this inside, ladies?' she said.

'But we need Nate too...' Anna started.

'We don't need Nathan to make a plan, do we?' She glanced back to Darcy. 'He'll only try to bring his own ideas into it.'

Anna and Nina exchanged a very definite look. 'Well, we don't need that,' Anna muttered.

Finally they allowed Veronica to shepherd them back towards the ballroom, still chattering and bickering. 'What about a pre-opening?'

'What on earth's a pre-opening?'

Nate waited until he was sure they were back inside and the courtyard was empty again, before he closed the gap between himself and Darcy. If this was a movie then interruption would have broken the moment, but it wasn't a movie, and Nate knew, without thinking about it, that if one of them was going to run, they'd have run already. They'd had their chance to step back. He was inches away from her now. 'Hi.'

She didn't answer. She just inched closer to him and tilted her head to his. Nate really didn't do this. Nate's encounters were brief and casual. His focus was work. There wasn't time to get involved. This would be getting involved. And in the morning it would drown him. Her lips were a fraction away from his. Who was he kidding? The morning was a lifetime away.

Nate Thomas bent his head and kissed her. However much it hurt to walk away tomorrow, walking away without ever tasting her would be a million times worse.

'That went really well...' The new voice was coming from the kitchen doorway. Darcy and Nate jumped apart before anyone could come out and see them. This was it – the final chance to step back from the brink. They could decide now to laugh a little out of awkwardness and embarrassment and in the morning agree to never mention it again. At least he imagined Darcy could decide that. Nate knew he was already way too far gone.

Instead, Darcy took his hand. 'Come on,' she whispered, pulling him towards the side entrance to the castle and the staircase that would take them up to her room before anybody saw they were here.

She was aware that Nate was following her. Her grip on his hand wasn't giving him a huge amount of choice. Everything about this idea was wrong. She was using him as a sticking plaster over a gaping wound, but the wound was too great for her to deal with now. She pushed the door to her room open and pulled him through.

'Are you sure about this?' he asked her again.

'Yeah.' That wasn't enough, was it? 'Are you?'

He exhaled hard. 'I'm sure I want to.'

There was a 'but' unspoken at the end of that sentence. 'But?'

'What about tomorrow?'

'Who cares about tomorrow?' She pulled him closer to her, gripping the open collar of his chef's coat. 'I need this. Now.'

'OK.'

She'd thought – in so much as she'd thought at all – it would be quick. The urgent animal act of two people desperately trying to fill a void or scratch an itch.

It wasn't like that at all.

As soon as Nate's lips met hers, time slowed and stretched around them. He peeled, rather than tore her dress away. She was undone one zipper, one clasp at a time, and only when they were both completely naked, did he pause for a moment. 'Shit. Condoms are in my room.'

No. She needed him. She needed him now. And then she remembered. Darcy reached for the drawer in her bedside table and pulled out a mini pack of condoms. 'Anna did a safer sex presentation at Ladies' Group.'

Nate's jaw dropped. 'I have so many questions.'

'Later,' she whispered.

'Later,' he agreed.

And then he was inside her, and the feeling was everything. It wasn't at all what Darcy had imagined when she'd begged him to make her feel something that would distract her from the pain. His body against hers, his lips on her skin, his hand wrapped around her hip, weren't a distraction. They were everything. They promised her that somehow everything was all right. All the pain and all the pleasure were here and she could encompass it all.

And then there was no thought, no pain, nothing at all but pleasure. And Darcy closed her eyes and clung to the moment for as long as she could bear.

Chapter 10

She woke to the depths of what felt like a raging hangover. Her head hurt. Her eyes were dry and sore. Her limbs felt heavy. She'd had one glass of fizz to calm her nerves. How did she feel so wretched?

'Morning.'

Slowly, so very slowly, she crunched open her eyes and turned her head towards the voice. Nate was sitting in the armchair next to the window, jeans on but unbuttoned, chest bare, crumpled T-shirt in his hand. Nate was in her room. She closed her eyes and opened them again. He was still here, looking at her now with an annoying little half-smile.

He was back in last night's clothes. In a thousand movies, Darcy had seen this scene – the woman waking up after the one-night stand and slowly remembering exactly what happened. This wasn't that scene. She didn't need to remember. Every second was printed on her mind and on her body. She was never going to be able to forget.

'I woke up early. I've got students at nine, and I didn't clean up properly last night. I was…' He half smiled. 'Distracted.'

Darcy closed her eyes. 'I am so sorry.'

'Don't be.'

But she was. The picture of herself in her mind from the night before wasn't pretty. She'd been emotional and pushy and an absolute cliché of a middle-aged woman in crisis pursuing a younger man. 'But I am. I was... awful.' Darcy pulled the covers up to her neck. 'I harried you into bed.'

Across the room, Nate shook his head. 'No. I was definitely a willing participant.' He stood, pulling the T-shirt over his head, and bending to pick his chef's coat from the floor. 'I have to go. Work. You know?'

She nodded. 'Go. And it's fine. We never have to speak about this again.'

Something flickered across his face, but he nodded and made his way to the door. Then he stopped, hand on the handle. 'We can though.'

'What?'

'Speak about it again.' He hesitated. 'Or do it again. If you want.'

'I...' She what? 'We can't.'

He nodded. 'OK.' This time he was halfway through the door before he stopped. 'Why not?'

'Because...' Because it was preposterous. Because she was turning into a joke. Because she was the dowager of the estate. That was her role. Professional widow. And just widow widow. She couldn't begin to explain. 'So many reasons. I'm a lot older than you.'

'How old?'

'You don't ask a lady that!' she pointed out.

'Well, if the lady is proposing it as a reason not to...' He grinned. 'Do "that" again, I think I'm entitled to see your full working.'

'Nearly forty. And you're...' She knew he'd told her. She told herself she wasn't rounding up. 'Twenty-six?'

'Twenty-four.' He shrugged. 'Nearly twenty-five.'

'You're fifteen years younger than me.' Darcy's head fell into her hands. 'I'm way too old for you.'

'I don't think so.' He sighed. 'What else?'

'Isn't that enough?'

'You said there were so many reasons.'

'You work here.'

'For Bella. You're not my boss.'

True. Damn. 'And you're only here for the next few months.'

'So? Doesn't that override your other objections? None of that matters if it's just short term, surely?'

That did kind of make sense.

'What else?' He leaned on the doorframe. 'What's the real reason?'

'All those things,' she insisted.

'And?'

And? She knew the real answer. It was deep inside her gut and at the very front of her mind. 'And I don't think I'm allowed to be happy again.'

'What?'

'It makes me sad to be happy. Because I was happy, you know. With Alexander. And every time I'm happy now it hurts so much because it feels so unfair.'

Nate nodded slowly. 'OK. Well, thank you.'

'For what?'

'Being honest.'

She forced a smile. 'Lucky escape for you then?'

'No. Don't do that.'

'What?'

'Don't pretend this was my decision.'

Nate pulled the door closed behind him. He'd thought the morning after would feel desperate but actually the despair was tinged with something else. Something both expected and entirely unfamiliar. He liked Darcy. He really, really liked Darcy. And even though she had very definitely given him the clearest of brush-offs, there was something exhilarating about the simple awareness that for the next few months he was here and she'd be here, and even if she held him at arm's length, he'd see her every day. Nate grinned.

'Good night?'

Nate stopped and turned towards the voice. Bella was standing in the hallway, behind him, mug of tea in hand. 'I was bringing this for Darcy, but it looks like she's already been... looked after this morning?'

Nate closed his eyes for a second. He was pretty sure Darcy wouldn't want what had happened last night broadcasting, but equally sure that Bella was too bright to see him coming out of a woman's room first thing in the morning wearing last night's clothes and put two and two together to make anything other than four. 'Look, it was a one-off. I don't think Darcy would want anyone knowing, so can you just...' He shrugged. 'Pretend you didn't see me?'

'Sure.' She held the mug out. 'Do you want this?'

'Thanks. I'd better get down. I missed clear-up last night.'

'I noticed.'

'Shit. I'm sorry.'

'No. No. You were otherwise occupied. And people helped.'

'Thank you.' Nate ought to be mortified that people had had to step in and do his job while he'd been in Darcy's bed all night, but however hard he tried he couldn't find the smallest hint of regret. Given the chance, and knowing for sure that he'd be out in the cold in the morning, he would do the same again.

'And if you'd checked your phone this morning, you'd also know that the group booking for today cancelled. They had lunch at a place on the McKenzie estate yesterday and they've had an outbreak of food poisoning.'

'Oh my God.' Food poisoning was every chef's nightmare. In the age of social media, news of an outbreak spread fast and you could swing from fully booked to the brink of closure in hours. 'They didn't eat here? You're sure?'

'Completely sure.'

'Thank God. Is everyone OK?'

Bella nodded. 'Sounds like they will be. Not great PR for McKenzie though.' She was grinning.

'Which you're delighted about?'

'No! Not delighted people got sick. Just…'

'We don't like Mr McKenzie?'

'We do not.'

'Pretty flash donation he made last night.'

Bella nodded. 'Yeah. Wouldn't have agreed to cover the ingredients if I'd known he was going to bid.'

'Cos he's gonna want lobster and prime steak and all the works, isn't he?'

Bella sighed. 'He's sent his menu request already. And it's all stuff we can't really afford. Not for twelve people who aren't paying us for it.'

Nate grinned. 'Then I'll have to see what I can come up with, won't I?'

'The lot said it was the winner's choice of menu though,' Bella pointed out.

'Leave it with me. I'm sure I can come up with something he'll think is the business without bankrupting you in the process.' Nate's mind was already whirring. 'Are you busy this morning?'

Bella pulled a face. 'Supposed to be resting again. Adam had a go at me when I told him how much I'd done yesterday.' She rubbed her belly. 'Can't believe I've still got another month of this.'

Nate grinned. 'Well, does sitting down in the Yellow Room and helping me plan a budget-friendly McKenzie-impressing menu sound close enough to resting?'

'So long as you make the tea,' she agreed.

Ten minutes later they were sitting in the Yellow Room with fresh mugs of tea and a plate of the less pretty cookie rejects from a course a few days before. Nate opened a notebook on his lap. 'OK. So we can do a lot with presentation, right? If I make it look Michelin star, is McKenzie going to know the difference?'

Bella shrugged. 'Based on the food in his cafes, I'd say no, but I don't actually know him that well. Hold on.' She wandered into the hallway and called through to Fiona in the estate office. 'Fi! Have you got a minute?'

Fiona followed her boss back into the room and Bella explained the situation. 'We're trying to come up with a menu for McKenzie that doesn't break the bank on ingredients.'

'But Bella reckons he wants the full three-star works,' Nate added.

Fiona pursed her lips. 'Of course he does. He'll be inviting people he wants to impress.'

'Like who?'

'I don't know. When we, he, was building loads of new stuff it would be councillors, people on the planning committee, that kind of thing, but I don't know now.' She paused. 'Probably the great and good.'

'What do you mean?' Nate asked.

'You know. The landed gentry. Like Adam.'

'Adam's not...' Bella started, and then stopped when she saw Nate's face.

'We're discussing this in his castle.'

'Yeah. Fair enough.'

'Maybe Iain MacWillis from Skye,' Fiona suggested. 'He might ask Adam.'

'He hates Adam.' Bella turned to Nate. 'He tried to buy Adam out of this place a load of times when he first inherited. Wasn't pleased to be turned down.'

'All the more reason,' Fiona pointed out. 'He'd love lording it over him while serving a dinner Adam's had to cover the cost of.'

'Can't we take our costs out of his donation?' Nate asked.

Fiona frowned. 'I'd love to, but I think ethically...' She looked to Bella for guidance.

'No. We said all of the bid money would go to the Community Hall appeal. I know McKenzie won't care but I don't want to do anything he can hold over us.'

'All right then.' Nate pulled them back to the menu. 'He's asked for lobster. Hard to see how we can do that on the cheap.'

'One lobster and a load of crabmeat?' Bella suggested.

'Can we get crab at a good price?'

She nodded. 'Yeah. I can probably get a deal on the lobster as well. I always use the same supplier whenever we do seafood stuff at the school, so we order enough to be in his good books.'

'OK. So we'll do some sort of lobster starter. That'll be smaller portions anyway and we can make it a mixed seafood thing and bring in whatever's a good price on the day?'

'Great,' Bella agreed.

'He asked for steak.'

Fiona sighed. 'Highland Wagyu? He had a thing about that. Reckoned it was the best and only the best for him.' She frowned.

Nate shook his head. 'What if we did beef three ways or something? Like a tiny amount of the Wagyu to keep him happy and then braising steak and a mini steak pie to bulk it out?'

'And you'd make it look amazing?'

'Like it was painted by Van Gogh himself,' Nate promised.

Fiona nodded. 'Then yeah. I think he'll go for that. And then something with peaches.'

Bella checked her list. 'How did you know?'

Fiona shook her head. 'Iain MacWillis loves them, and he won't show himself up in front of a proper laird.'

'We've got peach trees,' Bella said, 'but it's a bit early still. I'll check what Anna and Hugh can do.'

'Peach tarte tatin?' Nate suggested.

'Peach melba?' Bella suggested.

'Isn't that just peaches and ice cream?'

'Deconstructed peach melba with a something-or-other tuile? Then we won't need so much peach per portion.'

'And a shedload of spun sugar?' he added.

'Perfect.'

'And cheap.'

She smiled. 'So cheap.'

Nate started making an ingredients list. 'Could we do a hint of elderflower in the dessert? Would that work?'

'You can forage elderflowers,' Bella pointed out. 'And mushrooms for the steak pie. If you want.'

Nate found he did want. The menu in front of him, born out of necessity and the delicate balance between what their very generous bidder wanted and what Bella could afford to provide, actually looked pretty good, and he'd designed it himself, with an eye to local ingredients. 'This looks good.'

Fiona smiled. 'You've got a spring in your step this morning.'

Bella opened her mouth.

Oh no. 'Just excited about the menu. And foraging sounds cool. I've never foraged ingredients before.'

Bella and Fiona exchanged a look.

'Then you'll need a local guide,' Bella said.

'I thought you were resting?'

'Oh no. I'm not taking you.' She smiled. It was not a comforting smile.

—

Darcy stayed in bed for a long, long time. She didn't decide to stay in bed. In fact, she decided to get up, to take a shower, to get dressed, to find something to eat. She decided to do all those things many times. But still she stayed lying, dead still, in bed.

She'd heard people who'd suffered a loss say that sometimes when they woke up there was a fleeting wonderful moment when they forgot that their loved one was gone, and then the shock hit them all over again. Recently Darcy had found that her every waking moment was filled with exactly the same feeling of numbness. Everything – joy and pain alike – had felt distant to her.

Until Nate Thomas came along with his stupid grin and his incredible food and... and last night. The pure joy of last night. The tangle of limbs. The taste of him. The urgency with which she'd pulled him to her.

And after that the numbness was gone, replaced by something worse. All the fear and the loneliness and the anger she'd been holding at bay had flooded through the dam that Nate had broken down.

Finally, Darcy dragged herself out of bed, pulled on a dressing gown and made her way over to the window. From here the view went out across the north-western part of the estate and the sea. She could see the edge of the walled garden where Alexander had spent as much time as possible, and where she would sit, on sunny days, and watch him pottering while Dipper ran between them in search of treats and head rubs.

She could see a small boat pootling its way over to Skye, a journey she'd made a thousand times with Alexander. He loved it out on the water, and would point out the wildlife all around them.

Then there was the path leading past the walled garden up to the clifftop. That was where he'd proposed the second time. She'd known she would marry Alexander within a few minutes of meeting him. He was so polite and attentive and so utterly out of place in New York City. She'd slipped up the very next day and said, 'When we're married...' and stopped herself, horrified at having shown her hand. He'd simply nodded and muttered, 'Yes. Of course. Go on.' So while Darcy absolutely considered that the real moment of their engagement, he'd proposed properly on that clifftop right there, down on one knee with a long preamble about how he didn't understand for one moment why she would have fallen for someone like him, but that he would do everything he could to make her happy. She'd said yes before he'd even got to the question.

Everywhere here was a memory of Alexander. He was, in a very real sense, still here. And so long as she was here, Darcy was still his wife. She would always be his wife. And she'd betrayed that last night. A wave hit Darcy as surely as if she was in the ocean. A wave of guilt. She'd betrayed her husband. It didn't matter that other people might not see it that way. It mattered that she did.

It could never happen again. That was the only conclusion. She would apologise to Nate and then she would keep her distance. All the feelings in the world weren't enough to justify what she'd done. It was better to accept the numbness, keep busy, take one day at a time, and just keep on going like she had been before.

The knock on the door came just as Darcy finished slicking on her mascara. War paint to face the world, the painted illusion of feeling all right. Her stomach jumped. 'Who's there?'

'Fiona.'

Oh.

'Can I come in?'

Darcy pulled the bed covers over the crumpled sheets. 'OK.'

Fiona pushed the door open. She was carrying three clothes hangers of outfits in her free hand. 'Can you tell me which of these to wear?'

'What for?' Darcy suspected she knew what for already. Fiona was finally going on an actual date, wasn't she?

'Lunch with Pete, who runs tour boats to Raasay from Skye, and then coffee with Fabian, who says he lives off-grid near Torridon but he's on dating apps so clearly not that off-grid, and then dinner with Seb, who is a baker in Portree.'

'Nell's little brother?'

'I guess so.'

'Right. That's a lot of dates. When are they all?'

'Tomorrow.'

Darcy shook her head. 'All of them?'

Fiona nodded. 'It's efficient. Quick early screening and then decide who to invite to second interview.' She paused. 'Date. I mean on a second date.'

'I haven't been on a date for a long time,' Darcy objected. 'Maybe you'd be better asking Bella.'

'You're all stylish though.'

Darcy shook her head. 'I'm not.'

'You are. You have that whole model elegance thing going on. So come on.' She held up the first hanger. 'This is the casual option.'

It was jeans and a simple white T-shirt, with a pale blue jumper. 'It says feminine but practical. Not trying too hard,' Fiona explained.

'Does it?' Darcy asked.

'Well, that's the question. What does it say to you?'

'It's fine.'

Fiona shook her head. 'Fine. I see.' She moved the second hanger to the front. 'This is more smart-casual.' Black wide trousers, and a button-front shirt.

'Bit office maybe?'

'What if I undo an extra button?'

'I think the first one's better.'

The third outfit was, in Fiona's words, the 'more going out' option.

Darcy wasn't quite sure how to react. 'It has a lot of ruffles.'

'Are ruffles sexy?'

'I don't know. Maybe you'd be better asking a man about this?'

'I can't. Nate's off with Veronica and Adam's still in Edinburgh. What sort of clothes did Alexander like?'

Darcy tried to think. 'I don't think he really noticed clothes. He liked practicality – things that were weather appropriate.'

'Forecast is for sun and a light breeze.'

Of course Fiona had checked.

'Probably any of those will be fine then.'

—

'Well, come along then.' Veronica made her way across the walled garden. 'Don't dilly-dally.'

Nate was about to protest that he wasn't, and that she was walking at a fairly impressive long-distance racing pace, but he remembered that she was close to sixty years older than him and thought better of complaining. 'Sorry.'

'Right. So Bella said you need mushrooms, wild garlic and elderflowers.'

That sounded right. 'And anything else you can suggest that would go well with shellfish, or beef.'

Veronica nodded curtly. 'We'll need to take the Land Rover over into the woodland for those, but, as Adam's away, I thought a quick look at what's growing right here would be worthwhile. Old Man Strachan comes down and makes sure everything's watered.'

Nate was ashamed to admit he hadn't been in Adam's much-discussed kitchen garden before. Produce appeared in the kitchen, brought in, he assumed, by Adam or Bella, but this was his first time inside the walls. 'Wow.'

'There's been a garden here for decades, centuries even, but my son really brought it back to life. That's where Adam got his green fingers.'

'That was Alexander? Darcy's husband?'

Veronica nodded.

Nate couldn't help himself. 'What was he like?'

'Oh.' Veronica looked surprised at the question. 'I'm not sure. I'm not sure a mother is the best person to ask what someone is really like. We see what we want to, I suspect. He was clever though and he tried desperately hard to be a good laird.'

Nate paused over how to ask the next thing that was playing on his mind. 'He must have been quite a bit older than Darcy?'

'Fifteen years.'

'He was?' Nate blurted out the reaction.

Veronica raised a perfectly neat eyebrow. 'He was. It caused quite a lot of excitement when he came home with this twenty-five-year-old from New York.'

Fifteen years. Nate filed that little detail away.

'Anyway, you can see what's out here. Lots of stuff coming in now, so no need to buy greens at all, really. Or carrots. Or tomatoes in another day or two.'

Nate nodded. 'This is incredible.' He bent down and rubbed a mint leaf between his fingers. The smell was bright and fresh. He broke the leaf off and chewed. 'That's great.'

'Yes. The walls keep the warmth in, and it's temperate here from the Gulf Stream anyway.'

'I'd love to have a restaurant with access to something like this.'

'Well, for the next few months at least you have a cookery school with access to precisely this.'

That was true. He should really think about seasonality in the lessons. Could he build a whole course around that? Maybe do a session each month focusing on things to make with whatever was best right then. 'This is great.'

'Bella always says it's a chef's dream.'

'I guess.'

'Not your dream?'

'I always pictured myself staying in London. Head chef, then my own place.'

'I suppose that's what young chefs are expected to want.'

'Yeah.' Of course it was. It was about being the best, rising to the top — what else would he want?

'We should get on if we're going to find everything you want in the woods.'

'So where are we actually going?'

'Up into the hills a bit. Mushrooms and wild garlic like wooded, damp areas.' She gave Nate a once-over. He was wearing the sort of trainers that were really designed for walking to the pub in the middle of the city. 'Do you have walking boots?'

'Sorry.'

'Very well. We'll find you some wellingtons before we go.' She strode back towards the entrance way to the walled garden. 'Come along.'

About half an hour later, Veronica pulled the ageing Land Rover that seemed to be the estate's default communal mode of transport off the road, and along a track into the forest. 'Our land goes up to the ridge line.

Beyond that it's McKenzie, and you won't find anything worth foraging there. It's all what he calls "managed forest", which is really just the fastest-growing, highest-profit wood he can find. A wildlife desert.' She shook her head sadly. She started to walk into the woodland. 'Mushrooms for example have symbiotic relationships with different trees. If it's all the same thing you lose all of that.'

Nate followed Veronica through the forest, listening as she pointed out signs of different wildlife – scats on the ground, marks on the bark of trees, nesting sites hidden away from view. 'You really know your stuff.'

'I grew up here. My father used to...' She smiled slightly. 'Well, it was when the laird, my husband's father, still stocked grouse. Let's just say they didn't all make it through to the official shoot days.'

'He was a poacher?' Nate grinned.

'He believed that the land should serve all the people of the area, not just a few.'

Nate laughed. 'Wow! I didn't have you down as a leftie.'

'Oh don't be ridiculous. I'm not anything like that, but I agree that an estate has to serve everyone who lives and works on it. I always tried...' She shook her head. 'Not my business any more.'

Nate wasn't convinced that anything much went on at Lowbridge that wasn't Veronica's business, but he recognised the attempt to change the subject. 'I'm sorry you didn't win the auction. I mean I'm glad that we raised so much money, but...'

Veronica nodded. 'It would have meant a great deal to Margaret.'

'She's your partner?'

Another very small nod. 'Oh, I'm sure you've been filled in on that gossip already, Nathan.'

'Not really. I'm not a big fan of gossip.'

Veronica stopped and looked him over. 'Good. And yes. Margaret is my partner. It took us a long time to get here and now...' She stopped. 'Never mind. Mushrooms, of course, you have to be careful with so show me anything you're not absolutely sure about before you pick it. Wild garlic you'll smell before you see so that's straightforward.'

They picked mushrooms together, pausing now and then for Veronica to identify a particular variety or shake her head. 'Not poisonous but not nice either. I wouldn't.' She smiled slightly. 'Unless you've truly taken against Mr McKenzie.'

Nate hesitated for just a moment. 'Best not,' he agreed. 'Why would the meal have meant so much to Margaret?'

Veronica placed the basket she was filling down on the ground and took a deep breath. 'I don't know if you're aware... I mean, I don't know if people have noticed but Margaret is...' She shook her head. 'For goodness' sake, woman. She's been having little lapses. Of memory. She won't listen to me and go to a doctor but it's happening and it's getting more frequent.'

'I'm sorry.'

'But then sometimes she'll hear a piece of music or catch a particular scent and she'll be back to herself again. I think I thought that you could make us a really special meal – something that would remind her of when we first knew each other and perhaps that would help, and maybe it would be a memory I could hold on to, even when she can't any more. I think there are hard days ahead.' She shook her head. 'But no use crying over things.'

'I'll cook for you.'

'No. I was outbid.'

'Yes.' Nate was decided. 'I'll cook for you and Flinty. Whatever you want. I don't mind.'

'You don't have...'

'Make the donation to the community hall if it makes you feel better. Please.' The memory of his nan in those last few weeks before the social worker came and said she couldn't stay at home any more sat in the front of Nate's mind. 'But let me cook for you.'

—

Darcy finally dragged herself out of her room. She needed something to eat, but that meant the kitchen and the kitchen might very well mean Nate. Her mind was already constructing cute little scenarios where she wandered down, and he was toasting crumpets and poaching eggs for her, and then they sat around the kitchen island, eating brunch and... then the guilt came. She was picturing someone else in the space that was supposed to be Alexander's alone.

She bypassed the kitchen, and walked right out of the castle, past the coach house and over the Low Bridge to the village. She could skip breakfast. She could go for a walk and buy something at the village shop. She probably couldn't do that for every meal for as long as Nate was here, but it would do for now.

She slowed down as she saw Anna bustling towards her with Evie trudging along behind. 'Where on earth are you going?' Anna demanded.

'Just for a walk.'

'What about Evie's riding lesson?'

Anna had been the winning bidder for Darcy's lot the night before but they hadn't even discussed a time or date. Darcy had left the auction too quickly for that. 'What about it?'

'Well, I was just bringing her over.'

'Right. Now?'

'Yes.' Anna nodded like this was totally apparent. 'It says PE on her homeschool schedule. Riding's physical, isn't it?'

'Well, yes.'

Evie stared at her aunt. 'It's Sunday.'

Anna frowned. 'That was probably RE then. I should have taken you to Jill.'

'I think you were looking at Monday.'

'Oh well, we're here now.'

'We hadn't arranged anything.' Darcy wished she could claim parts of last night were a blur, but she remembered every detail. The thrill of hosting the auction. The pain that flooded in afterwards. And then every second of the night that followed. Every touch. Every gasp. Every breath.

Anna narrowed her eyes. 'No time like the present. You're not doing anything else, are you?'

Darcy opened her mouth to object. Why would Anna assume she wouldn't be doing anything else? Darcy had things to do. Darcy was... Darcy was not busy. 'It's fine.' She looked at Evie. 'Have you ridden before?'

'Not really.'

'So a little bit?'

'My parents got me lessons when I was about six, but I didn't go for very long.'

'OK.' Evie was wearing trainers with a flat sole. 'What shoe size are you?'

'Five.'

'OK if I lend you some boots?'

The girl nodded.

'Right. Come on then.'

Once Anna had taken herself back to the shop and Evie was properly shod in a low-heeled boot, Darcy led the way down to the stables. 'We'll do the lesson on Liberty. She's good as gold. Very calm for a beginner.'

Evie listened attentively while Darcy put the saddle and bridle on Liberty. She gave a quarter of an apple to Evie and instructed her to hold her palm flat. Liberty took it, and nuzzled gently in the hope of more. She really was very easy to win around.

'You can stroke her neck,' Darcy added. 'It'll help her get used to you. And you to her.'

Evie smiled a little as she ran her hand gently down Liberty's neck.

Darcy led the way out to the school area, fenced off and soft underfoot. She helped Evie mount, which she did impressively gracefully. 'It's coming back to you?'

'A little bit.' She patted Liberty again. 'She's a good girl.'

'She really is.' Darcy adjusted Evie's stirrups. 'OK. I'm just going to walk her round on the lunge rein.' She connected the long rope to the bridle and set Liberty walking in a gentle circle around the school. She had no doubt the horse could do this entirely on her own at this stage, but she watched their progress like a hawk anyway. Evie's position in the saddle was good, and she balanced well. 'Feel OK to take the reins?'

Evie nodded, and took control.

'Stick to a walk. See if you can go all the way round a couple of times and then turn around?'

Evie did.

'Brilliant. Good hands.'

'Thank you.'

'You seem like you've had more than just a few lessons.'

'Not really. I loved it though. The instructor said I was a natural.' Evie shrugged. 'Probably just being polite.'

'I don't think so.'

'Mum couldn't afford it any more anyway, so…'

'I'm sorry.'

'It's OK.' Liberty continued to carry her rider round in big looping circles. 'It's good though, isn't it? I remember when I was a kid they kept telling me I had to slow down and not get overexcited or stressed cos the horse could feel it. Do you think that's true?'

'Definitely.' It was more than that though. 'I find being with Liberty and Larry stops me feeling stressed.'

'I get that.' Another big loop around the school. 'You were great at the auction.'

'Sorry?'

'Doing all the onstage stuff. Proper rizz.'

'Er… thank you.'

'It was fun. More fun than online school anyway. Nate asked me to waitress for this fancy dinner he's doing.'

'You talked to Nate?' Darcy asked far too quickly.

Evie looked at her out of the corner of her eye. 'He rang the shop just before we came out and talked to Auntie Anna.'

'Well, good. I mean, you did well before so there's no reason he wouldn't ask you again, is there? He can. He should. Well, it's up to him. He didn't mention it. But why would he? I haven't seen him. Not since last night. Not at all.'

The look on Evie's face stopped Darcy's babbling. 'So, are you, like, banging Nate then?'

'No!'

'Right.' Evie rolled her eyes. 'Cos you talk about him a lot. A lot a lot.'

'No. I don't. Not until you mentioned him. You definitely mentioned him first. I didn't even...' Darcy grasped for a distraction. 'Do you want to try a trot?'

Evie nodded.

'OK then. You remember how to push her to a trot?'

'I think so.'

'OK. Pressure with the legs. Don't kick.'

Evie bounced a little awkwardly before settling into the rhythm.

'That's good.' Darcy watched her change direction with a figure of eight and trot back down to the school. 'Excellent.'

'Can I canter?'

'Down the long sides, but trot into the corner.' Darcy watched her charge. Her childhood instructor had been right about Evie being a natural. 'Keep your weight over your hips. Try not to lean forward too much.'

When Evie finally dismounted, Darcy asked her what she'd thought of the lesson.

'It was good. Do you have to, like, feed her now or muck her out or something?'

'I'll just rub her down under the cloth when I take the saddle off.'

'I could help with that.'

Darcy shook her head. 'I can manage.'

'I don't mind.'

'It's fine.' Darcy started to lead Liberty back towards the stables. 'You can get back.'

The girl didn't go anywhere.

'Or you can stay, if you want. I'll give Larry a rub down as well while I'm here.'

'OK. If I can help.'

Darcy narrowed her eyes. 'It must be a bit dull for you stuck up here all summer.'

Evie shrugged. 'It's fine. Auntie Anna's busy though, in't she?' Another shrug.

'What about your parents?'

'It's just Mum. She's busy too.'

'Right.'

'S'why I'm here.' Evie rubbed a hand down Liberty's neck. 'I could help with the horses. You know, if you wanted me to.'

'I…'

Evie folded her arms. 'Dun't matter.'

'No. That would be great. I'd appreciate the help.' In truth Darcy didn't need the help. Caring for Larry and Liberty seemed to be the only thing around the estate that she could do herself, but Evie was clearly at a loose end, feeling out of place and without purpose, and riding, even just a short lesson, had clearly brought her so much joy. Darcy could understand all of that.

Nate arrived back from his foraging trip to find Darcy walking across the courtyard. He called after her. She didn't turn back. She didn't come down for dinner that evening either. Bella explained that Darcy had said she had a headache and just wanted an early night. Nate laughed as casually as he could and said that meant extra portions for Bella and made some stupid joke about eating for two.

And then chewed his perfect, but now utterly tasteless, meal, while trying to keep a cheerful smile on his face.

The next day he saw her back disappearing through the archway towards the stable, and caught sight of her again in the doorway to the kitchen as he was saying goodbye to the afternoon students. By the time he came back she'd gone, along with a selection of cheese and a bottle of sparkling water from the fridge. He'd almost found the resolve to follow her and have it out when a slightly tearful Bella appeared clutching her mobile and the news that Adam wouldn't be back today as planned, but at the end of the week, after a work crisis in Edinburgh. Nate dispensed sandwiches and sympathy and pretended his attention was on the woman in front of him, and not the one he couldn't get out of his head.

On the third day he only saw Darcy once, riding off towards the village early in the morning. The sound of hooves in the courtyard while he was teaching later in the day confirmed she'd come back, but it was getting harder and harder to avoid the conclusion that Darcy Lowbridge was avoiding him.

On the fourth day the discarded biscuit packet and banana skin in the kitchen bin confirmed his suspicion that she was avoiding him to the point of sneaking into the kitchen after he'd gone to bed to find food. Nate was debating what to do when a phone rang on the worktop alongside him. Not his phone. He glanced at the screen. *Adam calling.* He grabbed the handset and called out into the hallway. 'Bella! Your phone's ringing.'

No reply. He swiped to answer. 'Hi. Bella's not here. It's Nate. Do you want me to ask her to ring you back?'

'Please.' The voice at the other end sounded tired. 'How mad is she with me?'

Bella's updates on Adam's expected return date had got a little more curt as time had gone by. 'Quite pissed off, I think.'

'There's just so much I need to finish before the baby comes, and if the project we're on falls through then...' Adam fell silent. 'Not your worry. And it won't fall through. I just wish I could be in two places at once.'

'Yeah. I'm sure she understands. I'll tell her you called.'

'Thanks. And sorry I haven't had a chance to check in with you. How are you getting on?'

'Fine.'

'Just fine?'

Definitely not just fine. 'Fine' was so far from covering how Nate was getting on at Lowbridge. 'It's been incredible. The produce you have up here, mate, is amazing. And the people have been so kind. I went foraging with Veronica.'

He heard Adam laugh. 'Brave man.'

'She was lovely.'

'She was?'

'Well, you know, she knows a lot about mushrooms.'

Adam laughed again. 'Glad it's going well. How are you getting on with Darcy?'

Nate felt his shoulders tense. 'How do you mean?'

'Bel said she was sitting in keeping an eye on your lessons.'

'Right. Yeah. She's fine. It's fine. We're fine.'

'Just fine again?'

'Sorry. It's all good.'

'Not desperate to get back to London just yet then.'

'Not just yet.' Nate hung up the phone with another promise to tell Bella to call her fiancé back. He wasn't desperate to get back to London at all. He'd told Veronica that was still his dream, but actually he hadn't thought about it since the night of the auction. He'd thought about his students. He'd thought about menu ideas. He'd thought about produce. But mostly he'd thought about Darcy.

Lowbridge was a lot more than fine, but the best part wasn't speaking to him, and he had nothing in his armoury. He'd made her perfect sandwich and her perfect dessert. He searched Darcy's name again and found the same article from when she'd first moved to Lowbridge. It offered no new clues as to what else might delight her.

Nate opened the fridge. They had cooked meat and cheeses and salad. Maybe it didn't have to be fancy. Maybe it was better if it wasn't. He didn't want her to think he was trying to seduce her. He just wanted her to talk to him.

Just after twelve he headed upstairs with what he'd intended to be a simple plate of something homely but nourishing. Actually, it was an overpacked tray of everything he could find or think of. The fear of getting it wrong had overcomplicated everything.

Nobody answered the knock on Darcy's door, so he knocked again and shouted, 'Look. It's stupid you never coming down for meals, so I've made you a tray of bits.'

No response.

'I'm just going to leave it out here and go back down.' He took a deep breath. 'I get that you don't want to talk to me. That's fine.' It wasn't fine. It was the only thing he could think about. He chopped tomatoes and he thought about her. He kneaded dough and he thought about her. He lay in bed, failed to sleep and he thought about her. 'I'll just leave the tray.'

He stepped back. A minute later the door to Darcy's room opened. Nate stepped forward. 'I'm sorry. I lied about just leaving the tray.'

Darcy glanced down at the food, and then up at the man. 'That's a lot of food.'

'I didn't know what to make.'

'You didn't have to make me anything.'

'I'm just sick of you avoiding me.'

'I'm not avoiding you.'

Nate sighed. 'So we're both lying. I guess that makes us even, at least.'

'I'm not...' It was clear from his expression that he wasn't buying her denials. 'I... just. Look, what happened. It shouldn't have happened.'

'Yeah. I think you've made that feeling clear.'

'I know I...' This was awful. 'I know I kind of insisted.'

Nate shook his head. 'I didn't take very much persuasion.'

'Even so, some drunk forty-year-old...'

'You're thirty-nine.'

'Nearly forty-year-old, pawing at you.' It was humiliating. 'I'm sorry.'

'Why?'

'You don't have to be polite. I know I made a fool of myself. You're very kind not to say so, but I'd prefer it if we could never mention it again.'

Nate nodded. 'OK. After this conversation we'll never mention it again, if that's what you want.'

His politeness was getting annoying. 'You don't have to pretend it's not what you want.'

He stepped forward again, so he was close enough to her to whisper. 'Let me be absolutely clear about one thing, Darcy. If you want to pretend it never happened, that's fine. If you don't fancy me, I...' His voice cracked slightly. 'Well, I don't love that, but that's up to you. If you don't feel ready for something new after your husband, that's fine too. If you just don't want to, then OK. But you don't get to pretend that this went nowhere because I didn't want it to. I loved, absolutely fucking loved, every second we spent together that night and I would do it all again a thousand times without a second thought.' He stepped back. 'I just wanted to be clear about that.'

Darcy couldn't respond. Her whole body was on fire, but it shouldn't be. It couldn't be. She wasn't someone who felt these feelings. Not any more.

'So, anyway, if you change your mind, you know where to find me.'

Darcy watched him walk away to the top of the stairs.

He paused and turned back. 'And if you don't change your mind then I respect that, but please come down for dinner sometimes. At least let's be friends?'

She couldn't be friends with Nate Thomas. It would be like trying to be friends with the sun. She could tell herself it was warm and safe but really it would burn. She couldn't say that. She shouldn't say that. Instead, she nodded. 'OK. Just friends.'

He didn't meet her eye. 'Sure.'

Darcy ate. The food wasn't Nate's usual offering. Not cheffy and not apparently precisely engineered to make Darcy feel something, but it was exactly what she needed.

She was hungry, hungrier than she remembered being for a very long time, and simple food, presented with love but no fuss, was exactly what she needed. She let Nate's peace offering satisfy one hunger at least.

And, when she'd finished, she acknowledged that she really had no choice but to bite the bullet Nate had shot at her. She couldn't avoid him any longer. He lived here. For the time being, at least. And she lived here. Her mind added *for the time being, at least* to that thought as well.

What was that? She rejected the thought. Of course she lived here. Lowbridge was home. That meant that she was going to see him. So she might as well get used to it again. She carried her empty tray down to the kitchen and walked straight into a very heated Bella. 'Tomorrow!' she exclaimed.

Nate was sitting at the kitchen island, phone in hand, staring at the screen. 'Tomorrow,' he replied.

'What's tomorrow?' Darcy directed the question to Bella, not looking at Nate, not admitting that every inch of her skin was alert to his proximity.

'McKenzie's big dinner, apparently.'

'And he only just set the date.'

Nate nodded. 'He's claiming his assistant told Fiona the day after the auction.'

Fiona was standing ashen-faced in the corner of the room. 'She didn't. I swear.'

'It's OK.' Bella rubbed her brow. 'I believe you. He's being a dick.'

'Yeah, but he's a dick who'll make a whole big fuss and try to get back his fifteen grand if I don't turn up and play the big fancy chef,' Nate pointed out.

'And we can't give him an excuse to do that, can we?' Bella asked.

'Definitely not.' Darcy was adamant. 'So can you do it tomorrow?'

'I could, I think, cooking-wise, but…' Nate glanced at his boss.

'We've got *Take your barbecue to the next level* in the courtyard all afternoon,' Bella explained. 'So Nate's supposed to be leading that.' She pursed her lips. 'I guess the plus side is that it doesn't really need the kitchen, does it? Apart from a bit of prep. So I could lead the cookery school and you could do your prep in here?'

'Are you OK to do the cookery school?' Darcy could hear the doubt in her own voice. Bella was eight months gone now. 'I mean…' How to put this politely. 'You can barely reach past your belly.'

'I'll use the big tongs. And Fi can help?' Bella looked at their business manager hopefully.

Fiona nodded. 'I can. And we could ask Nina? She won't let anyone burn the place down.'

'Right.' Bella turned back to Nate. 'Ingredients list for McKenzie?'

He pulled up the list on his phone. 'I was going to do another foraging run the day before, but no time for that now.' He sighed. 'If I called Veronica, do you think she'd go for us?'

'Can't hurt to ask.'

'Most of the rest we've either got or I can run over to Anna and get now. Can you call your shellfish guy?'

Bella nodded. 'I'll do that now. Are you OK with the prep on your own?'

Nate scrolled further down the list. 'It's a lot. I thought I'd have you with me, but yeah. I'll just have to start earlier and work faster.'

Everyone had a role apart from Darcy. 'I could help.'

'Help me?' She could feel Nate's gaze on her.

She nodded mutely.

'OK. That would be great. Start at nine and get as much as we can done in the morning? Then we'll have time to load everything up to take over to the McKenzie place without rushing too much.'

'Great. I'll see you in the morning.' She strode out of the kitchen, just stopping herself from breaking into a run. She could be around Nate Thomas. She could be totally normal around Nate Thomas. She could stop herself from staring at him, from reaching out to touch his hand, from running her fingers into his messy chestnut hair, from pressing her lips... Darcy made it to her room and slammed the door shut, against the rest of the castle, against people, against Nate, and against everything she was desperate not to feel.

Chapter 11

Nate watched the clock in his room tick around from five a.m., to six, and then to seven, counting down to nine a.m. and his date in the kitchen with Darcy. Not a date, of course. He was there to work. She was there to assist. And she'd made it excruciatingly clear that she wasn't interested in him. By eight a.m. he couldn't stay awake in his room any longer and headed over to the kitchen.

The room was full – Bella, Fiona, Veronica and Flinty were all around the kitchen island. As Nate came in from outside, Darcy made her own entrance from the hallway.

'Happy birthday!' Everyone shouted and clapped as one.

Nate frowned. He hadn't told anyone... His brain was racing to catch up. And something else was off. Bella darted forward, grabbed Darcy's arm and pulled her into the throng. 'Happy birthday! I know first thing in the morning is a weird time for a birthday party, but it's such a busy day. Sorry. But we didn't want to let it pass. I know we didn't really do anything last year because...' Her face dropped slightly. 'Well, you know why, but this year we wanted to do something.' She stepped back.

Over Veronica's shoulder Nate could see a perfectly iced chocolate cake with a 4 and a 0 candle on top.

Bella grinned. 'Cake for breakfast!'

Darcy blew out her candles and accepted gifts from Bella – 'and Adam,' she explained – and from Veronica and Flinty.

'I'm really sorry,' Nate apologised. 'I didn't know.'

'That's fine. Why would you? I don't know when your birthday is.'

Clearly. Nate shook his head. 'Not for ages. I don't really make a big thing of them anyway.'

Darcy frowned. 'No cake for breakfast for you then?'

'I didn't say that.' He took the plate Bella was offering him, and took a bite of cake. It was excellent. Slightly sweeter than he'd have made it, but moist and soft and rich with chocolate. 'This is really good.' He glanced at Bella. 'One of yours?'

She shook her head. 'Flinty.'

Veronica patted her partner's hand. 'Margaret has been making birthday cakes for everyone around for years.'

Flinty nodded. 'Chocolate's Darcy's favourite.'

Nate caught a slight hint of a frown from Darcy. 'One of my favourites,' she said.

'It's really good. There's a hint of a caramel taste somewhere?'

'Got good taste buds, this one. The recipe says caster sugar, but I do half and half with dark muscovado.'

Nate took another bite. 'That's it. I might nick that. Great idea.'

'You should try my carrot cake, lad.' Flinty beamed. 'I use oil instead of butter to keep it moist.'

'I'd love to. You should come and cook with me here. Teach me your cake-making secrets.'

'What do you mean? I cook here all the time.' Flinty shook her head at him.

'Of course. Well, maybe I'll come and see you.'

'I'd like that, lad.'

Over Flinty's head, Veronica mouthed a silent *thank you*.

Nate swallowed back a tear.

'Could I have a quick word outside, Mr Thomas?' Veronica asked.

Flinty looked up. 'What's this about?'

'Oh, just bringing in the things I foraged for you last night.'

'I'll help.'

Nate patted Flinty on the shoulder. 'No need. You stay and enjoy the fruits of your labours. I can bring stuff in.'

He followed Veronica into the courtyard.

'Thank you for being kind.'

'I'm not. That cake was fantastic.'

The dowager lady nodded. 'Baking seems to help her feel more herself. I suppose some things are so deep in memory that they don't go away so easily.'

'So what do we need to bring in?'

Veronica opened the back of the Land Rover. 'Just that one box. I could have brought it, but I wanted to talk to you about Margaret's meal. I think I know what I'd like you to cook.'

Nate arrived back in the kitchen with a list of traditional Scottish dishes he needed to learn how to cook to an impromptu birthday breakfast party that was winding down. Fiona was the first to excuse herself. 'I'd better get on. I've got some bits to sort out before our barbecue students arrive.'

Bella followed to set up the barbecues in the courtyard.

Veronica led Flinty away a few minutes later, despite her partner's protests that she needed to clear the upstairs bathrooms and put a load of laundry on.

And then he was alone in the kitchen with Darcy. For the rest of the day. The silence sat between them. It extended and thickened. Somebody needed to say something. Nate tried to think. Something, anything to break the tension.

'So I am forty now.' Darcy got there first.

'Sorry?'

'Yesterday when you said I was thirty-nine? Forty now.'

'Right. Yeah. Of course. Happy birthday.'

'Thanks.' She shook her head. 'I hadn't really planned to celebrate much.'

'Birthday cake wasn't your idea?'

Darcy shook her head. 'It was nice though.'

'Yeah. Nice that people care.'

The silence came back, softer this time, but still swirling between them.

'I guess we should get on?' he suggested.

'Yes. What do you need me to do?'

How to put this nicely? 'Well, I've seen your attempt at chopping neatly and I thought maybe the things that the massively overpaying customer won't see?'

Darcy's face looked genuinely upset.

'I'm joking.'

'It's fine.' Her voice was tense.

'It's not. What's wrong?'

She shook her head. 'Nothing. Let's get on.'

'OK, so if you could start the prep for the steak pie?' He took a folder from the countertop and pulled out a recipe. 'Step-by-step instructions, but just shout if you're not sure about anything. Anything at all. You don't need to make pastry. There's some pre-made in the fridge.'

'You shop-bought the pastry?'

'No! I made it late last night. I've been...' He shook his head.

'What?'

'Just not been sleeping well, the last few nights.' He risked a hint of a grin. 'Something's got me all distracted.'

The silence shot back in, pointed now, and pushing for a response.

'I'll start on the pie filling,' was all he got.

—

Darcy tried to tell herself that the quiet while they worked was a companionable, easy quiet. It wasn't. It was awkward, and charged. Nate had come close to saying outright that he couldn't sleep for thinking about her.

Darcy pushed the thought away. He hadn't said that at all. He'd said he was distracted. That could be with anything. Work, most probably. The cookery school was busy and this big meal for McKenzie was probably just one more thing he could do without. It was her brain filling in the gaps, and coming up with the fantasy that he was thinking about her.

What he'd said yesterday wasn't a fantasy though. That was burned into her soul. The urgency and the certainty with which he'd told her that he loved being with her and that he'd willingly, happily, enthusiastically do it all again, was real.

It just wasn't right.

The silence still sat heavy around her. The silence was making the space for all these thoughts, all these feelings to rush in. She needed to banish it. 'What's your favourite meal?'

'I love everything.'

'Well, sure, but what's the thing you really love?'

The sound of Nate's knife tapping rhythmically against his board stopped for a moment. 'It's really hard to say. I guess I wasn't really introduced to any of this until I started in kitchens, so I'm a bit of a latecomer to good food.'

'What did you eat when you were a kid then?' Darcy was picturing turkey twizzlers and dino nuggets.

'Whatever I could get my hands on.'

'Oh, growing boys? Always hungry?'

'No. It wasn't that. It was more whatever I was given.' The chopping started again, slightly slower, but there providing a punctuation and a distraction as he spoke. 'I didn't grow up in a nice neat family. I was in care for a long time, so different foster families, and then some time in a group home. It was complicated with my parents.' He took a deep breath. 'They were both addicts and they'd get a bit better and there'd be all this hope that maybe I'd be able to go back to my mum or dad. And my nan was always dead set on that, so every time adoption was mentioned she'd push back and say my mum was in rehab or in some new programme, but it never worked out.'

'I'm sorry.'

'Yeah. Well, it was complicated but it ended up meaning I was never anywhere long-term. And you get a bit... Oh God. My therapist had a word for it. It's like an attachment thing or a displacement thing or something. If you're never quite sure that the people who are supposed to look after you are going to look after you it can turn into wanting to hoard resources, or overeat, or actually undereat.' He shrugged. 'Brains are weird.'

'I'm sorry.'

'Again?' He put the knife down and turned towards her. 'You don't have to be. It was a shit start, but we're not defined by how we start. And I found cooking and Guy took me on as an apprentice and yeah… I think if you have one person who really believes in you, then sometimes that's enough.'

'Guy believed in you?'

Nate realised his eyes were moistening. He wished he was chopping onions right now so he could pass it off as a reaction to that and nothing more. He didn't normally talk like this, but there was something about having a task, and being alongside her rather than sitting eye to eye, that made it easier. Once, in an early session, the Owl had made him meet in Hyde Park and they'd walked around and around. That had been the first session where Nate had really opened up. Not having to look the other person in the eye made it easier to talk, the Owl had told him.

He thought about Darcy's question. Guy had believed in him. He'd helped him through his early years in the kitchen. He'd called in favours to get him stages at great restaurants in France and in Spain and then he'd welcomed him back to La Mer, when other London restaurants quite understandably looked askance at the kid from nowhere with the patchy CV and history of losing his rag with his colleagues. 'He did.'

'Past tense?'

'Maybe.' Was it past tense? Nate had been sent here as a punishment. He'd been absolutely clear about that in his own mind, whatever Guy said. 'He's shunted me out to the wilderness.'

'Excuse me?' The outrage in Darcy's tone was teasing rather than deeply held. 'Lowbridge is not the wilderness. All human life is here.'

'It's not exactly London.'

'Or New York,' she conceded. 'But still. It's got everything I need.'

'Has it?'

He saw her forehead crinkle just slightly before she replied. 'It had.' This time she didn't even let the silence take hold before she changed the subject. 'There must be something you remember eating from being a kid that makes you smile though? Like your pastrami on rye?'

'Not really. Free school dinners and whatever the foster carer thought kids might like.'

'So what about school dinners?' She grinned. 'Tater tots and sloppy joes?'

'What and what?'

She shook her head. 'That's what it was in my day.'

'Not "in your day".' He wasn't having her generating this huge imagined chasm between their ages. 'In your country. That's not old. That's just American.'

She paused. 'Oh. Maybe. I guess I thought I'd just grown out of them, but maybe you don't have them here.'

'What even are tater tots?'

Darcy gasped in mock outrage. 'They're potato, and, well… I guess it's sort of diced or grated and then formed into little mini tube things and cooked.'

'Like fried?'

'I guess.'

Nate nodded. 'I don't think we had those at any point in time. Definitely an American thing, not an age thing.'

'You were missing out,' she insisted. 'There must have been something though that you remember.'

And there was. Of course there was. 'It's stupid.'

'Tell me.'

'Strawberry jam sandwich. The cheapest, worst, probably-never-seen-a-strawberry jam' – he glanced at her – '*sorry, jelly* you can find and the most overprocessed sliced white bread in the shop.'

Darcy laughed. 'I can see how you ended up a top chef.'

'It's the only thing I remember anyone making just for me.' Nate spoke before he could stop himself. 'It was in a group home rather than a foster family and some of the kids were rough, you know?'

'OK?'

'I was one of the youngest. About twelve, I think, and there was another kid, Lucy, the same age. I'd just had an awful day. School was...' Nate shook his head. School had been hard. Nate's scattergun concentration never truly calmed until he'd found cooking. 'School was shit. And then one of the older lads had kicked off when we got home. Just a crap day. And Lucy made me this sandwich to cheer me up. But like that was all she could find, and the knives were locked away, so even if she'd found decent bread I don't think she'd have been able to cut it.' He laughed. 'And it had way too much butter on it, cos there was nothing to spread it with. I guess she must have tried to kind of smear it with her hands. And then big blobs of jam where she'd just dolloped it out of the jar.'

'Lovely.'

'It was. Best sandwich I've ever tasted.' He hadn't thought about that memory for years. 'I think it was the first time I knew that something made with love always tastes better.'

'Alexander used to make me egg on toast when I was ill.'

'Made with love?'

Darcy nodded. 'He wasn't much good in the kitchen. With Flinty around you didn't need to be, but if I had a cold or, you know, was just under the weather, he'd make me a poached egg on toast.'

Nate could see the glisten of tears at her eye now as well. He put his knife down, and reached for her hand. 'It's OK to talk about him, you know. It's good to remember.'

Darcy shook her head. 'I've been trying not to. It hurts when I remember.'

'It'll hurt more later on if you don't.'

Darcy pulled her hand away and wiped her cheek with the back of it. He saw her physically compose herself and put her smile back in place. 'You can tell you've been to therapy,' she joked.

He certainly had done that. 'I feel like just being here is therapy sometimes.'

'I knew Lowbridge would get to you eventually.'

'Maybe.' It wasn't that. It was just the break. A change, before he went back to his real life. Even as Nate thought it, his brain itched a little bit, but that was still the plan. Of course that was still the plan. 'Just short-term though.'

She didn't reply.

'Can I ask you something?'

'Sure.'

'Before, when I said your chopping wasn't great, you looked really upset?'

'No.'

'Really?'

'I... it's silly.'

'I don't mind silly.'

'Just lately I haven't been feeling much use around here. I guess I just heard it as another thing I'm not good for.'

'I didn't mean—'

'It's fine. You're right. It's everything else, really. I'm almost wondering if I need a change. Maybe I won't stay at Lowbridge forever.'

It sounded even less convincing when Darcy said it.

—

'Are you sure you're OK driving this thing?'

Eight hours later, Darcy and Nate were packing cool boxes and plastic crates into the back of the Land Rover. Nate nodded. 'I mean, how hard can it be?'

Darcy shuddered. 'That car takes against people.'

'Veronica drove me up to the woodland in it and it seemed fine.'

'Yeah. It likes her. And I think it's just scared of Flinty. It takes me about eight goes to change gear.'

Nate shrugged. 'Well, unless you think we can fit all this on the back of my bike, I don't have a lot of choice.' He checked the time. 'Better go. I'm picking Evie up on the way.'

He climbed into the driver's seat and started the engine. He didn't drive a car very often. In London his motorbike was much better for winding through the traffic, and even with that he walked and got the bus or Tube most of the time anyway.

'Nate.' Darcy laid a hand on the top of the open window. 'I enjoyed today.'

Something inside him lit up a little. 'Yeah. Me too.'

Nate made his way through the village – Darcy was right, the gear change took a bit of getting used to – and picked up his waitress for the evening from outside the village shop. The sat nav led him perfectly out of the village, along the loch side and then up into the woods to the entrance to the McKenzie estate. He handed his phone to his passenger. 'There's instructions open on my email to get to the place.'

She tapped and scrolled. 'The executive dining court?'

'Yeah. Sounds homely, doesn't it?'

'Sounds horrible,' Evie muttered.

It was horrible. Nate tried to keep his disapproval off his face. He'd been schooled in Guy Fforde's approach to designing spaces for eating and knew he followed three very simple rules. The light needed to be bright enough that guests could see what they were eating and ordering but not so bright they felt exposed. Seats should be comfortable enough that people were enticed to stay for dessert, coffee, or just one or two more drinks. And the music should be soft but not without personality, and should never distract from diners' conversations.

The executive dining court was a multi-use meeting room by any other name. The décor was at least not dull. But it was tartan. So much tartan. The lights were bright and unflattering. And the muzak sounded worryingly like a bagpipe tune imagined by an AI that had never heard of Scotland.

John McKenzie strode across the room to greet them. 'Welcome to a proper Highland estate.'

Nate had only been at Lowbridge a few weeks, but he still bristled. On behalf of Bella, and Adam and Darcy and Veronica.

'Let me show you the kitchen. You're going to love it. A step up from what you've been working with lately.'

Nate couldn't deny that that was true. Whoever decked this place out had spared no expense, but, he thought, also been royally ripped off. The dining space could never seat more than thirty or forty, and there was space in this kitchen for a small army of chefs to cook for a very large army of diners. 'Do you do a lot of big events here then?'

'We do. But they're mostly catered from our main guest eatery. This is for more exclusive visitors only.'

Double royally ripped off, Nate thought.

John McKenzie frowned. 'It's just the two of you.'

'Yep. Evie will be serving you and your guests. There's twelve of you in total?'

'Ah.' John McKenzie was all bonhomie and back slaps. 'Bit of a cock-up at your end by the sounds of it. We're up to fifteen. I did let your…' He frowned as if searching for an unfamiliar name. 'Fiona is it, know. And one of them's vegetarian. That won't be a problem, will it?'

It absolutely would be a problem, but Fiona had warned him that McKenzie was liable to try to pull something like this so he could claim Nate hadn't kept his side of the bargain and demand his contribution back from the community hall appeal. The tension that Nate had become accustomed to not feeling over the last few weeks burned in his chest. He smiled blandly. 'Not a problem at all.'

He'd been aware that this was the sort of crap McKenzie would try. That should have meant that he was prepared for the frustration that always came as the curtain raiser to anger, but tonight the feeling blindsided him. A wave of shock replaced the rising rage. He'd had a moment or two, when he was finding his feet as a tutor, but since then he hadn't felt this way at Lowbridge. The calm of his current life was rapidly being replaced by the urge to fight or fly. And doing either would be letting everyone – Bella, Fiona, the whole village who needed their community hall – down. But if he didn't fight or run away he was stuck with the Owl's third option – freeze.

He staggered his way back to the kitchen, observing, as if from outside his body, that the walk took all his effort. Once there, he placed both hands on the counter to anchor himself and forced himself to breathe. He had plenty of time to finalise and plate the meals he'd been planning to serve. Coming up with two extra portions of everything, and designing a full set of vegetarian alternatives was a very different proposition. The Owl would tell him to take his time, identify the source of the anger that was rising, and then use 'I' statements to verbalise his feelings before he erupted. The source of his anger was pretty clear, and 'I' statements wouldn't get him a vegetarian starter before service time.

What else did the Owl say? *Ask for help.*

He grabbed his phone. The signal was sketchy but it was there. He rang Bella. Engaged. He tried Fiona instead. Voicemail. Darcy. She answered.

'What can I make as a veggie starter and main out of only the things we prepped today?'

'Something with carrots.'

'What?'

'I did too many carrots.'

She had. That was true.

'Did you take the ones I chopped weird?'

Nate rifled through the boxes. 'Yes. I didn't realise I'd brought these.'

'Sorry. I just put everything in.'

'Don't apologise. That's good. Carrot soup. I can steal some seasonings from…' He had no idea where from. 'Wild garlic!' Veronica had given him a mountain of that. 'Wild garlic and carrot soup? Is that even a thing?'

Darcy laughed. 'I guess it is now. I'm sure you'll make it wonderful.'

The tension in his mind eased a little at her voice.

'Great. Main course?' *Think, Nate. Think.* 'The mushroom sauce for the beef. If I thicken that and don't put all the pastry on the mini steak pies' – which he was going to have to vigorously deconstruct anyway to make them go round the extra guests – 'I could do some sort of mushroom tart?'

'Sounds good.'

It sounded utterly uninspired. Mushroom tart was in Nate's view the vegetarian option of last resort. It absolutely said that the chef had not thought about the vegetarian in question for more than two minutes, but in this case that was absolutely true, so he was just going to have to make the best of it.

'No problem. You'll make it wonderful. I know you will.'

He felt his shoulders drop a fraction. The anger was passing. The red heat wasn't spreading across his skin. He wasn't going to lose it. He wasn't going to run away. He could get through service. 'Thank you.'

Nate got to work. Fifteen starters pulled together from the ingredients for twelve and sent to the dining room. He was plating the mains when the itch came back. He could see his own hands moving, dressing plates, but it was like he was watching something he had no part in from a long way away. It felt like a routine his body knew how to go through, but his mind was elsewhere. The Owl had called it burnout. This wasn't the same. He wasn't feeling the overwhelming tension any more. This was like a memory, or an echo, of that feeling.

'What do you need me to do?'

Evie's voice pulled him back into his body. She was relying on him to take charge. 'Right. Sauce.' He pointed at a pan on the stove. 'In jugs. You can pour it into the big jug on the side first if it's easier.'

And he was back, focused, in the moment, getting the job done. 'How's it going out there?'

'They like the food.'

That answer felt oddly specific. 'And apart from the food?'

'Can't keep their hands to themselves. And they're still sober.' Evie shook her head. 'Sober-ish at the moment.'

'Right. I'm serving the mains then.'

'No. You've got too much to do in here.'

No way. He wasn't sending a sixteen-year-old into a lion's den.

'They're old and slow. I'm fine.'

'Evie.'

'Whatever. We'll do it together then. You can keep an eye.'

'Fine.'

By the end of main course, Nate wanted to get himself a very large whisky and his waitress a medal. McKenzie's guests were, as Evie had implied, loud, rude and in two cases inappropriate with their words and looks towards their waitress, even when Nate didn't let her near enough for them to touch.

'I'll do the desserts on my own,' he told her.

'I have a plan,' she insisted.

'Don't do anything stupid,' Nate called after her disappearing back. 'I'll be out in a minute.'

Two minutes later, when Evie hadn't returned to the kitchen, Nate made his way towards the dining room. He picked up his pace at the sound of raised voices.

'How dare you!' John McKenzie towered above Evie. 'This is a private dinner. I will be talking to my solicitors about getting my donation back from your silly little—'

'What's going on?' Nate asked.

'It's fine. I'm handling it.' Evie had a new sense of purpose about her. 'Mr McKenzie is all up in my face because I filmed a bit of the party.'

That didn't sound good. Evie held out her phone. Nate grabbed it, before McKenzie managed to intercept. He hit play.

'See?'

Nate nodded. He saw very clearly not just two of McKenzie's guests, but also the esteemed estate owner himself, either pat Evie on the bum, or take a very obvious peer down her cleavage as she leaned over to serve dessert.

'I see.'

'So what I thought was I've had such a lovely evening' – there was a clarity to Evie's voice – 'that I wanted to put it on my TikTok, you know, so my friends, and, well, anyone in the world, really, can see what I've been up to.'

Nate nodded. 'I'm sure people won't mind that.' He looked around the group. 'Evie is staying in the area for the summer. I'm sure nobody would mind her posting something as a memento. So people can see how she's been volunteering at this charity event.' A few people – the people at the far end of the table away from all the drama – nodded.

McKenzie was puce. 'She will do no such thing.'

'Well, I want to post something.' Evie's voice was innocent now. 'OK. I know what would be even better.'

Nate was curious. 'Go on.'

'Well, as this is for charity, wouldn't it be great if we could post about some additional donations on the night?'

Nate suppressed a laugh.

'Like if Mr McKenzie and' – she turned and pointed at the two worst offenders – 'let's say these two gentlemen each offered another five grand to the community hall fund?'

'That would make such a fantastic TikTok,' Nate agreed. 'Don't you think?'

There was a moment where this could so easily fall apart. Nate could hear the tension under Evie's confident tone, and he was very aware that they were an actual child and a jumped-up care leaver with an attitude problem in a room full of serious entitlement. John McKenzie could laugh them out of here. Evie might post her video but half the comments would be about how she was asking for it and nobody could take a joke any more, and probably the other half would be worse.

McKenzie didn't blink. Neither did Tweedles Dum and Dee still seated at the table.

A woman at the far end did. 'What a lovely idea.'

Nate looked towards the voice. He recognised the redhead in the jet-black dress. She'd been with McKenzie at the auction. 'Mrs McKenzie?'

She nodded. 'My husband's generosity is one of his best qualities. Always willing to spend money to make things right.' There was an edge to her voice. 'I'm sure he'd be delighted to contribute more to the appeal. As would his friends.'

A few of the other women murmured their assent, along with a large red-faced man sitting alongside Mrs McKenzie. 'Great.' Nate smiled. 'Let me get Fiona on the phone right now and you can do a card payment while we're all here.' There was no way he was having cheques handed over that could be cancelled in the morning.

The intervention did the trick. The offenders plastered smiles of mock sincerity and joy on their faces and read out their card details to a delighted Fiona.

Mrs McKenzie sidled in next to Nate. 'Is that Fiona MacCellan they're talking to?'

Nate nodded.

'And she's doing well over there?'

'Yeah. She's great.'

Mrs McKenzie nodded. 'Would you tell her I don't blame her for anything? And…' She patted the heavily jewelled necklace at her throat. 'Thank her for this. It's bespoke. As I say, very generous man, my husband, when he needs to make amends.'

'I'll tell her.' He wasn't sure it was his place to add anything. 'I really don't think she knew he was…' He nodded at Mrs McKenzie. 'Knew that you…'

'No. I do sometimes slip my husband's mind. Anyway, you must meet our other guests. Iain!'

'Hello! MacWillis.'

'Iain has a little place over on Skye.'

Nate was starting to understand what these people meant by a 'little place'.

'I do. I do. And I'm very impressed with what Adam and that wee lass have done over at Lowbridge. Do tell them to give me a call. If you're doing food like this, we must do something together.'

'That would be great.'

He leaned in. 'And tell your waitress she deserves a medal. Was just about to punch one or two of those fellows myself but turned out she could take care of business very well on her own.'

Across the room, Evie was posting her new TikTok thanking the group for their very generous donations, and sullenly deleted the other video in front of Mr McKenzie.

As they loaded the car, Nate had to ask. 'Are you sure you're OK?'

'Yeah. It's not my fault, is it? If men are dicks.'

'Course it's not. That doesn't mean it's not upsetting though.'

'Not upset. Angry.' She climbed into the passenger seat. 'I'll get them back.'

'More than you did already?' Nate asked.

'Five grand's pocket change, innit? To them.'

Nate didn't know, but based on Mrs McKenzie's jewellery collection, probably.

'So I'm gonna post the other video anyway. After the money's definitely gone through.'

Nate grinned. 'Backed up to the cloud?'

She nodded. 'Course it is.'

'You know if you post it, you'll get comments.'

Her face darkened. 'Like toxic manosphere crap.'

'Yeah.'

She slumped slightly. The bravado she'd had in the room in front of all those people ebbed away. 'Had a bit of that at school last term. That's part of why Mum sent me here. She wanted me away from that crowd but…' She held up her phone.

'You carry the crowd in your pocket?'

She nodded. 'Doesn't bother me as much here though. Like, there's other stuff to do. The waitressing, and helping Darcy with the horses.' She shrugged. 'Makes all that stuff feel further away.'

'We could send the video to the police?' he suggested.

'Would they do anything?'

'I don't know. Maybe the ones who touched you. But probably just a caution. At most. I don't know.'

She sighed. 'You don't win, do you?'

'What do you mean?'

She was looking out of the window into the dark now. 'You just gotta keep on fighting.'

Nate dropped her off after securing a promise that she'd think about what she wanted to do with the video and talk to Anna or call him if she needed to. 'I'm going to tell Auntie Anna. And I don't mind you telling people what happened. I'm not embarrassed or anything.'

'Good. You shouldn't be.'

He waited for her to get inside and started up the engine to make his way back to the castle. His gear shifts were bordering on smooth now and he was starting to think he might fall into the rare group of people the Land Rover liked.

Darcy was sitting in the kitchen, glued to her phone. She looked up as he came in. 'Bella sent me the TikTok. Another fifteen grand?'

'Yeah. Wait until you hear how.' He told her the story of the lecherous dinner guests and Evie's magnificent response.

Darcy shook her head. 'Wow. I wish I'd been that bold at her age.'

'Me too.'

'What were you like at her age?'

Nate thought back. 'Sixteen? Just before I started in my first kitchen. I was a mess. What about you?'

'I was a child. And then two years later I was modelling, out doing jobs on my own.' She shook her head. 'You meet some creepy men doing that.'

'I'm sorry.'

'Long time ago now. I was just going to make a coffee. Decaf. Do you want anything?'

Nate was bone tired after a full day cooking, but he was also buzzing too much to sleep. 'Decaf would be sensible. Thank you. Did you have a nice birthday?'

Darcy hesitated. She'd had a wonderful day. She hadn't felt the ease in someone's company that she'd felt by the afternoon working alongside Nate since... 'Well, I spent most of it chopping vegetables for some kid who thinks he's a chef.'

'I'm not a kid.'

He was a kid. 'You're twenty-four.'

'Twenty-five,' he said quietly.

'What? When was your birthday?'

He winced slightly. 'It's today.'

'What?' He hadn't said a thing. He'd eaten her cake and wished her happy birthday and not a word. 'Why didn't you say?'

'I didn't want to take over your day, and like I said, I don't really make a big deal of them anyway.'

'But it's your birthday.'

'Really. It's not a big deal.'

She poured coffee for both of them. 'Why don't you make a thing of them?'

'Why would I?' His voice had an edge she wasn't used to. 'I'm sorry. It's just... Growing up how I did, birthdays were always just one present organised by a foster carer or a social worker or whoever who's barely had a chance to get to know you so it's never anything you really want, and then that's kind of it. There's no fun family memories, you know.'

'I'm sorry.'

'It's fine.' He shrugged. 'Well, not fine exactly. Just what it is. Can we talk about something else?'

Darcy could have kicked herself. She was the one supposedly keeping him at arm's length and here she was probing his deepest emotional scars. 'Sorry. Erm, what was the rest of the evening like?'

Nate's expression didn't lighten. 'Weird. I don't know. The food was good. McKenzie was a dick, but I'd been warned he might be so that was all OK. I mean, it wound me up but it was fine… after I'd talked to you.'

'I don't think I helped, really.'

'You did. I was ready to whack him with a frying pan and walk right out.'

Darcy wasn't entirely sure she'd have opposed that approach to John McKenzie if Nate had asked her.

'Talking to you brought me back down to the moment though, you know?'

'Yeah. I do know.' Working in the kitchen alongside him had been exactly that. Darcy had felt secure in her moorings, just for a few hours. 'It went OK after that though?'

He frowned into his coffee. 'I think I was expecting to enjoy it more. Cooking proper restaurant food again. Being the big star chef. That's what I've been working for my whole life.'

'It's just one dinner,' she suggested.

'Maybe. I didn't want to be there though. In that kitchen, plating up, it didn't feel like the place I need to be.' He rubbed his hand across his eyes. 'Ignore me. I'm knackered.' He raised his mug. 'I'll take this back to my room if you don't mind. I'm glad you had a nice birthday, Darcy.'

Darcy's heart lurched a little bit as he walked away. Nobody should be unhappy on their birthday. That was what was pulling at her heartstrings. Just that. Nothing more. Even so, she wanted to do something.

And she knew exactly what, but the castle kitchen – beautifully stocked by Bella and Nate – would provide none of what she needed. Anna and Guy would be fast asleep, but Evie... Evie was at the shop and she'd only just been dropped off. Darcy was prepared to bet she'd still be awake. She grabbed her phone and her jacket and jogged out of the kitchen.

Nate sat on the end of his bed and tried desperately to convince himself that he felt the way he was supposed to feel. Tonight had been a step back into his real life. High-end cooking at an – albeit charitable – premium price, with his name as the Michelin kitchen chef driving the whole thing. That was what he dreamed of. He wanted a restaurant with his name above the door. He wanted the best reviewers in the country flocking to eat his food. He wanted the same reviewers to pan his rivals with comments about how they were poor imitations of the great Nathan Thomas. That was his ambition. That had been his ambition since he was sixteen years old.

So why had tonight left him cold? He told himself it was the issue with how the guests had treated Evie, but he'd dealt with guests who couldn't keep their hands to themselves a hundred times before. He told himself he was just out of practice after the slower pace of the cookery school, but that should have meant the adrenalin was flowing more than usual, not less. He told himself it was the uninspiring surroundings of the McKenzie estate, but he'd cooked with Guy for banquets in tents and corporate events in faceless convention centres and felt the buzz every time.

Something had changed. And it had changed before he'd even come here. He'd lost himself that last night at La Mer. What had the Owl called it? Burnout. Lowbridge was supposed to fix that. He was supposed to go back into the kitchen all better. And so long as he didn't step into a kitchen and try to be that version of Nate Turner, it felt like he was all better.

Nate buried his head in his hands. He didn't want things to change. He was on a path. It was a path he'd been on for years. It had given him purpose in a life that had been beyond his control since the day he was born. If he let go of that, who was he?

A knock at the door pulled him out of his spiral. He opened it to see nobody. He glanced down the hallway and caught a glimpse of Darcy Lowbridge disappearing from view. 'Darcy!'

She didn't come back. He looked down. On the floor in front of him was a plate with a sandwich on it. He knew without looking what the filling would be. Cheap white bread, too much butter, terrible jam. There was a Post-it note stuck to the plate.

Happy Birthday, Nate

He carried the plate into his room and sat down on the end of the bed, where he picked up the sandwich with both hands. He took a bite. It was precisely as he remembered it. Processed, plasticky, slightly wet, far too sweet. But made for him because somebody cared.

And for a moment he was twelve years old again, sitting on a staircase in a group home trying not to make a sound in case another kid came and had a go, or an adult came and yelled at him for whatever he'd done wrong that day. Nate had always done something wrong. He never meant to, but things got on top of him, and he either zoned out or lashed out.

The thought caught him unawares. He either zoned out or lashed out. Was that what had happened on his last night in Guy's kitchen and again tonight? He'd learned not to lash out, but he'd felt the same sense of overwhelm and disconnection and he'd zoned out instead. Nate had thought the whole idea of burnout was ridiculous, but what else would you call it when someone's brain shut down and just walked their body out of the room in the middle of a work shift?

He took another bite. He hadn't felt like that for weeks – until tonight – and he should have. Lowbridge had been nothing but new experiences and new people. If he was going to get overwhelmed, all those things should trigger it, but, for the first time he could remember, Nate felt calm.

He took a third bite of his sandwich. It was objectively awful. He ate the whole thing.

Chapter 12

'Stovies?' Anna shook her head vigorously. 'You don't learn how to cook stovies.'

Next to her Nina frowned. 'Well, you must do. Babies don't know how to make stovies.'

'A properly brought-up baby would,' Anna countered. 'Stovies isn't a thing you learn. Stovies just are.'

'Right.' Nate cleared his throat loudly. 'Imagine I'm a particularly badly raised toddler who doesn't know.'

'Stovies is leftovers, really, so it depends what you've got.'

'I've got leftovers from McKenzie's thing last night.'

Nina nodded. 'Right. Well, bring them out. And potatoes, lots of potatoes.'

Nate gathered likely looking ingredients and let Nina take the lead. 'Basically it's a potato stew. So always potato, lard and onions.'

'Onions?' Anna asked. 'You don't need onions.'

'They add flavour.'

'I mean if you've got some, but you can do without.'

'Fine. Potatoes and lard.'

'Beef dripping.'

Nina glared at her friend. 'Potatoes and fat.'

'Right. I'm sensing there's a lot of individual variations.'

'Well, aye. The idea is to use up what you've got, so it depends what you've got.'

Nate understood. 'Do you know how Flinty would have had this? When she was little.'

Nina nodded at Anna. 'Best ask your Hugh.'

'He won't remember.'

'He might. Anyway, you knew them when you were kids, didn't you? What sort of things did you eat?'

'Well, leftovers from the roast.' Anna said this like it was obvious.

'So beef?' Nate asked.

'Or lamb.' She thought for a second. 'I remember Maggie loving a beef roast on a Sunday though, so maybe beef.'

Nate noted that down. 'I've got some leftover stewing steak. It's not the same but…'

'That'll do for your practice,' Nina confirmed.

He tried his best to follow both Nina's instructions and Anna's contradictions as best he could to create the potato stew rich with beef dripping and a little bit of stock. Nina tasted first and then Anna.

'Needs more salt.'

'Too salty.'

'I'll take that as being just right then.' Nate grinned.

Anna frowned slightly. 'This is for Maggie. For her meal from the auction?'

Nate nodded. 'I know Veronica didn't win but she bid loads so it felt a bit unfair. And this is costing pence to make. Not like McKenzie's blowout, so…'

Anna nodded. 'It's good of you. I know she's…' She glanced at her friend. 'She's been struggling a bit lately.'

Nate wasn't sure how much Veronica confided in the other women in the village. 'I think Veronica is hoping a meal like this will help her feel more herself.'

Anna and Nina exchanged a look.

'I think that might take a bit more than a nice dinner,' Nina said.

That was true. Of course it was true. Whatever was wrong with Flinty, one good lunch wouldn't fix it, but it might bring a moment of joy.

'I do think food can help though,' Nate suggested tentatively.

'Well, food helps everything,' Nina agreed. 'Everyone knows that.'

'But, like, with memories and things. Or with pain. Eating something that brings back a memory or takes you to a happy place.' Nate could hear how stupid he was sounding. He shook his head.

'No. Go on, lad,' Anna instructed.

'I just think it can do more than words or explanations. Like it puts you back into the memory. Brings it to life.'

Nina nodded. 'I think you might be right. We had makowiec this Christmas.'

'What's that?'

'It's a sort of poppy-seed cake. Polish. My dad's favourite and he made it every year. Making it again was like having part of him back.'

That was it. The food and the memory and the people you were remembering were all one thing.

'So you think Flinty might remember herself a bit if you make this right?' Nina asked.

Nate shrugged. 'I think that's what Veronica hopes.'

The trio were quiet for a moment.

'My father lost himself at the end,' Anna added quite suddenly. 'You end up saying goodbye a thousand times to each little part of them.'

'I'm sorry,' Nate said. 'It was like that with my nan, I think. They'd already stopped me living with her by then but when I went to visit it was like she knew me a little bit less every time.'

'That's hard.' Nina stirred the stew. 'How old were you?'

'Fifteen when she died.'

Anna shook her head. 'But then everyone goes at some time, don't they? And all at once is just as cruel. No time to prepare or say the things that need to be said.'

'There's no good way,' Nina agreed. She tapped her spoon against her bowl. 'The rest of us just make the best dish we can with whatever's left behind.'

—

Nate was clearing up after his guests had gone when Darcy came into the kitchen. 'What's that? It smells great.'

'My first attempt at stovies. I'm going to make it for Flinty and Veronica.'

'Your first attempt?'

'I had expert help. Nina and Anna came over to talk me through it. Turns out they do not agree and there is no clear recipe. So that was lots of help.'

Darcy laughed. 'I'm surprised they stopped bickering long enough to teach you anything.'

'Well, barely. I think they wanted to help for Flinty though.'

Darcy knew what he meant. She didn't want to know what he meant. She kept her expression blank.

'I think they're both worried about her.'

Darcy shook her head. 'I'm sure she's fine.'

'I'm not. And I know Veronica's worried. She's forgetting things, losing her thread in the middle of conversations.'

No. Darcy would not have that. Flinty was a constant. Everything had changed at Lowbridge. Adam was the laird now. Bella was running the place. Fiona was here making everything hang together. And Nate had just rocked up and slid into place as though he'd always belonged. And Alexander. Her Alexander was gone. Too much had changed. Flinty had to remain the same. 'I don't want to talk about it.'

'Sometimes it's good to talk.' Nate laughed. 'Yeah. I know. Too much therapy. I ended up having a good chat with Nina and Anna about losing people though. Grief counselling through the medium of food.'

Darcy wasn't laughing. 'Is that what you've been doing for me?'

'No. No. Of course not. I just…'

Just what? 'Why do you keep cooking for me?'

'Well, why did you cook for me?' he shot back. 'I mean, if you can call that cooking.'

'I didn't like you being unhappy.'

He stood up and closed the space between them in one stride. 'Same. I mean, not at the start. I started out just trying to impress you cos you were checking up on me and reporting back, and then it was because you were so bloody hard to impress. But then, now, I just want to make you happy. I like you being happy. I like the idea that I'm the person who makes you happy. I like the man I am when I'm trying to make you happy.'

And there was that feeling again, the same feeling she'd had when he'd stood outside her room and told her he was not in favour of her plan to never ever spend the night with him again, the same feeling she'd had when she'd run out into the night to find terrible over-sweet jam at midnight, the same feeling she'd had for every second he'd spent in her bed. And she was powerless against it. Darcy raised her head, almost angrily, almost in defiance, and challenged him with her eyes to bring his lips to hers.

He did. Of course he did. What else would either of them do but kiss? She let herself melt into him, tasting him, wrapping her arms around his body, opening her lips to invite him in. She knew where this led. She knew where he wanted it to lead. She pulled back. 'We can't.'

'I think we've proven that we absolutely can.'

'We shouldn't.'

He stepped back. 'Why not?'

'You're twenty-four.'

'Twenty-five.'

'Sorry. Still. I'm a lot older than you.'

He hesitated. 'How old was Alexander when you met him?'

'That was different.'

'Why?'

'Because...' Why was it different? She hadn't minded one bit being the younger party. Alexander was sophisticated and thoughtful and mature in comparison to the boys who chased after models out on the town. 'Children, for one thing.'

'What about them?'

'Well, I'm forty. I don't even know if I can...' Her voice tailed away. Alexander and she had tried, but he'd baulked at the idea of investigations and tests so they'd ended up having to accept that it wasn't for them. 'What if you decide you want kids? In five years or ten years?'

Nate leaned back on the worktop. 'Well, I wasn't really thinking ten years ahead. More about ten minutes.'

'Exactly. Because you're twenty-five.'

'No. Because you are hot and I am human. But, if you're asking, I'm not sure I do want children. Serious answer. I've never really had a dad in my life so I'm not sure I'd ever feel confident to be a good one myself. And if, in five or ten years' time, we decided we could give that to someone then I'd probably want to look at fostering. Good consistent foster homes. You have no idea what they're worth if you haven't lived it.'

'Oh.' Darcy didn't have a response to that.

'So how else is it different?'

'Alexander was different.'

'Different to me?' Nate asked.

'No. Well, yes.' Actually, hugely yes. She couldn't imagine two more different men. On the surface at least. The motorcycle-riding ambitious young chef would have been an anathema to her husband. But the man who went foraging with Veronica, who cooked her dishes from her childhood to make her smile, who agreed to cook a perfect dinner for a woman with... Darcy's brain still refused to think about Flinty's condition. That man was someone Alexander would have thought a lot of, Darcy knew. 'That's not what I meant. I meant I'm different to Alexander. He was somebody.'

'You're somebody.'

'I'm not. I'm just left over.'

'What do you mean?'

'I mean Alexander had a place here. He was someone. He was the laird. I'm not anything. I'm a washed-up ex-model, ex-lady of the manor, ex-bookkeeper...'

'I'm not primarily interested in you for your CV.'

He was kind, but kindness wasn't enough to make this work. 'I'm not anybody.'

He stepped towards her. 'I disagree.'

'And I'm old.'

He shook his head. 'You're not old.'

'Older.'

'I don't care.'

'I do. Like, what do we even have in common? I'm NSYNC and tater tots and you're... I don't even know what.'

Nate shrugged.

'Seriously, what was on kids' TV when you were growing up?'

'I dunno. *Mr Tumble. Tracy Beaker Returns*.'

'See.' That was her point. 'I have no idea.'

'You've never heard of Tracy Beaker?'

Well, obviously she'd heard of Tracy Beaker. 'Not Mr Tumble though.'

Nate shook his head. 'That's not age. That's being American.' He sighed long and hard. 'Look, I don't want to pressure you, but I think the age thing's an excuse. And I think you know that. You've said it's the same gap as you and Alexander, so what is it?'

She owed him the truth. This wasn't something she could pretend was all in her head any more. It wasn't a one-off that would never be mentioned. He was being honest. He deserved the same. 'Alexander.'

Nate moved towards her. 'Go on.'

She stepped back. 'I'm not ready to forget him. I'm sorry. I'm not ready to forget my husband. I don't know if I ever will be.'

—

This time Darcy caught herself wondering if he'd bring her another beautifully plated dish. She even wondered what he'd prepare for her, and then pushed the thought down hard. It was stupid to think someone like Nate would continue his charm offensive when she'd made it clear that whatever charms she possessed were off the table.

But despite that she found herself listening for the knock at the door. No knock came. Of course it didn't. Why would he bring her food when she'd rejected him out of hand?

She'd told the truth though. She hadn't denied what he made her feel, but she'd told him about the other part – the thing she'd have to let go to be with him. She wasn't ready to let Alexander go. She wasn't ready to be truly without him. She knew now that she'd held herself in a sort of stasis to avoid the pain of remembering him, and the pain was awful. Worse than she could possibly imagine but the memories were everything. Worth every pang, and every tear, and every step deeper into despair.

Of course Nate wouldn't knock on her door. She should be glad that he didn't.

Discarded on the bed beside her, Darcy's phone pinged. She picked it up to swipe away the notification. One new message. From Nathan.

> Come down to the kitchen, Darcy.

She ignored it.

Her phone pinged again. One new message. From Nathan.

> Please.

She dragged her body down to the kitchen. 'Nate, I don't want to...'

He held up a hand, and nodded towards the island. 'I thought it was silly just leaving food at each other's doors. And I didn't trust myself not to knock it and break the yolk.'

The plate on the table was a simple poached egg on toast. 'You didn't have to...'

'I know.' Nate shook his head. 'I don't expect you to forget him. I never would. I... That's all. Enjoy your egg.'

He turned towards the door to the courtyard.

'You're not staying?'

He shook his head. 'This one's just for you.'

Darcy took a seat and picked up the knife and fork. The yolk was perfectly runny and the white perfectly firm. She wondered for a second how many goes Nate had taken and then she remembered how startlingly good at his job he was. She took a bite, balancing the soft, slippery egg on a piece of toast, dripping with salted butter. It wasn't exactly how Alexander made it at all. But it had the spirit of the eggs he used to bring her. It was a dish that simply said, 'I want you to be well.'

That was what her husband had always wanted. He wanted Darcy to be content and to be well. And she wasn't. She hadn't been for more than a year. There was no one in the kitchen. Darcy hopped off the stool and listened out for sounds in the hallway. Nothing. Nate had left her to it, and nobody else seemed to be around. She pushed the door closed and opened her mouth. 'Alexander.' She felt silly. Maybe it would be enough to just think this through. Or maybe she could write it down. No. Darcy was determined. She'd come this far. Some things did need to be said out loud. 'Alexander, I miss you.'

That was a start, but it was bland. Of course she missed him. What was it she needed him to know? 'I miss you bringing me eggs when I'm sick. I miss you getting distracted in the middle of a conversation. I miss shouting at you because I realise too late that you're not listening. I miss you getting irritated with me because I'm looking at my phone when you're telling me about an interesting butterfly. I miss...' She lowered her voice even though there was nobody in earshot. 'I miss your body. I miss kissing you. I miss the smell of your cheek, that little hint of shaving foam, you know?' Darcy's eyes were wet now. 'I miss the looks we used to exchange when your mother was being all disapproving about something. I miss just telling you about my day. I miss having you here. And I've been pretending I don't because it's so horrible to think about every little thing I lost when I lost you. But...' Now her eyes were streaming. 'I can't live like this. I need to be able to remember you but still be happy today. I need to remember that you always wanted me to be well. I need to try to be well, to live well. I'm sorry.'

You have nothing to be sorry for, my darling.

Darcy jump turned towards the voice. There was nobody there at all, but she could talk to him nonetheless, and so she did.

—

Nate headed towards the coach house, but found he didn't want to go to his room and sit staring at the same walls wondering if Darcy understood any of what he was trying to tell her. Instead, he turned towards the road and continued across the Low Bridge into the village. On the other side of the stream he was accosted, immediately and with the vigour of a well-planned ambush. Nina and Anna came at him from both sides.

'Nate's already said he'll cook for it, won't you?' Anna blocked his path.

'For what?'

'The re-opening.' That seemed to be the whole explanation.

'Not the re-opening. The pre-opening.' Nina corrected her friend. It didn't help.

'The re-opening of what?'

'Pre-opening.'

'Still, of what?' Nate asked again.

'The community hall.' Nina shook her head as if tiring of having to explain. 'She's right. You said yes.'

'You did. Out in the courtyard. After the auction.'

What?

'You were with Darcy.' Nina paused. 'Perhaps you were distracted.'

Just a bit. Nate shook his head. 'No. I remember. The community hall opening. I thought it wasn't going to be for months.'

Anna folded her arms. 'It's not the opening. It's the pre-opening.'

'And you're cooking for it,' Nina added.

Nate was starting to catch up. 'So at the community hall?'

Nina nodded. 'Well, just outside it. The roof's not safe yet.'

'Right. So presumably there's no kitchen?'

'There's a tea urn.'

'That hasn't been used for years.'

'It's a tea urn,' Anna shot back. 'They don't go out of date.'

'But no proper kitchen,' Nate continued. 'So there's no kitchen and we can't go inside in case the roof falls in.'

Anna sighed. 'I suppose that puts the tea urn off-limits too.'

'If we have it before summer's over, we can put tables on the car park,' Nina suggested.

'And you can cook in a tent?'

'A big tent. We could borrow the one they had for the fete in Lochcarron.'

'So a marquee really. That's practically indoors.' Anna sounded entirely confident in this solution.

'How many people?' he asked.

'Twenty?' Nina replied.

'Maybe thirty.'

'No more than forty.'

Anna nodded. 'Let's say fifty to be safe.'

'So you want me to cook for fifty people in a tent next to a car park with no kitchen?'

'And probably no tea urn,' Anna added.

Nina smiled brightly. 'I'm sure you'll work something out.'

'And if we find a hard hat, someone might be able to bring the tea urn out for you.'

Nate had no idea what this place was doing to him, but it seemed like there was no choice but to just go along with it. 'Sure,' he agreed. 'Why not?'

-

Darcy felt lighter as she walked out of the kitchen. None of the pain or sorrow had gone away, but it was sitting less profoundly on her heart. The other decision she'd confirmed in her mind was more difficult though. A few weeks ago it would have been unthinkable, but everything had changed since then.

And now she was decided, there was no point putting things off. She headed straight for the estate office. Fiona was there, as expected, but Veronica was with her. Both looked up. 'Veronica is just going through my invoicing,' Fiona said brightly.

Darcy felt a stab of solidarity for the woman she'd too often viewed as her replacement. Veronica's frequent checks on Darcy's own books had been the bane of her life. There was no system so efficient that Veronica Lowbridge couldn't find at least one mistake. 'It's good you're both here. I want to talk to both of you. Bella too. Do you know where she is?'

'Yellow Room, I think,' Fiona replied. She prised her laptop out of Veronica's hands. 'If you want to talk to us all, why don't we go through?'

Bella was in the Yellow Room, but so were Anna and Nina. And so was Nate, staring slightly wide-eyed at the three women. Bella looked up. 'Nate's going to cook for the community hall re-opening.'

Fiona frowned. 'Re-opening?'

'Pre-opening,' Nina corrected.

Nate nodded. 'Anna and Nina feel that, even though the building is unsafe and has no working kitchen, waiting to actually open before having an opening party is leaving things far too late.'

'I hope you're not being sarcastic, young man,' Anna said.

'Not at all. And even if I was, who am I to argue?'

'Who indeed?' Veronica confirmed. She turned back towards Fiona and Darcy in the doorway. 'Anyway, we are all gathered.'

Darcy hadn't planned to do this with Nate here as well. She had definitely been going to talk to him on his own. There were things she ought to say to him, things she wasn't going to say in front of her husband's mother.

Right now she had to deal with telling the people in front of her she couldn't be whatever the new version of her was going to turn out to be here. She didn't know how. She opened her mouth.

'Ooh.' Anna nudged Nina. 'Is it about your dates, Fiona?'

Fiona shook her head.

'She's gone all shy. You can tell us.'

Bella nodded. 'Yeah. Come on. Give us the details. How was three-date day?'

Fiona slumped a little. 'I'm not sure I'm cut out for dating.'

'So it wasn't an effective screening process?' Bella asked.

Darcy found herself moving back into the doorway. Maybe she didn't have to tell them today.

'No. It was a very effective screening process. Pete was too stupid to remember to take his wedding ring off.'

The group winced as one.

'Fabian wants to marry me and live in a yurt and raise llamas.'

'Well, that's nice,' Anna nodded approvingly. 'What's a yurt?'

'A big tent,' Nate explained.

'Oh no then. That won't do at all.' Anna changed her mind abruptly but definitively.

'And I don't really know anything about raising llamas.'

'What about the last one?' Bella asked.

'He didn't turn up at all.' Fiona almost smiled. 'And I think he might still have been the best of the three.'

'Maybe a more traditional approach to dating?' Bella suggested.

'Like one bloke at a time,' Nina clarified.

Fiona shook her head. 'I think I just need to tweak my parameters and maybe add some more data to my spreadsheet.'

Veronica cleared her throat. 'We actually came through because Darcy had something to tell us.'

The moment to run away had passed. All eyes turned towards her. She took a deep breath. She couldn't meet anyone's eye. She certainly couldn't meet his. But she had made up her mind. Finally, after months of inertia she was going to do something. She had to tell them sooner or later. 'Right. Well, OK. Sorry if this is out of the blue, but I've decided I'm going to move away from Lowbridge.'

—

The silence that followed wasn't companionable, or charged, or awkward. It was simply shocked. Darcy continued in order to fill it. 'Since Alexander died I've been a bit in limbo. And I need to move on, but I don't think I can do that here. Everywhere has a memory, so I think it's best if I find somewhere new.'

'No.' Bella shook her head. 'You can't go.'

'I agree,' Veronica added. 'You're part of Lowbridge.'

Darcy had been expecting Bella's objection. She was surprised by Veronica's. 'I mean, we haven't exactly always got on.'

'Nonsense. I've treated you like my own daughter.'

Veronica didn't have a daughter, which was, perhaps, for the best.

Fiona joined in the objections. 'She's right. You're part of the place.'

Darcy's gaze was fixed on the one person who hadn't said a word. Eventually Nate stood up. 'So when do you think you'll go?'

'I'm not sure. As soon as possible.'

'Not waiting for anything?'

She wasn't sure how to respond.

'You can't go until after the baby comes,' Bella pointed out.

'Right. Well, I'll see.' The baby. There was a baby coming. To whom she was what? Not grandma or nana. Adam wasn't her son. Not Auntie Darcy. Not really anything at all.

'Nothing else?' Nate asked.

'I don't think so.'

He nodded. 'Right, well, I hope you're very happy then.'

And that was it. He stalked out of the room, leaving Darcy with the objections and horror of the rest of the group. 'Excuse me.'

She ran into the hallway and after Nate. 'Nate!'

'What?'

'I'm sorry. I was going to tell you on your own.'

'Why?'

'Because...' Darcy closed her mouth. Because she'd led him on and let him down and she needed him to understand that this was for the best. If anything, she was doing him a favour.

'We're on our own now.'

They were. 'I just wanted to say sorry. For everything that happened. I took advantage of you.'

He shook his head. 'This again? No. You didn't.'

'I just never thought you would really be interested in me.' She couldn't help but picture that night together. 'I thought you just felt sorry for me.'

'That's not how I generally express sympathy.'

'No.'

'Why do you keep doing this?'

'Doing what?'

'Making like I couldn't possibly be interested in you?' He wasn't raising his voice, but he was angry. She could hear the tension in every word. 'It's so...' He shook his head. 'It's so frustrating. I can't work out if you think so little of me or so little of yourself.'

'I don't think so little of you.' In fact, she thought too much of him. 'But I can't do this. Everything here reminds me of Alexander.'

He nodded. 'So go, but wait a bit.'

'For what?'

'For me.'

Her face must have shown her shock.

'See the baby. Let me finish my job here and then we can go together. Wherever you want.'

It was so tempting. She could run away with her hot young lover – go somewhere new and be with him. She shook her head. 'I'm not ready.'

'But if you wait a few months?'

'No, Nate. No.' It was the only answer she could give. If she stayed for him, everything he made her feel would fill her, overwhelm her, burst her open, and she'd be raw to the elements. She was keeping a lid on the pain of losing Alexander, but it was taking all her strength to do it. There was no way she could contain any more feelings within herself. What she would feel for Nate, if she allowed it, would be simply too much.

'Right. OK.' He stepped back. 'That's that, then.'

'You'll go back to London when Bella comes back to work?'

'That's the plan.'

Of course it was, but Darcy found she didn't believe it. 'I think you fit here.'

Nate didn't argue. 'I think that's what they were all trying to tell you.'

—

Nate left her in the castle hallway. He fitted here. Darcy thought he fitted here. That was madness. Nate was group homes, and housing estates, and London, and noise, and rushing, and Lowbridge was quiet, and open space, and time to talk and listen and put down roots. There wasn't a place on earth less likely to find a slot that fitted Nate than Lowbridge.

And especially without Darcy here. She might have been a place where he fitted. That wasn't an option now, and worrying about it now wasn't an option either. He checked the time. Veronica would be waiting for him to walk back to the village. Today was stovies-for-Flinty day.

They walked together over the Low Bridge and into the village. The water lapped against the shallow pebble beach. 'Quite a surprise that Darcy sprung on us,' Veronica commented.

'Yeah.'

'A surprise for you too?'

'Why wouldn't it be?'

Veronica shook her head. 'I don't know. I just wondered if she'd told you her plans.'

'No. I think I'm the last person she'd tell anything.'

Veronica was quiet for a moment. 'Well, that's a shame,' she said eventually. 'Here we are.'

She led the way inside a small cottage in the terraced row at the beginning of the village just after the pub. Inside was bright and clean, but Flinty was dusting it nonetheless.

'Margaret, the place is perfectly clean.'

Flinty gave her partner a very definite look. 'And how do you think it stays that way?'

'You clean the same number of hours here as when you were doing a whole castle.'

'Yes.' Flinty nodded happily. 'That's why it's so clean.' She glanced at Nate. 'Why's the lad here?'

'He's going to make us dinner.'

'Stovies.'

'Ah, don't be daft. You can't trust a wee English lad to make stovies.'

'I've had lessons. Anna and Nina. They were very definite about how to do it.'

'And dead wrong, mind.' She looked at him. 'Did they put the onion in first?'

'There was some debate about that.'

'See. Dead wrong.' She nodded at the bag of ingredients in his hand. 'Well, hand it over, pet. Let's get on with it.'

'No, Margaret. He's going to cook for us.'

Flinty's expression didn't change. 'And I said not to be daft. Come on, lad. I'll let you help if you don't get in the way.'

He exchanged a look with Veronica, who simply shook her head in defeat, and followed Flinty through to the tiny cottage kitchen. Among the things she disapproved of over the next two hours were the potatoes he'd brought, the way he chopped said potatoes, the dryness of his roast beef, the herbiness of his herbs – that one left Nate entirely confused as well – the size of his onion, and the handle of his chef's knife.

As he dished up the stovies though, she nodded. 'You did a good job, lad. We'll make a cook out of you yet.'

'Thank you, Margaret.'

'Ach, call me Flinty. Everyone does.'

'All right, Flinty.'

'Not quite everyone.' She smiled a smile that was more for herself than him. 'Veronica, lass in the village, always calls me Margaret. Just her, though.' She shook her head. 'Not that it matters. She's off to marry the laird's boy.' She narrowed her eyes at Nate. 'About your age. You must know him.'

'I'm not sure.'

'Well, anyway, off to marry him. For the best. For the best.'

Nate caught the smallest movement out of the corner of his eye. Veronica was leaning on the wall on the other side of the door, absolutely still. He handed the ladle to Flinty. 'You can dish this up. Two bowls.'

'I know. I know.'

He didn't know what to say to Veronica. 'Are you OK?'

She nodded. 'Yes. Yes. I will be. This is better than sometimes. She's thinking about me. That's nice, in a way?'

'Of course it is.' Nate had no idea if it was or not, but he knew what she needed him to say.

'Oh.' Flinty was behind him in the doorway. 'Veronica?'

'Yes.'

'What are you doing here?'

'You're making me stovies.'

'Why aren't you at the castle?'

Veronica hesitated just for a second. 'Because today I'm here with you.'

Flinty nodded. 'Well, sit down then. I'll get another bowl for the lad.'

Nate shook his head. 'You two eat. I'll just clear up through here.'

'All right then. He's a good lad. He's not your lad?'

'No, Margaret. That's Nathan. He works at the castle.'

Nate pulled the door to and set about tidying up the tiny kitchen, but the voices from the next room carried through to him.

'You look older.'

'So do you.'

'Oh.' And then quiet, and then a much smaller, less confident voice. 'I'm not very well, am I, V?'

'No. Sometimes you're not.'

'Will you take me to the doctor?'

'Of course.'

'I keep thinking it's back then and you're about to head off and marry your laird.'

'And I did.'

He heard Flinty laugh. 'I told myself I was going to march over there and stop it. So you could be mine and I could be with you every day.'

'Well, you can't go back and change the past.'

'You married him.'

'But you came to the castle and looked after us, so I was with you every day.'

'I don't remember.'

'That's all right. I do. I can tell you all about it.'

Nate let himself out of the back of the cottage and walked the short way around to the street. Instead of turning back towards the castle, he jogged over the road and onto the narrow strip of shingle at the shore of the loch. The water lapped at his feet as he stared out towards the islands. So much space. So much quiet. Space for all the things he'd buried under the noise and the constant distraction of work, to rush back into his life. Space to feel creative. Space to make friends. Space to fall... Nate stepped back from the shore. Darcy was leaving and she'd been very clear about how she felt, or, more importantly, didn't feel. Whatever he might have dreamed could fill all the space he found in his life, it wasn't going to be her.

For the first time since he'd arrived in Scotland, Nate grabbed his phone and scrolled through his contacts to the Owl, and tapped out a message.

> Are you free today at all?

The response was unexpectedly quick.

> Back-to-back cancellations actually. Give me ten minutes?

And an online meeting link.

Nate picked up the pace and jogged back to his room in the coach house. He'd never quite got on with online therapy. There was something about meeting face to face that felt more confronting and made it harder for him to hide and prevaricate, but needs must. He suspected Nina was the closest thing Lowbridge had to a therapist and he didn't want the things on his mind to be village gossip for the next month.

The Owl appeared on the screen in front of him. 'Nathan, how's everything going?'

He took a deep breath. There was no point doing this if you didn't do it properly. 'You know I'm in Scotland.'

'Yes.'

'Where Guy sent me to do penance for being a shiftless twat who gets overwhelmed in the middle of service.'

'Is that how he put it?'

Nate shook his head. 'Anyway, I'm here and it's... it's everything. It's brilliant, and I'm teaching people, which I never thought I'd be any good at but I love it, and the produce is unbelievable. And I'm loving cooking here, apart from... I did this one night for this really fancy dinner and I hated it. It was exactly what I've trained for. Restaurant quality, elegant presentation, all that stuff. And I wanted to run away, but then I just cooked stovies.' He laughed. 'I didn't even cook them. I got shouted at by a tiny Scottish woman while she cooked stovies and I tried not to get in the way and it was incredible. It was like the cooking and the eating was part of her, and her story and her life and she had all these memories and the person who asked me to cook for them just… just loves her so much and the meal was part of all that. But it was stovies. It's spuds and leftovers. You can't put a fucking aromatic steam on spuds and leftovers.'

'Would you want to?'

And that answer was simple. 'No.'

'OK.'

Nate stopped him. 'That's not everything. I slept with someone, and, well, I…' The whole point of this was that he had to say it all, however exposed he felt. 'I'm in love with her.'

He was in love with Darcy. Of course he was. She was part of him as sure as breathing or cooking or missing his nan.

'I love her and she doesn't want me and she's leaving.'

He saw the Owl's eyebrow raise the tiniest fraction of a pixel. The Owl never reacted. At all. 'Right. I'm wondering if we need to book in more than one session?'

—

'What are you doing?'

Darcy jumped at the sound of Bella's voice in the doorway to the Blue Room. 'I thought you preferred the Yellow Room.'

'Not enough cushions to get comfy any more,' she sighed. 'I've come to steal some from in here. What are you going?'

'Deciding where to go.'

'No.' Bella put her fingers in her ears. 'I shan't listen to this.'

'Bel? Please. I need to move on.' She needed to get away, at least. Everything here was too much. 'You've got to let me.'

Bella dropped her hands and sagged into the sofa next to her. 'Oh bloody hell. This is lower down than I remembered. You're going to have to get a tow truck to get me up from here. Show me what you're thinking then. Might as well if I'm stuck in the couch.'

Darcy had a pile of index cards in front of her, each with a place name at the top.

Bella picked up the first one, headed *New York*, and started to read from the lists below. '*Pros: close to family. Bustling. Exciting. Cons: Can't take horses. Close to family. Noisy. Overwhelming.* OK then.' She picked up the second card. '*Edinburgh. Pros: Could visit Lowbridge (and Liberty and Larry!)* Big pro that. *Could see Adam when he's in the city.* Right. *Cons: Expensive.* Yeah. What are you going to do for money?'

Darcy sagged a little deeper into the cushions. The details of what next weren't high on her mental agenda. Getting away from here was. Once she'd got away, she'd stop feeling all of this. She'd be able to just be. 'I'll get a job,' she said. 'Admin or bookkeeping, I guess. You'll give me a reference.'

'Yeah. Of course. You wouldn't need one if you stayed here.'

'Bel!'

'Sorry.' Bella flicked to the next card. '*Lake District. Pros: Bit like Lowbridge. Might be able to find stables. Cons: Hard to find work?* You are aware that a lot of your pros are to do with how like here it is, or how much you can visit here, aren't you?'

Of course she was. 'But I need somewhere I can find a role for myself. Not just as someone left over from a different time.'

'You're not...' Bella started.

'I've made up my mind.'

'Fine.' She turned to the last card. '*Ottery St Mary.*' Bella gave her a look. '*Pros: Sounds adorable. Otters? Cons: Where is Ottery St Mary?* Cornwall, I think.'

'Well, Cornwall's nice.'

'I don't think it's particularly full of otters though, if that's what you're hoping.'

'I was a bit.'

'And Cornwall is a long way from here.'

It was. Maybe that was what she needed though.

'I'm adding that to the con list,' Bella insisted. 'You're not going to go before the baby comes, are you?'

Darcy shook her head. 'I promised.'

'And Adam promised he'd be back before the baby came, but still no Adam.'

They were a week out from Bella's due date. 'He's back tomorrow.'

'In time for the community hall thing. Or so he claims.' Bella nodded glumly. 'It's not his fault. He's working, working, working so we have enough money to stay afloat and he can be here when she's born.'

'She?'

'Just a vibe.' Bella shook her head. 'We really honestly don't know. Adam keeps saying he, so one of us is going to be surprised. It won't be the same without her Nana Darcy here when she's growing up, though.'

'I'm not really her nana though, am I?' She wasn't Adam's mother.

'Course you are. You are if I say you are. Or Auntie Darcy. Whatever you want.' Bella nodded decisively. 'You're family.'

Something pulled at Darcy's gut. She wasn't Adam's mother. She'd only met Bella a year ago. Whatever Veronica said, she wasn't the daughter she never had. They'd been Alexander's family. They didn't need her.

'We need you.'

Darcy did a double take. Bella couldn't read her mind. Coincidence. That was all. 'I'll visit,' she promised. 'Lots. I just need to find my own path for a bit.'

Bella nodded. 'If you say so. We're just going to miss you. That's all.' She shifted in her seat. 'Come on. Help me up then.'

She helped Bella out of the low slouchy sofa, and gathered up armfuls of cushions to reinforce her pregnancy-comfortable seat in the Yellow Room. Then she made her way to the estate office. Fiona wasn't sat at the desk. Instead she was on the chair in the corner, a chair Darcy had sat in many times chatting to Alexander, bent over her tablet. She looked up. 'Do you think it's reasonable to ask bicep circumference before agreeing to a first date?'

Darcy frowned. 'What?'

'Well, you can ask if they work out but that's quite broad? I, personally, don't find super-built buff guys that attractive, but I do want someone who takes care of themself. So like maybe a runner, or like someone who does sport.'

'Why don't you just ask what their hobbies are?' Darcy suggested.

Fiona shook her head and jabbed at her screen. 'That doesn't give a clear data point. It's anecdotal, not empirical.'

'Yeah, but isn't dating more of a...' How to put it? 'More of a vibes thing? Than a data thing?'

'No. No.' There was a catch in Fiona's voice. 'It can't be. There has to be a way to make it safe.'

'What do you mean, "safe"?'

Fiona let the tablet drop onto her lap and looked up at Darcy. There were tears brimming in her eyes. 'So it won't hurt so much.'

'Oh sweetie.'

'With John I tried to be everything he wanted, and he...' Fiona shook her head. 'I let him take over everything. How I dressed, what I spent money on, when I went out. How do I know I'm choosing someone better this time?' She picked up the tablet. 'Like, there has to be a better way. A way to get all the information and be sure you're making the right choice.'

Darcy shook her head. 'I don't think it works like that.'

'Why not?'

Why not? 'Because falling in love with someone is just something that happens. I don't think you can plan for it. You just have to be open to it when it does.'

Fiona shook her head. 'I don't trust myself. What if I pick the wrong person again?'

'Then you'll get out again. And you'll see it sooner this time.' She crouched down and wrapped her arm round Fiona's shoulder. 'It's OK to have standards. It's OK to expect to be treated well. But the person who makes your heart go all silly probably won't be someone who ticks all the boxes on your spreadsheet.'

'You're braver than me.'

'How do you mean?'

'When you met Alexander, you threw yourself in, didn't you? I remember. Everyone was talking about it. Adam's hot new American stepmum.'

Darcy pulled a face. She knew she'd caused a bit of excitement when she'd arrived.

'But moving across the world cos you're head over heels…' Fiona leaned her head into Darcy's shoulder for a moment. 'That's brave. And now you're being brave again. Taking yourself off, heading out and looking for what you really want.'

Was that what she was doing?

'Well, you can be brave too. Maybe forget about finding the perfect man and just get out and meet people and see what happens. You might have fun on the way.'

'Maybe.' Fiona took a breath in, wiped her eyes and stood up. 'I mean, I can have a few little criteria.'

Darcy shook her head. 'Can I stop you?'

'Nothing major. Six foot would be nice. Maybe a little older than me but not too much. I'd like someone who had their own business. Entrepreneurial, you know – that's attractive. And I do like runners. Kind. Well-travelled. Cultured. Nice hair.'

'That's quite a lot of criteria,' Darcy pointed out.

'Well, I'll agree that they're not dealbreakers.'

'Being kind is,' Darcy said. 'That's a dealbreaker.'

'OK.' Fiona sighed. 'Why's it so hard? I just want somebody who gets me, and who likes being with me.'

'That sounds nice.'

Darcy left Fiona to get back to work and wandered over to the stables. Liberty was out in the paddock. Evie, who was becoming a fixture around the stables, must have turned her out in the morning. Liberty ambled over to

Darcy and nuzzled for a treat. 'Fiona thinks I'm brave,' Darcy told her. 'What do you think?'

Liberty didn't offer an opinion. She never did.

Chapter 13

The Community Hall Pre-Opening Gala was taking place, as suggested by Nina, in the small car park in front of the not-yet-open hall. Nate had a kitchen set up, pulled together with impressive organisation by Fiona and a whole team of Strachans, in a tent borrowed from the Scouts in Strathcarron. He had work benches, and a whole row of burners fed from portable gas bottles. It wasn't what he was used to, but from where they'd started it was impressive. Outside, there was space for tables for forty-five villagers and visitors from the surrounding area. Fiona had put tickets on sale at £10 each, instructed Nate not to spend more than half that per person on ingredients – which with Bella's contacts and Adam's garden he'd just about managed – and somehow magicked up the tables, chairs and kitchen set-up with the rest of the money and a lot of begging and borrowing. If she wasn't so distracted trying to distil the equation for the perfect first date, that woman would probably be ruling the world already.

Nate walked along his row of helpers like a general surveying his troops. And he found his troops to be ready and attentive (Evie), distracted by their phone (Young Strachan), bickering about the bunting across the parking area in front of the community hall (Anna and Nina), ignoring him entirely and already putting up trestle tables in entirely the wrong place (Jill and Hugh), or simply absent (Darcy). His phone rang in his hand. *Bella calling.* He answered. 'How's it going?' she asked.

'Chaotically,' he answered.

'Good. Welcome to your first big community event in Lowbridge.'

'What about the talent auction?'

'For that we got them on our turf, so we could take control. You're out in the field now.'

And didn't he know it. 'Is it always like this?'

'Remind me later and I'll tell you the story of the boy-band singer and the massive piece of Edam at the Christmas lights switch-on.'

'I can't wait.'

'Hold on. Fiona's here. Let me put you on speaker.'

He ran through the plan for the day one more time with the only two people in Lowbridge who seemed to have any understanding of the idea of a schedule.

'The menu is incredible, Nate,' Bella reassured him at the end of the call. 'He's going to love it.'

'Who is?'

'Everyone,' she said. 'I said they're all going to love it.'

Nate stared at the handset as the call went dead. That definitely wasn't what she'd said but he didn't have time to worry about what she'd meant now. He had tables to move, chairs to set up and a mountain of cooking to do, a lot of it outside and a lot of it at the last minute.

'What do you need me to do?'

He didn't need to turn to know who was talking. Even without the only New York accent between where he was standing and, well, actual New York, he knew she was close by the hint of cocoa butter on the breeze. 'Anything you can. Tables need setting up.' He handed her a crumpled drawing of the layout they'd agreed, and that was now being completely ignored. 'Nina and Anna are supposed to be on food duty but they're doing something with decorations that I don't even understand. Young Strachan and Evie need to start bringing drinks over from the pub and...'

She laid a hand on his chest. Nate stopped. Not because it was calming. Because his senses had shut down to everything but the awareness of her touch. 'What needs doing first?'

'Tables. Then drinks.'

'OK. I'll sort that out. You do what you can to corral your sous chefs.'

Nate's menu for the evening was something he was genuinely pleased with. Bella was the only person he'd shared the whole thing with and even she didn't quite have the full picture. He called over to Evie. 'Do they have a printer at the shop?'

She nodded.

'If I give you this' – he held out a memory stick – 'can you print out twenty and bring them back to me without showing anyone else?'

'Course.'

'Thank you, Evie.'

She paused. 'Did Anna tell you my mum's coming tonight?'

Nate shook his head.

'She came up yesterday for the last week of the holidays.' Evie looked happier than he'd seen her all summer. 'And she says we'll both come back up at Christmas.'

'Great. That's great.'

Across the re-purposed car park, Darcy finally seemed to be getting the tables set up in the right positions, and Hugh was starting to put out chairs. Anna was still fussing with the bunting but Nina came over. 'Shall I go and crack on with the first course while Anna's busy?'

Nate frowned. 'Did you put the bunting up wrong so she'd do that and you wouldn't have to cook with her?'

Nina looked outraged. Or at least she tried to.

'Go on. So long as it gets done, I don't care what dark arts you use to get us there.'

That meant he was free to focus on dessert. He retreated into the marquee they'd set up as a temporary finishing kitchen. The dessert tonight had to be perfect. For years Nate had told himself every dish had to be perfect, but in the last few weeks his understanding of perfect had changed. Sometimes the thrill of somebody knowing they'd made something themselves for the very first time was closer to excellence than having the potato seasoned to perfection. Sometimes the memory associated with a dish was as important as the dish itself. Sometimes the KitKat you broke in half and shared with a friend who boosted you up was more perfect than the Michelin-star dinner eaten with a companion who made you feel less than.

Sometimes what you cooked for someone mattered less than the thing you wanted the food to tell them. *You're safe. You're loved. You're cared for. You will always be cared for.* Communicated through the medium of stovies, or egg on toast, or a jam sandwich.

Nate's plan today was to put everything he knew about food before he came to Lowbridge, and everything he'd learned since he got here, together in one brilliantly fun, tasty, heartwarming meal. And he was excited. More excited than he'd been about food for a very long time.

Villagers who weren't involved in the organising started to arrive. Old and Young, but not that young, Strachan strolled over, Young Strachan holding the arm of Mrs Timberley from the pub. Netty's husband arrived, along with Kenny, the tour operator and Jill's friend who was a boy. A couple of cars pulled up across the street, spilling out families from Lochcarron who'd become wrapped up in Lowbridge via the cookery school, or supplying the shop, or coming to parents and tots at the castle. Soon the whole community was gathered, and even though it was still early and the sky was bright and clear, Darcy switched on the fairy lights that were strung among the bunting, as she passed through the crowd handing out drinks and welcoming people as they arrived.

The estate Land Rover pulled up, and Bella and a tall slim man Darcy didn't know started unloading pans and trays from the back. Bella beckoned her over. 'Is Adam here?'

'Sorry.'

'He rang when he was leaving Edinburgh. He should be here by now.'

'I'm sure it's just traffic.'

'I know. I just...' Bella looked tired. 'You know.'

'I know.'

'Anyway, this is Guy.'

'Nate's boss?' Nate's link back to London. That shouldn't feel like a knife to her. Nate would go back home. She was leaving anyway. What he did next was not her concern. She'd made that very clear. 'Does he know you're here?'

Guy and Bella exchanged a look. 'He does not.'

'Right. OK.' Darcy wasn't sure at all how that would go down. 'Well, I'm sure he'll be delighted to see you.'

Guy scanned the crowd. 'And where is he?'

'Back in the kitchen.' And operating, Darcy suspected, at a level of stress that would be multiplied by Guy's appearance, not reduced. 'Why don't you get a drink and let Bella and Nate cook for you for a change?'

Guy nodded. 'Why not indeed?'

Bella mouthed a *thank you* in Darcy's direction and set off for the kitchen tent.

Nina appeared, pushing a huge, lidded pan in a child's pushchair a few minutes later. 'This was way too much to carry. I don't know what I was thinking.' She nodded at the pram. 'This was my Pavel's. No idea why I kept it. I can't have thought it would come in handy, but it has.' She followed Bella into the kitchen as well.

Darcy checked on Evie and Youngest Strachan, checked everyone had a drink and looked around for the next problem. She could see… nothing. Nobody looking lost. Nobody with an empty glass. Nobody moving the place cards around to sit next to their ex. Everything was in hand.

Fiona appeared at her elbow. 'This looks great.'

'Yeah. Nothing really for me to do.'

'What?'

'Well, it doesn't need me, does it?'

Fiona shook her head. 'Haven't you been here all afternoon?'

'Yes, but just sorting out little niggles and calming people down, and then greeting people when they arrived.'

'And that's why it's all running so smoothly. You're good at this. Without you I bet Nate would have been running in and out of the kitchen all day fighting fires and the whole thing would be a mess.'

'I don't know.'

'Well, I do. Good front of house is what makes hospitality businesses sing. The chefs get all the glory but fire the maître d' from one of those big fancy places and it'd fall apart within a week.'

'I think a week is optimistic, Miss...?' Guy Fforde stepped closer.

'Miss MacCellan. Fiona.'

'You are quite right. Finding good front-of-house staff is the bane of my life. Our job is to make our guests happy. The food is only one part of that.'

Fiona beamed. 'You're Guy Fforde.'

'Yes.'

'I ate at La Mer once.' Was Fiona showing a slight blush at her cheek? 'Only once a long time ago. I saved up and it was incredible. To think you turned a local bistro into a whole empire. It's so entrepreneurial.'

'Well, I've always been blessed with get-up-and-go. Too much energy, you might say.' He smiled, leaning towards his new companion. 'I had to take up running to burn some of it off.'

'Oh.'

'It's good to keep fit, isn't it?'

Fiona was definitely looking more than a little starry-eyed. 'Actually, I read your book about growing up in kitchens.'

'Oh gosh. Did you? I think you may have been the only one who did.'

'It was fascinating. I really understood what you said about family expectation versus finding your own way. I get that...'

Darcy stepped away from the increasingly animated tête-à-tête. There was a seating plan for the meal. She had been very clear that it wasn't to be messed around with. But what did one small tweak matter? She grabbed Fiona's name card and popped it down next to Guy Fforde. Well, it couldn't hurt, could it?

Nate checked the time. He knew, from experience, that the last ten minutes before any service were frenetic and disorganised but that somehow everything came together in the end. The good ladies of Lowbridge were testing that belief at this moment.

'You're putting too much salt in that.' Anna was turning her nose up at Nina's pan.

'I've tasted it and I am not.'

'Well, I can see just from looking that you are.'

'Oh.' Flinty picked up a spoon from the side. 'Let me taste. Did you do these with lard or beef dripping?'

Veronica clapped her hands together. 'Ladies, why don't we take our seats and let the professionals finish off.'

Nina folded her arms. 'I'm a professional. I cook for the pub every week and...'

'Indeed. Perhaps tonight though' – Veronica smiled – 'you ought to be out there as chair of the Community Hall Fund Committee.'

'She might be the chair, but I'm the president,' Anna pointed out.

'Which is an honorary position,' Nina shot back.

'Perhaps you should both be representing the fund, though, at such an important gathering as the...' Veronica hesitated.

'Pre-opening party,' Nate supplied.

'Of course. How could I forget?'

Veronica shepherded them away. Nate caught Bella's eye. 'Ready?'

She nodded.

'Are you OK? I can get Darcy in here, or manage with Evie and Strach if you want to go and sit down?'

Bella shook her head. 'I'm fine. Just a bit of a back twinge. Honestly, sitting down is worse. I'm just not a practical shape at the moment.'

'OK. Shall we start then?'

'Yep. Are you going to introduce it?'

'What?'

'Like, say a few words about the menu. If you don't say something Nina will. And then Anna will because Nina did and then Nina won't want her to get the last word and so... And we'll never eat.'

'Fine.' He rang the handbell Fiona had come up with as the lowest-cost and -tech way to call the servers to the kitchen tent, and waited for Evie and Strach to appear. 'Did you print that stuff?'

Evie nodded. 'On the drinks table, under the 7 Up.'

'OK. Let's do this.'

He led his team out into the fresh air. He'd barely had time to check on progress out here, beyond a few heads stuck into the tent to reassure him that everything was fine and Darcy had it all in hand. The outdoor dining area looked spectacular. Old trestle tables, covered with white linens and transformed into Lowbridge's version of open-air fine dining. As they came out, all eyes turned towards them. 'Right. Hello, everyone.'

He was greeted with a chorus of 'Hello, Nate' like he was the head teacher at the beginning of primary-school assembly.

'Thanks. So tonight is the pre-opening party for the community hall, which, thanks to some very kind donations from people here tonight, from visitors to Lowbridge, and also from our neighbouring estate owner, John McKenzie, who sadly can't be with us tonight...' And who, according to what Nate had heard from Fiona, didn't get out very much at all after his wife had offered him the option of a very short leash indeed or a very expensive divorce. Poor chap. 'Anyway, we are now able to start refurbishments on the community hall next week.' He read from the list Nina had thrust into his hand. 'New roof, new disabled toilet with modern flush mechanism.'

'It's water-saving,' Nina shouted.

'Great.' Nate scanned down the list. 'And new restaurant-standard kitchen set-up.' He paused. 'Sorry. Right. Anyway, that's what the party is for. But I just wanted to say a couple of very quick things about the menu tonight. Good food should speak for itself.'

'Hear hear!'

Nate turned to the voice. Guy Fforde was nodding vigorously. What on earth was he doing here? Nate turned back towards Bella, who was staring intently at her shoes, or at least at where her shoes would have been if they weren't obscured by her belly. 'And I hope this menu does, but I did just want to say that this menu is my thank you to everyone in Lowbridge for looking after me, and teaching me some of your dishes and, well, everything, over the last couple of months. I'm not going anywhere until Bella's little one is out in the world and a good bit bigger, but I wanted to take this chance to say thank you. So thank you.'

He nodded to Evie and Strach, who set out around the tables first with the menu cards Evie had printed for him, and then with the first course.

'We're serving family style,' he explained as serving dishes of stovies were popped down into the middle of the tables. 'And remember this is only the first course so don't fill up too much. This course is called Lowbridge Memories.'

He'd asked Nina to cut the potato small to encourage people to take smaller portions, and added a little bit of venison to the beef for a gamier flavour. He took a moment to walk between the tables as people dug in.

Flinty was smiling. 'Oh, stovies. Haven't had stovies for years,' she said to Veronica. 'I make the best stovies. I should make them for you one day.'

Veronica nodded. 'I'd like that.'

Nate swallowed down the lump in his throat and moved on. Reverend Jill was leaning towards Kenny the tour guide, who was not to be referred to as her boyfriend, in a definitely more-than-just-mates sort of a way. All around people were eating, chatting, having a good time and creating brand new memories.

He stopped next to Bella. 'Your dish next.'

'Well, your dish.'

'You made it.'

'To your recipe.' She paused. 'With a bit of extra lime zest.'

'What?'

Bella shrugged. 'Just lemon was a bit one-note.'

Nate shook his head. 'Shocking behaviour.'

The main course was fish. Thick juicy langoustines and smooth silky salmon, with a fresh, zingy salad and green salsa. Nate had dedicated it in his mind to Bella and

Adam's baby and tried to come up with a dish that tasted of excitement, and freshness and hope. On the menu it was called Lowbridge New Beginnings.

'I just hope they like it.'

'They or someone in particular?' asked Bella.

Was it that obvious? He'd tried all the way through his introduction not to stare at her. He'd kept her name off the menu even though the whole meal was for her, and about her and the dessert was nothing but her. 'Well...'

Bella nudged him. 'I guess you're about to find out.'

Nate looked up. Guy Fforde was bearing down on them. What did Bella mean? Oh. Of course. That was who he was supposed to be trying to impress, wasn't it? That was the whole reason he was here at all – to prove to Guy that he was ready to step up.

'I can't believe you're here.'

'Bella called and said how well you were getting on and I haven't seen her for years and this place sounded incredible.' He looked around. 'Which it is. So why not?'

'Well, thanks for coming.'

'This is your menu.'

Nate nodded. 'I didn't cook everything myself. Bella did a lot of the main. And Nina from the village helped with the stovies.'

'But it's your menu?'

Nate nodded.

'It's spectacular.'

'Thank you.'

'It's everything I hoped and more.'

'Hoped?'

'When I suggested you come here. To find your own style. To find your food. If this is your food, then London had better look out.'

Nate decided he wasn't going to tear up. The validation was Flinty loving his stovies. It was Bella considering his main a squeeze of lime away from acceptable. It was Darcy moaning in delight over banoffee pie. Or pastrami on rye. Or a poached egg on toast. But still. Guy Fforde was a great chef and a good man. 'Thank you. That means a lot.'

'So now I have something to ask you.'

Right. 'OK?'

'La Mer. If you want it, it's yours.'

'I...'

Of course he wanted it. It was more than he'd have dared to dream of a few weeks ago. Head chef at La Mer, carrying on from Guy Fforde himself and taking La Mer into the next phase. There'd be profiles in the nationals. Every reviewer in the country would come by. It was the very top, and he was twenty-five years old.

'So what do you say? You can come home.'

Home. La Mer was home. It was the best home he'd had. He'd found a place there that needed him, and he'd become the chef it needed in return. He could go home. 'Wow.'

—

Darcy saw Guy approaching Nate. It would be good news. No one who'd eaten the food he'd put in front of them this evening would doubt that. Nate deserved to be at the very top of the culinary tree. That would be his next step.

She staggered away from the party and ran through the village towards the Low Bridge and then up beyond the castle. She had to be away from this. He was going to go. She couldn't watch it happen. She couldn't be there for the congratulations and the pats on the back. She ran past the walled garden, breath catching in her throat, and up onto the clifftop to the spot where Alexander had proposed. Only then did she stop. Darcy stared out to sea for a moment and then sat down cross-legged on the cool grass.

She'd come here, to the place where they'd officially agreed that they were together until death parted them, without thinking, but now she was here she knew why. She was here to say goodbye. But there was no rush. The pain of missing Alexander was still with her but it wasn't jabbing at her, forcing her to howl in pain or retreat in fear. It sat more comfortably now in among a whole smorgasbord of emotions. Sadness at the idea of leaving Lowbridge. Hope for a different future. Gratitude, belated though it was, to Nate for showing her that she was still alive somewhere inside the bubble she'd created to keep her feelings at bay.

Eventually she slipped the wedding ring off her finger. She wasn't about to throw it dramatically into the waves. Nate was right. She didn't need to forget. She could carry Alexander and his ring with her – perhaps on a chain around her neck, perhaps in a box deep in a drawer – she didn't know which quite yet – but she could carry him with her into the next phase of her life.

–

Nate watched as Evie and Strach carried the desserts out to the guests. This was the part of the meal he'd put the most heart into. This was the thing he truly wanted to say. On the menu he'd just called it Love. Nothing less, nothing more. In his notes it had another name though: Darcy.

It was chocolate, with a hint of coffee, and a hint of whisky, and then something else. Something he waited for the diners to discover.

'Oh!' Veronica was the first to put a hand to her lips. 'Gosh.'

At the next table, Jill giggled, followed by Kenny. And then another gasp, and another laugh. Nate scanned the tables for her. How was she reacting? Did she understand?

Her place was empty. He leaned towards Veronica.

'This is wonderful. So fun.' She smiled. 'It's comforting and warm but surprising at the same time.'

Nate nodded. 'It is.'

'Is that popping candy?' Veronica asked.

'I wanted something unexpected.'

'It's wonderful.'

'Erm, do you know where Darcy is?' he asked.

Veronica looked at him for a second. 'I'm sorry. I think she must have slipped away.'

Nate's heart dropped. 'OK. Never mind.'

He headed back to the kitchen tent. He could still go after her. He could try to tell her one more time. He could...

'Oooooh.'

The noise was coming from inside the tent. Bella was leaning against the worktop, blowing breath out in short sharp puffs.

'Are you OK?'

'Yep. Fine.'

'Cos you look like you're...' This couldn't be happening. 'You look like you might be in labour.'

'No.'

'Right. Then why are you breathing weird?'

'Can't be in labour. Adam's not here.'

'Don't think that's how it works.' Nate needed to think. Childbirth was not an area of expertise, but he had watched *Grey's Anatomy*. 'Have your waters broken yet?'

'Maybe?'

'Bella.'

'Yes.'

'Fuck. When?'

'This afternoon, but I was in the middle of doing the salmon so I just cleaned up and carried on.'

'Bella!'

'What?'

'Oooooh.' She let out another cry somewhere between a moan and a roar.

'Right. That was only three or four minutes after the last one. You're properly in labour.' This was definitely beyond his capabilities. What Nate needed was someone who could cope with anything. He stuck his head out of the tent and shouted in a way he hoped sounded both urgent and casual. 'Veronica! Could you pop over here for a minute?'

Attracting Veronica obviously attracted the attention of Flinty as well. And Nina, and that attracted Anna. And Jill. Soon there was a small birthing committee in the kitchen tent.

'We need to get her pants off,' Anna announced.

'She can't have it here,' Nate protested.

'I think you'll find she can.'

'I'm not having anything without Adam here,' Bella screamed.

Veronica shook her head. 'No. She's still got a little bit of time. Right. Jill, can you set about trying to find out where on earth Adam is? Nathan, phone an ambulance and ask them to come to Margaret and my cottage, and then bloody well go and find Darcy. She won't want to miss this. Nina, you've delivered babies before.'

Nina nodded. 'Mostly guinea pigs, but the basics are the same.'

'And Netty's lad,' Anna pointed out.

'True. And he got a first, so…'

Veronica turned her attention to Bella. 'Can you walk to the cottage, love? It's closer than the castle and you'll be more comfortable than here.'

Bella nodded.

'Right. Let's go then.'

They half walked, half waddled, through the gathered villagers of Lowbridge, Veronica pausing only to issue Fiona with instructions for managing the rest of the party, and made their way the short distance to the cottage.

'Ambulance is on its way,' Nate confirmed. 'Any guesses where Darcy might be?'

'She wanders up on the clifftop,' Flinty murmured absent-mindedly.

'Right.' Nate set off at a run towards the castle, and then on beyond the walled garden. God bless Flinty. Darcy was right there, sitting on the earth on the top of the cliff. 'Darcy!'

She startled as he called out. 'I was having an emotional moment there.'

'No time.'

'Excuse me?'

Nate bent double, desperately trying to catch his breath. 'No time. Bella's having the baby.'

'What? Where?'

'Flinty's cottage. Come on.'

Without waiting for a reaction, he grabbed Darcy's hand, pulled her to her feet and set off at a run back down the hill towards the village.

When they arrived, Jill was talking animatedly on the phone in the doorway. She yelled through the door. 'Adam has broken down, just the other side of Lochcarron.'

Veronica shook her head. 'Well, maybe the bloody ambulance can pick him up.'

'I don't think they do that,' Anna pointed out.

'No. I know.'

'If you cut across the McKenzie land you could get over there and back in less than an hour,' Flinty suggested. 'Well, I could anyway.'

Nate didn't think anyone who'd seen Flinty drive would doubt it.

'You had a drink though, didn't you? With dinner,' Darcy jumped in.

Flinty frowned.

'I'm sober,' Nate volunteered.

'Good.' Veronica was back in control. 'Darcy, you get in there and hold Bella's hand. Margaret, you go with Nathan and show him the way.' She pressed the Land Rover keys into Nate's hand. 'You bring that boy here before this baby comes or so help me, God.'

'I will.'

Another roar came from the living room.

Nate downgraded his ambition. 'I'll try.'

They hurried back to the Land Rover and set off along the road.

'Turn in here,' Flinty instructed.

'That's not a turning.'

'Aye, it is if you're determined.'

Nate navigated his way through a gap in the trees and found himself on a widening farm track. 'OK.'

'Left here.'

'Still not a turning.'

'Do as you're told, lad.'

And so he did. Time and time again Flinty directed him down the side of a particular tree, or past a particular stump that looked, in the darkening air, entirely identical to every other. 'How are you doing this?'

She shrugged. 'Just going the right way.'

'How do you remember?'

Her face hardened slightly. 'Don't remember. Just know. How do you get around London?'

'Tube. Or bus.'

'But how do you know which way to go?'

'Well, there's maps and...'

Flinty shook her head. 'No, lad. You're a local. You don't look at the map for journeys you've done a hundred times, do you?'

'Course not.'

'This is the same, but with trees where you've stuck up buildings.'

They came out on a small lane that led down to the road and a few metres on, just around a bend, they found Adam, leaning on the side of his much newer, supposedly much more reliable four-wheel drive.

'I never thought I'd be this happy to see this old thing.'

'Don't you talk to me like that,' Flinty snapped.

'I meant the car.'

But Flinty was smiling. 'Let the laird drive, lad. He knows his way about the damn site better than you.'

Adam accepted the keys Nate chucked to him. 'But nowhere near as well as Flinty, I'm afraid.'

Darcy wasn't so much holding Bella's hand as having her own hand squeezed into a bone-cracking new shape.

'Where is Adam?'

'On his way. Nate and Flinty have gone to pick him up.'

'You said that an hour ago.'

'It was twenty minutes ago.'

Another roar and another bone-crushing squeeze.

Nina frowned from her position at the business end of proceedings. 'OK, sweetie. On the next contraction it's time to push.'

'No.'

Nina shot Darcy a look.

'Bella, it's time. And I know you didn't want to be doing this without Adam, but he's going to be here really soon and you are going to have a beautiful baby and once the baby's here you won't care exactly how all this happened. You'll have your baby. And Adam will be here. But you just need to be brave and listen to Nina for the next little bit. I'm sorry.'

Bella shook her head.

'Come on. For the baby.'

'OK.'

Another roar of pain but this time there was a new intensity.

'Push,' yelled Nina.

After what felt like far, far too long, the roar subsided.

'Perfect. One more.'

'I can't.'

'You can,' Darcy promised her. 'Just one more.'

'No. I can't.' Bella's face was streaked with tears. 'I can't.'

'Yes. You can.' The voice in the doorway was the one voice Bella needed to hear. He looked over Nina's shoulder. 'Bloody hell. So this is happening.'

Bella released her hand and Darcy stepped back to let Adam take her place at his fiancée's side. 'I'm here. I'm here. I'm sorry.'

One final roar split the quiet, and then softly at first and then louder, a baby cried.

Darcy staggered out into the hallway to find Veronica, Flinty, Jill, Anna and Nate huddled around the door.

Inside the room, Nina's voice rang out. 'A little girl.'

Followed by Bella's exhausted shout. 'I told you so.'

Blue lights finally lit up the street outside, and paramedics jumped out. Veronica pursed her lips. 'What time do you call this?'

—

Nate slipped away. This was family time and there was clearing up to do at the party before he could get to his own bed. Nina and Anna followed not very long after.

'Did they pick a name yet?' he asked as they joined him in the kitchen tent.

'Well, they haven't said' – Nina preened slightly – 'but I think they might want to give a little nod to someone who helped them out a lot tonight.'

Anna nodded. 'I hope they do.' She patted Nina's arm. 'You did well tonight.'

Nate resisted the urge to raise an eyebrow at the unexpected détente.

'Oh, thank you. I'm just glad there weren't any complications, and the paramedics got there in time to check everything was as it should be.'

'The meal was wonderful tonight as well,' Anna added. The miracle of new life had clearly put her in a complimentary mood.

'It really was.'

'A team effort.'

Nina looked back over her shoulder towards the not-yet-renovated community hall. 'It would be good to be able to do more things like this here. You know, not just teas and scones for the tourists.'

There was the very edge of the shape of an idea in Nate's mind. It had been there at the castle when he'd made stovies with Anna and Nina. It had prodded again when he'd cooked in Flinty's kitchen. It had practically screamed at him when Guy Fforde had offered to make all his dreams come true. But he still couldn't quite see it.

'Well, we can do functions,' Anna said. 'Weddings, even?'

Nina shook her head. 'Who'd get married here when there's a castle half a mile down the road?'

'Atheists,' Anna muttered. 'Non-believers.'

'They still believe in castles.'

'Well, I don't know. Wakes. Christenings. Birthday parties. Whatever people want to have a do for.'

Events that mattered to people. Evenings they'd remember and look back on. Nights that would be referred back to in family stories and village gossip for years to come. The idea was starting to take shape.

Nate cleared his throat. 'I mean, you do need to use that fancy kitchen for something. What were you thinking when you ordered it?'

'I'm not really sure. It was a really good deal, so I just sort of thought we'd come up with something.'

'Build it. They will come,' added Anna.

'Like *Field of Dreams*?' Nate murmured.

Anna looked blank. 'No, dear. Like the community hall.'

'Of course.' A kitchen with no chef. An idea that was still only half formed in his mind. It wasn't much, but it wasn't nothing either. 'I might have a suggestion.'

—

At two a.m., Darcy eventually set off to walk back to the castle. Bella was tucked up in bed in Flinty's tiny second bedroom. Adam was still wide awake on the sofa staring at his new baby in delight and terror. And Darcy was dead on her feet. She stumbled through the door and into the kitchen corridor. Veronica was already there.

'I thought you'd gone to bed?'

'Oh, it was terribly noisy and crowded, and Flinty needs her sleep. And I thought Adam and Bella would appreciate the privacy. We came over an hour ago.'

'I don't think they know that.'

Veronica looked unconcerned. 'Well, they were a bit preoccupied. I did hope to see you though.'

'Why?'

'Because you missed dessert.' Veronica pushed a bowl across the countertop to her. 'I think you should try it.'

She was far too wrung out to eat. 'It's two a.m.'

'Nevertheless.'

Darcy didn't have the energy to argue with her mother-in-law, so she took the spoon Veronica was offering and took a taste of Nate's last creation. It was rich and chocolatey with a hint of caramel and coffee. She closed her eyes and luxuriated in the flavour and then something tingled and popped on her tongue, and then again. She laughed. The sweet made her smile and involuntarily giggle out loud. 'This is brilliant.'

Veronica nodded. 'I thought so. I had quite a fight to save a piece for you.'

'Why did you?'

'He called it Love on the menu card, but it made me think of something else.'

Veronica was wrong. Love was exactly what it made Darcy think of. 'Of what?'

'Well, it seems so smooth and sweet, yes?'

Darcy nodded.

'But then there's that little kick. That little bit of something under the surface that people perhaps don't see on first glance.'

'There's more to it?'

'Precisely. When Alexander first brought you back here, I thought you wouldn't cope at all. I thought you'd run back to New York within a week, but there's more to you than meets the eye.' Veronica smiled. 'Nathan's dessert – it rather made me think of you.'

—

And at two thirty in the morning, Darcy was alive, more alive than she'd felt for years and she was running. Running out of the castle, over the Low Bridge and along the street to the community hall. Veronica had told her Nate had headed back to clear up. She wasn't even sure he'd still be there. She rounded the corner into the car park. It was deserted.

Not quite deserted.

Nate Thomas was standing with his back to her, folding what appeared to be the final trestle table.

'Nate?'

He turned. 'Darcy? Is something wrong?'

She shook her head.

'You're all flushed.'

'I've been running.'

'It's the middle of the night. What? Why?'

'Because I tried your dessert.'

—

Nate's voice caught in his throat. There were a thousand things he wanted to say – how it wasn't quite perfect, how it didn't quite catch her, how nothing ever could do her justice, but he knew already that he would spend the rest of his life trying.

'Veronica said it made her think of me.'

Nate smiled. Trust Veronica to get it.

'And I would have said that was silly, and a dessert can't make you think of a person. But then I tried it.'

'And?'

'And I understood what she meant.' Darcy shook her head. 'Not that it made me think of me. It made me think of you.'

Oh.

'It was sort of warm and comforting but then surprising all at once. And I wanted to eat it all in one go, but I also wanted to make it last forever.' She smiled. 'I ate it all in one go.'

'I can make you more.'

She shook her head. 'You don't have to say that.'

'It's true.'

'But you're going, aren't you?'

Going where? Darcy was leaving. Nate was staying at the castle, covering Bella's leave, making the best of every day and trying to tell himself that it was better to have loved and lost or some such nonsense. 'What do you mean?'

Darcy took a deep breath in. 'Just let me say this. I know I have no right, because when you asked me the same I told you no. But would you stay here with me?'

'Yes.' He didn't hesitate. He didn't feel the panic rising. He wasn't worrying about what he was giving up in London. Of course he would.

Her face broke into a smile. The gap between them closed as he knew it would, and she was in his arms, lips pressed to his.

'Wait.' Nate pulled himself away, forcing his body to act against every instinct. If there was going to be a night, he needed to know about tomorrow. If it was only one night, he knew already that he would take one night, but if the sun was going to rise to Darcy walking away forever he wanted to know now. 'I thought you were leaving.'

—

That had been the plan. 'I thought there was no place for me here. No role, you know.'

'I wasn't enough?'

That stung. 'It wasn't that.' There was so much going on inside Darcy's head. She tried to put it into words. 'All the time I've lived here, I've had a role. I was the lady of the manor. I was the hostess. I was Alexander's wife. Without that I was feeling like I didn't belong.'

'So what changed?'

'Well, tonight. I loved tonight. I loved being out here, greeting everyone, hosting, organising. And then I'm going to be Auntie Darcy.' Now all the thoughts were rushing together. 'And I know I'm not an auntie auntie but when I said that, Adam said I could be auntie or nana or anything I wanted, but that I'm definitely going to be Izzy's godmother and they won't take no for an answer.'

'Izzy?' he asked.

'Isabella. After Bella but different.'

'I like it.'

'Isabella Nina though. Cos Nina would probably try to stuff her back up if she didn't get a mention after all that.'

Nate didn't argue. 'Do you really want to talk about baby names?'

'No.' She shook her head. 'I was feeling like I wasn't needed here.'

'And now you feel needed?'

'Now I feel like I can find a role for myself.'

'That's great.'

'It's not what I came to tell you though.' This was the harder part. This was the part that broke her heart and healed it all at the same time. 'I felt so guilty about letting Alexander go.'

'You don't need to.'

She held a hand up to stop him. 'I know. And I know I don't have to forget him, but I do feel guilty. But I love you more.' She'd wondered if saying the l-word for the first time would be smaller the second time around. If anything it was bigger. The first time she'd fallen in love she'd been almost careless with it. She'd had no idea how much love could hurt. She'd thrown herself in without thought or fear. This was different. 'The idea of losing you is worse than anything else. So...' She breathed out. 'That's it. I came to ask you to stay. That's all. Stay. With me. Here.'

Nate took a step back towards her, and then stopped. 'What about everything else you said?'

'Like what?'

'That I'm too young.'

'You'll grow out of it.'

'And Alexander? You said you weren't ready to move on.'

'I can still remember him, can't I?'

'Of course you can. You loved him. Still love him.'

But love wasn't finite. It was bigger and messier and more complicated than she'd ever needed to imagine before. 'But there's room to love you too. Just as much. Differently but the same.'

'Izzy rather than Bella?' he asked.

'Exactly.'

—

It sounded so straightforward. Maybe it was. Maybe he could simply jump in. There was no reason not to, but Darcy's heart had been torn apart before. If he was going to accept it now he had to do so with care. 'I have something to tell you.'

'OK?'

'Guy was here tonight.'

'I know.'

'And he offered me a job. My dream job. Head chef at La Mer.'

Darcy stepped back. 'I understand. It's your dream.'

'It was more than that.' This was what he'd only realised tonight. 'It was home – the longest I've ever stayed anywhere. Guy...' He shook his head at the cliché. 'It sounds stupid to say he was like a father, but he took care of me, believed in me.'

Darcy nodded. 'It's OK. Go and be brilliant. I'm still glad we met.' She turned away.

What? Nate lunged forward, grabbed her hand and spun her back to him. 'I turned it down.'

Confusion covered her features.

'I turned it down,' he repeated. 'You really thought I'd say yes to you if I knew I wasn't going to be here?'

'I...' She shook her head. 'I was scared. Why though? You were desperate for that job.'

'Because the Owl was right, and Guy was right. I was burned out. And if I went back it would be the same. I'd work and work and I'd constantly be trying to reach a goal somewhere over there.' He looked at Darcy, stroking her hand with his thumb. 'And here, I feel like I'm already where I'm meant to be. It's not out of reach.' He pulled her closer in. 'It's right here.'

'We're both staying?'

'We are.'

'So?'

There was one more thing. It could wait, but why should it? Nate wasn't chasing dreams any more. He was living them, right now in the moment. 'I need you to know that if I'd said yes to Guy and you'd come to me right now – then I would have changed my mind in a heartbeat to stay with you.'

'Really?'

'Always.'

'Why?'

Nate had never said this before. His nan was the sort who showed her love gently, through actions, not words, and since then he wasn't sure he'd ever truly loved or been loved. Even the idea of it had been too huge to contemplate. He took a moment. 'Because I love you,' he said.

And then he kissed her, and this time neither of them was going to pull back.

Epilogue

Six Months Later

Darcy Lowbridge stood outside the Lowbridge community hall and admired the sign that was being hung above the entrance.

> Home to Darcy's – memory cafe and
> community kitchen

Inside the door there was a longer explanation of what they did.

> *Food evokes memories. If you've lost someone, or if you or your loved one's memories are getting patchy, then come to us. Tell us your favourite meal. Tell us what it means to you and how you like it cooked, and we will do whatever we can to give that memory back to you.*
>
> *Bring us your stories, your memories and your recipes and we will bring them to life.*

Darcy made her way from table to table, pausing to rehang a dropped bauble from the Christmas tree in the corner. Evie, her mom and Anna were sitting on the bench seats drinking milkshakes and talking about family holidays to Newquay when Evie was just a little girl.

In the centre of the room, Nate was sitting with a man Darcy didn't know yet nodding intently as the stranger talked. He beckoned her over. 'Rob, this is Darcy, our front-of-house manager. Just let her know if there's anything we can do to make your dad more comfortable. Rob's dad used to work on fishing boats out of Portree. He was asking if his dad could come in and cook some fish up with us.'

Darcy nodded. 'Sounds great.' She grabbed the big diary. 'When would you like to come in?'

She confirmed the booking.

'Thanks. Oh, where's the loo before I go?'

Darcy smiled as brightly as she could. 'The John McKenzie Gentlemen's Toilet is just down there, past the noticeboard.'

'The what?'

'Named for one of our most generous sponsors.'

Rob looked blank.

'Just read the plaque above the urinal,' Darcy told him. 'It'll all make sense.'

She headed back to the kitchen.

Nate was pouring coffee into mugs. He held one out to her. 'For you.'

'Thanks.'

She leaned back on the counter and sipped the coffee.

'Anyone home?' Guy Fforde pushed open the kitchen door.

Nate checked the clock. 'I thought your train back was lunchtime.'

'Your business development manager persuaded me to stay another night.'

Darcy smiled. Fiona's search for Mr Right seemed to be at an end.

'But she's working so I wondered if I could make myself useful here.'

Nate laughed. 'There's a bag of potatoes need chopping.'

'Lead me to them.' Guy shrugged off his coat and went to wash his hands. 'My trainees are going to love it here.'

'Should we add that to the sign?' Darcy asked. 'Memory cafe, community kitchen and training school.'

Nate shook his head. 'Bella's leading the training, really.'

'But they'll work here too, and Adam's talked my ear off about getting them into the garden for a real field to fork understanding of ingredients,' Guy pointed out. 'And you're going to take them out foraging.'

'Only if they're good.' Nate grinned. 'If they're cocky little brats like me I'll set Veronica on them.'

Guy's idea to send all his trainee chefs to Lowbridge for a stint with Nate and Bella to, in his words, 'Get back to what food's really about before I fill their head with all the swanky stuff,' and his willingness to put a chunk of his own money behind the endeavour, was a large part of what made Nate's idea for the community hall work financially, and Darcy could see how much Guy's obvious pride meant to Nate.

She followed Nate out into the foyer, as he checked out of the window for new arrivals.

'What time is the photographer coming?'

'Two.' Nate rubbed his eyes. 'Do I look all right?'

'You'll do. What about me?'

'Perfect.'

What else was he going to say? 'What was the reporter like?'

Nate had spent an hour on the phone earlier in the morning to a reporter from *Highland Life*. 'Fine. Loved the memory cafe idea almost as much as she loved the whole falling-in-love-with-the-lady-of-the-manor thing.'

Darcy pulled a face. 'Oh, it's going to be all "Chef's recipe for love", isn't it?'

Nate laughed. 'Chef cooks up a Highland storm…'

'Chef stirs up a…' Darcy shrugged. 'No. Can't think of a third one.'

'Well, so long as it promotes the cafe, I don't care what they write.'

Darcy moved towards him and slid into the space Nate instinctively created in his arms. 'You never thought this would be your life, did you?'

'Which part?'

'Any of it? A tiny community cafe in the Highlands. Making cakes for dementia sufferers.' She paused. 'Me.'

'But I love it.'

'Which part?'

'Every part.' Nate bent his head to her cheek and pressed his lips to her skin. 'This part.' He moved to her neck. 'This part.' Down to her shoulder. 'This part.'

'People, please!' Bella was lugging her baby buggy through the doors. 'This is a food service area.'

Darcy and Nate pulled apart in time to see Bella lifting baby Izzy out of her pushchair. 'Babysitting time.'

Darcy hurried around the counter and pulled Izzy into a snuggle. 'My favourite time.' She checked her watch. 'You've got an hour, and then I have to head back to the stables.'

'Persuaded Nate to take a riding lesson yet?'

Darcy shook her head. She'd offered to continue Evie's riding lessons whenever she came back up to Lowbridge, and somehow it had spiralled. This afternoon was a private lesson for Reverend Jill. Nate remained insistent that he preferred horsepower to actual horses.

She left Nate and Bella discussing cookery school schedules and cafe hours and who was covering for who when, and balanced Izzy on her hip. Nate said he loved every part of his new life. For the first time in forever, Darcy felt exactly the same way.

A Letter from Amelia

Hello again dear and lovely readers.

I hope you've enjoyed this return visit to Lowbridge – or indeed your first visit to Lowbridge. If you haven't been here before, please do go back and catch up on *A Recipe for Love* and *Cooking up a Christmas Storm*.

Stirring up a Love Story was a difficult book to write. I loved returning to Lowbridge and catching up with Nina, Anna, Bella, Adam and the whole village. I loved being able to introduce you all to Nate. His transition from cocky but brilliant chef to the community-minded cook he becomes might be my very favourite transformation the magic of Lowbridge has given us. And I was delighted to be able to give Darcy a happy-ever-after ending, given that I so cruelly tore her world apart back in *A Recipe for Love*, but exploring loss in so many different ways in this story put me through a bit of an emotional wringer as I was writing it.

I think Veronica and Darcy's stories have always existed in parallel to one another. They've been rivals. They've been united by loss and also pulled apart by it, and now we see Darcy processing her own loss while Veronica is living with a very different type of loss, as someone she loves is taken from her inch and inch and little by little. That story in particular was emotional to write, but I wanted to find something hopeful and uplifting in the life Flinty and

Veronica still have together. There is still joy for them to find in the moment, and there are still memories locked away in places, in music, in scent, and, of course, in food.

I hope all the little stories in this novel find the reader that they speak to, and that whether you're a Darcy or a Nate, a Jill or a Fiona, a Bella or an Evie, a Flinty or a Veronica you find the promise of your own personal happy-ever-after somewhere in the heart of Lowbridge.

And I'd also love it if you chose to keep in touch. You can find me on Instagram under my alter ego of @MsAlisonMay and on YouTube @AlAllyAlison, but the best way to keep up to date with everything I'm up to and what stories are coming next is by signing up to my monthly reader newsletter here: https://alison-may.co.uk/newsletter/

And now it's time for some thanks. Writing and publishing a novel is never a solo endeavour so huge thanks first of all to my truly excellent editor, Jennie. She has a slight obsession with the practicality of imaginary business plans in escapist romcoms, but I'm trying my very best to knock that out of her. Thanks as well to Becca for her brilliantly thorough copy-editing insights, and to the whole team at Hera – Keshini, Dan, Kate, Vicki and everybody involved in publicity, sales, marketing, cover design, editorial and proofreading. I have huge appreciation for you all.

Much love as well to my friends and family who put up with me mid-tricky draft. Thanks to Emma-Claire Wilson and Alex Stone, who were my emotional support team through much of the last six months. Thanks, as always, to the glorious human beings of the naughty kitchen – Annie O'Neil, Daisy Tate, Imogen Howson, Janet Gover, Jeevani Charika, Jessica Thorne,

Kate Johnson, Rhoda Baxter, Ruth Long, and Sheila McClure – there are less of you than that list of names implies, but we authors can be greedy like that. Massive thanks and general appreciation to you all.

And finally, in his traditional place in the last line of my acknowledgements – an afterthought or a saving of the best until last, depending on your perspective – thank you EngineerBoy. Still, and indeed, again.

Amelia x